W9-AUO-847

THE FENG SHUI DETECTIVE

THOMAS DUNNE BOOKS ⚲ ST. MARTIN'S MINOTAUR NEW YORK

THE FENG SHUI DETECTIVE

風

水

NURY VITTACHI

THOMAS DUNNE BOOKS.
An imprint of St. Martin's Press.

THE FENG SHUI DETECTIVE. Copyright © 2002 by Nury Vittachi. All rights reserved. Printed in the United States of America. No part of this book may be used or reproduced in any manner whatsoever without written permission except in the case of brief quotations embodied in critical articles or reviews. For information, address St. Martin's Press, 175 Fifth Avenue, New York, N.Y. 10010.

www.minotaurbooks.com

Book design by Jonathan Bennett

ISBN 0-312-32059-0

First published in Australia under the title *The Feng Shui Detective Goes South*, by Duffy & Snellgrove

First U.S. Edition: January 2004

10   9   8   7   6   5   4   3   2   1

CONTENTS

THE FENG SHUI DETECTIVE

S
A
T
U
R
D
A
Y

DYING IS VERY BAD FENG SHUI

THERE WAS something seriously wrong with the apartment, but he did not have the faintest idea what it was. He closed his eyes, tilted his head upward and inhaled deeply, seeking to strike some sort of harmony with his environment. He held his breath—for one long minute.

Then he let it out again. As the air flowed from his lungs, he tried to empty himself and become one with his surroundings.

A tiny but sharp feeling of discord remained. "Not good, not good," he mumbled to himself.

But *why* was it not good? He opened his eyes and scanned the clean, bright rooms again, his brows knotted and lips pursed. What was so bad about the place?

He became aware that his discomfort was perturbing his client.

"Something wrong, right?" Cady Tsai-Leibler said, pausing over her teapot.

Before he could answer, there was the noise of glass shattering in a room nearby. Without moving, the young mother shouted: "Melly? Did you break something? Be careful, okay?"

"Okay, Mama," said the voice of a small girl over the sound of pieces of glass being swept across a tiled floor by a shoe.

Mrs. Tsai-Leibler lowered her James Sadler designer teapot and went to investigate.

Happier to be alone, C.F. Wong cast his eyes around the room again.

The 1,712-square-foot apartment in a subdivided house in the rural part of Singapore's Ridley Park seemed perfect. It had been carefully selected by its new owners for its position. The building stood on a gentle slope on a plot overlooking one of the old black-and-whites. It had a breathable open space to the front and was pleasingly, if rather boringly, proportioned as a series of rectangles on three stories. But it just didn't feel right.

"Must think," said the feng shui master, flopping down in a seat on the small balcony that looked over a tastefully designed Chinese garden.

According to the technical demands of the ancient beliefs of geographical placement, it was fine. The block was a rectangular construction on an almost square podium, and belonged to the K'un orientation, with its door facing southwest. The main room faced due west of the center. This was one of the more prosperous directions for the main living space, and was known as the Direction of the Celestial Physician.

There was a potential clash with the flow of *ch'i* moving from the kitchen to the second bedroom which was directly opposite, but nothing that couldn't be fixed with the judicious placing of suitable objects to catch and divert any unsuitable rush of water or fire energy.

The salmon gloss the woman of the house had chosen for

the main room would have been uncomfortable for many people, but he realized that it was perfect for her. Calida "Cady" Tsai-Leibler, an executive secretary of Hong Kong origin married to a dentist from New York, was a wood person born under the sign of the ram.

"*Mutyeh si?*" he breathed, tapping his knuckles against the side of his forehead. *What was the matter?*

The family had owned the apartment for three weeks, but had only moved in two days earlier. Although much of the furniture had been unpacked and laid out, the main living area remained pleasantly uncluttered. Wong was pleased to see that Mrs. Tsai-Leibler had gone for an American-style open plan design, rather than the jam-packed every-inch-used style which was characteristic of Hong Kong flats. The apartment, as it stood, had a series of pleasant routes through which *ch'i* could flow and pool itself. So what was wrong?

A door swung open and Mrs. Tsai-Leibler's husband entered the living room. A large, unsmiling man with a glowering forehead, his presence immediately made the room too small.

"Finished?" Gibson Leibler growled, directing his comment at his wife rather than at the feng shui master. His face said: I hope so.

"Mr. Wong's just taking a last look round," Cady Tsai-Leibler piped, suddenly emerging from her child's room.

Dr. Leibler, still facing his wife, said crisply: "I think the apartment is fine." The clear implication was that his was the only opinion that counted.

"It's mostly fine, yes?" the meek woman said, turning to Wong with a note of pleading in her voice. "I mean, maybe there's just something small-small a bit wrong we can fix. But mostly it's okay . . . ?" She trailed off. She appeared to have shrunk several inches since her partner entered the room.

Dr. Leibler, a tall, overweight man in his mid-thirties, turned to face Wong. "I think the apartment's fine, Mr. Feng Shui Man," he said. "What do you think?"

"Ver' nice," said Wong, nodding like a dashboard toy. "Clean, bright, quite good."

"So we don't need to change anything." The voice was little more than a low rumble.

Was it a question? Wong looked at the expression on the man's face and realized it was a statement of fact.

"Mr. Wong likes the apartment," the dental surgeon's wife fluted nervously. "He thinks it's fine, most of it." She said the last three words almost under her breath.

The feng shui master nodded again. Then his head tilted to one side. "Only one thing wrong," he said.

Dr. Leibler's face muscles dropped slightly, causing his fake, barely-there smile to disappear. "And what would that be?" he asked, his chest expanding.

"I don't know," said the geomancer, looking around desperately.

The obvious visual demerit of the apartment was the wrought-iron bars on the windows, which made it look like a prettified prison. Wong knew that isolated dwellings could be popular targets for cat burglars in Singapore. The previous owner had placed bars on every window, and a steel-grilled outer door at the entrance to the flat. Yet such fittings were extremely common in the security-conscious city-state, and residents failed to find them ugly or objectionable in any way.

Numbers tumbled through the feng shui master's mind. He had earlier checked the birth dates of Mrs. Tsai-Leibler, her husband, and her child, comparing them to the construction date of the building. This was an unusually old block by local standards, first built in the 1950s, but substantially rebuilt in 1972 and again in 1991. There was no clash in the dates that could not be easily fixed with some minor acts of physical mitigation. Also present in the apartment was a quiet, rather broody-looking young Hong Kong woman named Madeleine, who had been introduced to him as Mrs. Tsai-Leibler's cousin. But he'd been told she was only staying a week. Nevertheless, he had given her birth chart a perfunctory examination and found no clash with the dates attached to the property. It was rare to find an apartment that was absolutely perfect for a family, but this one was close.

Yet he remained irritatingly aware there were always two major aspects to any reading of a dwelling place: the technical reading and the non-technical one. The first he did with his *lo pan*, plus books, charts, magnets, and a close study of the floor plan of the house and map of the surrounding area.

The second was simultaneously much easier and much harder. It was done without tools, and consisted of measuring the *settledness* of the dwelling. For this, a feng shui master had no tools but his own spirit. The apartment: Was it still? Was it disturbed? Was it fresh? Was it aged? Was it empty? Was it occupied? Was it ready? Was it going to be comfortable for the person who was going to use it? Dweller and dwelling needed to be in the same key, the same register. Yet most people had little awareness of the signals sent out by their inner selves, let alone any ability to detect anything about the spirit of their homes or offices. It was something he had to do for clients, at high speed during brief visits—never an easy job.

"Something very small may be wrong, right?" the still-shrinking Mrs. Tsai-Leibler prompted. "You don't like the salmon walls? I can change them. First I thought lime green. Lime green, is it better?"

"Color no problem, Mrs. Tsai-Leibler," said Wong, who

had the curious feeling that she was actually becoming transparent.

"Pink? Beige?" she offered, pronouncing it "beej" in a Hong Kong accent. She clearly wanted to bring the session to an end.

Wong looked around. What was wrong? Was it the light? It was late afternoon, and a rich but diffuse stream of super-heated tropical sunshine poured in through the French windows in the living room and the picture window in the master bedroom. But the angle was steep and the glare did not proceed more than two meters or so into the main seating area. The apartment welcomed the sun without trapping it. The light was not a problem.

Was there something outside he had missed? He scanned the horizon for the twentieth time. Although there was no obvious geological dragon guarding the premises, nor was there anything overtly negative. As well as the old black-and-white house set slightly to the west, there was lush vegetation and some exceptionally fine fruit trees visible straight ahead and to the east. It was a stately view by which the home could only be enriched. The malevolence was not external.

"Mr. Wong noticed that the tap in the kitchen leaks, and the shower head drips," Mrs. Tsai-Leibler said to break the uncomfortable silence.

Her husband folded his arms. "So I suppose that symbolizes money or good luck flowing away," he rumbled with a sneer in his voice. "So do we need to put a goldfish in the bathtub? What does a feng shui man do when his tap is dripping?"

"Call a plumber," replied Wong, pronouncing the "b."

The dental surgeon stared at the visitor, apparently attempting to work out whether he was being mocked. But the geomancer's face showed no emotion.

"There are two dead bulbs in the apartment and the door to the second bedroom sticks," the woman of the household tentatively added. "And one of the wall sockets has no electricity."

Her husband scowled. "You don't need a feng shui master to point these things out. They're all common sense stuff."

"Well you said you'd check all those things weeks ago and you didn't do anything about them," she snapped, showing a surprising flash of anger.

"I've been busy," the large man replied, unrepentant. "I would've gotten around to it."

"It took you six weeks to replace the bulbs in Melly's old room, and then you got the wrong ones."

"I'm a busy man."

Wong butted in. "I can arrange man to fix socket, lightbulbs, can get plumber if you want."

Dr. Leibler ignored him, having refocused his hostility at his tiny, cowering wife.

The geomancer prattled on. "Many feng shui advice is like common sense. If your environment not functioning, if doors in your house sticking, for example, then doors of opportunity in your life maybe also sticking, you see? Fix dripping taps in house: this makes you change attitude, fix metaphorical dripping taps in your life, get tighter control, understand or not? Partly, feng shui is about attitude. About taking control. Take control of physical environment. Make you take control of nonphysical elements of your life. See or not?"

The dentist turned to stare at the geomancer, evidently surprised at this relatively long utterance from the ethereal, taciturn visitor. The interruption had halted the argument.

"Let us *yum cha*," Mrs. Tsai-Leibler said, trying a different tack. "Drink some tea. We can all relax. Then we finish." She made big eyes at her husband for approval.

Gibson Leibler scowled at the tray of teacups and then walked over to the kitchen, from whence he returned clutching an open bottle of chilled Anchor.

Wong looked down at the pungent, sweet-smelling liquid in the cup she had placed into his hand. It wasn't what he would have called tea.

His hostess noticed. "Sorry. We don't have *ching cha*," Mrs. Tsai-Leibler said. "This is herb tea. Popular in America. Mango Kiwi Zinger flavor. I think you like it."

The geomancer smelled the tea—and suddenly looked up and smiled. "I have it," he said.

"You have Mango Kiwi Zinger tea?" asked Ms. Tsai-Leibler.

"I have the answer," said the feng shui man, putting down his cup and springing to his feet.

Dr. Leibler watched the unwelcome visitor carefully.

Wong smiled. The flat *smelt* wrong. There was a barely detectable odor in the building. And it was a wrong odor, a bad odor, an evil odor, a tiny but uncomfortable smell that disturbed the otherwise perfect tranquillity of the spot.

He strode around the living room, flaring his wide, flat nostrils to locate the source of the smell.

"You worked out what's wrong with apartment?" Mrs. Tsai-Leibler asked, suddenly interested again.

"Yes," said Wong, a broad grin of relief breaking out on his face. Mystery solved—and just in time. He inhaled deeply to confirm his suspicions. He sensed a low but unmistakable mix of smells: the heady tang of something like paraffin, the sharp odor of carbon, and the sour smell of ash. "The house is on fire," he explained.

"Oh dear," said Mrs. Tsai-Leibler. The teapot fell from her hand and shattered on the floor.

Gibson Leibler leaped to his feet. He sniffed once, and

then raced to the door. He threw it open—and had to sharply pull his fingers away from the hot handle. Almost immediately, there were flames crawling up both sides of the door. He let out a lengthy string of expletives in a furious wet splutter.

"Don't!" scolded Cady Tsai-Leibler. "Melly can hear."

Wong stared. Flames were springing from soaked rags that had been laid in a line across the front door of the flat.

The feng shui master watched with horror as a viscous liquid gently rolled across the floor from the front door. Dr. Leibler tripped awkwardly backward on his heavy feet. It was evident that just minutes earlier someone had sloshed the contents of a container of some sort of highly flammable oil under the gap at the front door and then lit the rags.

As they watched, the growing puddle suddenly burst into flame, slowly rolling toward them like lava. The air in the room was instantly scorching.

"Mummeeee!" Melody screamed, coming into the room and leaping into her mother's arms.

Cady Tsai-Leibler screamed even more loudly than her daughter and raced back toward the balcony, awkwardly clutching the tall child with both hands.

Dr. Leibler cursed again and stepped backward, away from the flames. "Where's the fire extinguisher?" he barked.

"Not have," his wife shouted, reverting back to Chinglish in her panic. "Wait. Outside is one."

There was no way they could get anywhere near the front door, let alone to the corridor outside. "Call the fire department," her husband shouted. "Then go out the back door. I'll see if I can find a bucket or something." He raced into the kitchen and threw open all the cabinet doors.

"Phone fire department," Mrs. Tsai-Leibler said to herself, dropping the child at her feet and reaching for the phone on a side table. It didn't work. Then she was breathlessly scrabbling through her handbag for her cell phone. She jabbed at the numbers with frightened fingers and had to clear the tiny screen twice to try again. Eventually getting an answer, she barked out the address. "Hurry, hurry!" she said. "We don't have much time."

She turned her face, suddenly tear-stained, to the feng shui master. "*Ho marfan!* I think they can't come in time. No road through front garden, only small path. We must get out of the window or something. Aiyeeaah!"

But the windows were barred. The only open space was the balcony—but being on the third story, it would be too high to jump from.

Madeline Tsai, the young lodger, wandered in a slightly dazed way into the room. Clearly she had been asleep, despite the fact that it was almost lunchtime.

"House is on fire," Cady shrieked.

Her cousin, who appeared to be in her late teens, seemed oddly unperturbed by the blaze around her. She calmly strolled toward the door, approaching within a meter of the flames, and picked up her shoulder bag. Drug-taker, Wong decided. Her skin was dry and dehydrated like that of an ecstasy-user.

Dr. Leibler noisily returned to the main room, his heavy form bumping against the side of the kitchen door. "There's nothing to use to fight the fire with. We'll all go out through the back door." He looked at his wife and child, both frozen with terror. He added, in a shout: "Do you hear me? NOW."

Cady Tsai-Leibler and C. F. Wong looked at each other. Neither wanted to deliver the bad news to the angry man in front of them. The Hong Kong woman spoke first: "This flat doesn't have back door."

Her husband reacted unexpectedly well. He spoke calmly:

"Okay. Get your valuables together. We'll go over the balcony when the fire department arrives."

She raced around the room, putting her cell phone in a bag that she slipped over one shoulder and then started looking for her shoes.

"My bag my bag my bag!" shouted Melody, who had been ordered to stand on the balcony. The child was jumping up and down. She pointed to the corner of the room, where a pink backpack with a Winnie the Pooh motif stood against a wall.

Her mother, braving the flames, picked it up and threw it onto the balcony. The child immediately unzipped the top and looked bereft. "My Miffy pencil case isn't inside."

"Just GO!" her father shouted.

"I want my Miffy pencil caaaaaase," she squealed, suddenly bursting into tears. "I *want* it."

Her mother saw the missing item under a chair. "Here," she shouted, throwing it to her.

The child squeezed it to her chest, and then started crying. "I wanna go home," she bawled.

Madeleine Tsai stood watching the chaos from the balcony. "Aiyeeaah," she breathed. She appeared to be gradually waking up to what was going on.

"Do something, Mr. Wong!" Mrs. Tsai-Leibler screamed, as the heat became more intense.

"I am, I am," said Wong. He was scrabbling through the mess on the table. "I try to find my papers."

"Forget papers," she said. "*Gau meng!* Save you. Save *us.*"

She raced into the bedroom. Seconds later, she raced out again, her arms full of silks. She raced to a window and threw them over the balcony.

"You see Hello Kitty clutch purse somewhere?"

"Forget the child's stupid things," her husband shouted.

11

"Not Melody's," said Mrs. Tsai-Leibler. "It's mine."

"*Geez,*" the American said.

"And my DKNY top," she squealed. "Can't find it."

The flames advanced steadily across the living room.

"Must jump out," she shrieked.

"No," said Wong. "You hurt yourself. Stay."

"We'll be fried if we stay," said her husband.

Right on cue, there was a roar as the chair nearest the front door ignited, and flames started to lick at a small rug in the center of the room.

"Where's my digital camera?" said Gibson Leibler.

"Where my earring box?" said Cady Tsai-Leibler.

"My computer. We need to save the hard disk. And my laptop. Where's my laptop?"

"My Cartier panther brooch."

"Where the hell is my Palm Pilot?"

The couple stared at each other.

"Must find my papers," said Wong. He was sure he had put them on the dining table, but they had vanished.

"Forget the papers," said Mrs. Tsai-Leibler. "Get important stuff." Then a thought seemed to occur to her. She turned to Wong: "I moved them to that chair so I could put the teapot on the table."

"The man's mad," said Dr. Leibler, who had absently picked up a hammer to fight the fire with, and then found himself unable to think of anything to do with it.

Wong found his papers on a chair. He sat down and started flicking through them one by one.

They were running out of time. Dr. Leibler was formulating a plan. "The old guy'll jump down first to the balcony below," he said, pointing to the feng shui master. "Then you hold on to Melly and I'll gently lower you guys to the apartment below."

He looked at the feng shui master's skeletal arms and

changed his mind. "He won't be able to catch you. Maybe I should jump down and catch you instead. Or Madeleine. One of you could lower Melly first. Do you think you could handle the weight of this child, Mr. Wong? Maybe Madeleine should go first."

"Shh!" said Wong. "I am reading."

The flames roared again as Mrs. Tsai-Leibler reopened the French windows and joined her child, having found her favorite DKNY top. The heat was blistering.

Gibson Leibler stared at Wong. "Don't you understand what is happening? We are going to die unless we get out of this place immediately. We are going to DIE. Dying is very bad feng shui I am sure, Mr. Wong."

Wong turned a piece of paper over and smiled. "Found," he said.

He walked into the heart of the burning living room with the paper in his left hand. "This apartment qualifies as a K'un dwelling because it faces southwest. But its water sources come from the south," he shouted over the crackling of the flames. "Just here, in fact."

"Mad," said Dr. Leibler again. "Totally."

The feng shui master pointed to the wall and mumbled some numbers to himself in Cantonese, working out that the spot he wanted was five feet to the left of the corner of the room: "Ng chek jor."

Then he picked up the hammer that the dental surgeon had abandoned. He swung it at what appeared to be a protruding joist running between the wall and the ceiling. The blow had almost no effect. He swung again, this time cracking the salmon gloss with a thud. A third, heavier swing caused several inches of red undercoat and white plaster to fall away. A fourth produced the sound of metal on plastic. The fifth produced a slight hiss as the hammer fractured a pipe. The sixth cracked open the pipe, producing a shower of water that spurted from the wall, soaking Wong. The fire on the carpet behind them hissed as a spray of water droplets hit the flames.

Wong continued to hammer at the pipe until a torrent was gushing into the center of the floor.

❖

Recently, 3,000 years ago, the floating people of old China lodged on the water and dined on the wind.

Each family lived on a platform in a bay. When a boy grew up he would stand at the edge of his platform and call. The girl he loved would call back. Then he would build a bridge from his platform to hers.

If his family liked the girl they would help build the bridge. Their homes would be joined and the two families would become one.

One day a floating boy heard a whisper from over the horizon. It was a girl from far away. They called to each other a long time. They decided to get married.

His family said no. She belonged to a different people and was too far away.

But the boy was determined. He started to build a bridge to the horizon. He dug deep into the seabed to make a strong foundation. His family did not help. They said the tradition of marrying neighbors gave strength to the community. They called his bridge "the whisper bridge." They told him to stop.

But he did not listen. He built the bridge for eight years.

When it was complete he met the girl who whispered from the horizon and they were married on the great bridge.

The following year, a great storm blew up. It destroyed the platform homes of the floating people. But the whisper bridge remained.

And so it is with us, Blade of Grass. That which takes a long time to build, takes a long time to destroy. To do what cannot be done is difficult, but once it is done, it cannot be undone. To make sure an old tradition retains its power, it must be changed.

*(Some Gleanings of Oriental Wisdom
by C. F. Wong, part 342)*

CRIMES COMMITTED BY DEAD PEOPLE

C. F. WONG blew on the paper to dry the ink. He was at his desk, writing in his journal. The chapter on which he was working was a series of anecdotes from the sages on the subject of ingenious solutions to unusual problems. From time to time, he looked up and stared out of the window. It was morning in the Singapore financial district.

During rush hour the constant background grumble from the vehicles on Church Street and Cross Street turned into a pained roar. Double-decker buses would grind their engines as they lumbered along, consuming the road in jerky, stop-start mouthfuls. Many vehicles existed in a permanently overheated state, whirring noises from their automatic cooling systems adding a high-pitched shriek to the massed mechanical choir. Taxis, attempting to cut from lane to lane, would inevitably find themselves wedged over dividing lines, their engines shivering and drivers yawning.

Providing contrast was a smattering of private cars, inevitably German, ferrying wealthier executives to their offices. The luxuriousness of these late-model limousines contrasted dramatically with the austerity of the other main group of minority road users: elderly men in dirty singlets cycling with baskets of flapping fish for factory canteen lunches.

Every two minutes or so, there was a periodic rise in the sound level as green traffic lights unleashed more vehicles from side roads into the already jammed main thoroughfare. The racket would grow into a hellish cacophony that made pedestrian conversation difficult. Occasionally, there would be a break in the rhythm as the *ticka-ticka-ticka* sound of pedestrian signals added a light counterpoint to the general low-pitched rumble of the road.

The structure of the central business district of Singapore, as a series of steep glass canyons, meant that the morning arrived in waves. Some junctions quickly turned into sun-traps, bathed in bright, yellow heat, while the areas around them remained misty, receiving only diffused light from pale, stone-and-glass buildings. The taller mirror-walled skyscrapers, backlit by the strengthening day, would be visible only as gray silhouettes until at least ten o'clock. That was the time when most people had arrived at their offices, and peace, relatively speaking, returned to the streets of the Lion City.

During the time of the northern Song Dynasty, 960 to 1279, two royal families fought over property. Each had a share of a great inheritance.

One of the princes went to Prime Minister Zhang Qixian and said: "My brother's share is bigger than mine. I have a list of what I have. It proves what I am saying is true."

But the man's brother also went to Prime Minister Zhang Qixian. He said: "The opposite is true. My brother's pro-

portion is bigger than mine. I have a list of my possessions.
It proves what I am saying is true."
Zhang Qixian took the two lists to examine and compare.
The fighting brothers waited and watched.
Then Zhang scratched out the names at the bottom of each
scroll. He replaced each name with the name of the other
brother.
He gave the lists back. He said to the first brother: "Now
you have more than your brother." And he said to the sec-
ond brother: "And you have more than yours."

If you can win a battle by accepting your enemy's arrows,
Blade of Grass, your victory will be untouchable from any side.

(Some Gleanings of Oriental Wisdom
by C. F. Wong, part 343)

He wrote feverishly, knowing that moments of creative tranquillity within the Telok Ayer Street offices of C. F. Wong &
Associates were rare and inevitably fleeting. Glancing at his
watch, he saw that it was one minute past ten o'clock. He
had been working quietly alone for almost three hours. How
kind the gods were, to bless him with staff who were always
late! Long might their bad habits continue. He clapped his
hands together and performed a short, grateful bow in the
direction of the nearest temple, which was a few hundred
yards south of his office. While not overtly religious, Wong
had a deep-rooted habit of performing lip-service to the
Taoist rituals he had learned during his childhood in Baiwan, a village in Guangdong Province, China. He could not

pass a temple, even on the other side of the road, without a quick bow and a cursory wave of closed palms.

Ten o'clock! He looked out of the window for a moment and blinked. One of these days, he thought, his receptionist-secretary-clerk-office administrator Winnie Lim might miss the entire morning—or not turn up at all. Perhaps she would go—what was the phrase in English? A wol? Or was that a type of bird?

Then there was the nightmarish intern that his main client, Mr. Pun, had forced on him recently. He would never forget the horrific moment a gawky young female *mat salleh* had appeared in his office speaking a bizarre and incomprehensible sub-dialect of English.

"My dad's like 'My mate Mr. Pun's gotta real feng shooee master and you can work for him,' and I'm like '*Wow*,' " she had said.

It had taken him a long time to establish any sort of proper communication with Joyce McQuinnie, who came from British–Australian parentage but seemed to speak only a strange language called "Teenager." An early breakthrough had been when he had realized that her word for *yes* was "Whatever." More recently, he had worked out that her term for *no* was "As if."

On arrival at Telok Ayer Street, her first action had been to rearrange her desk and chair to get more light. Who but the most insensitive person would unilaterally move the furniture in a feng shui master's office? From then on, she spent her days talking in an unknown tongue to her friends, and laughing the way that only men were supposed to laugh. He found it almost impossible to *think* let alone work with McQuinnie in the office.

And it wasn't just the noise that was a problem. Every day at 11 A.M., she would disappear for ten minutes before returning with a drink she called latte—a cardboard bucket of foam that made the office stink of bitter coffee and cow's milk. To add insult to injury, at midday she would sniff his aromatic *nasi kandar* lunchbox and turn up her nose with a pronounced "*Eeeewwww!*" For her own lunch, she would order sandwiches so overstuffed that she couldn't get them in her mouth. Most afternoons, her desk would be liberally sprinkled with bits of shredded lettuce—*raw* lettuce, if you can imagine.

Worst of all, she insisted on accompanying him on many of his assignments, where her loud and garish presence—she wore shapeless clothes and too much jewelery—would unsettle his clients. A developer named Tak had politely asked her how her studies were going. She had replied: "Oh, they used to be like *okay* but dad kept moving and everything went like pear-shaped, totally."

Old Tak had turned to Wong. "Pear-shaped? Is that good feng shui?"

Wong had been unable to think of a reply, so had nodded sagely.

He shuddered at the memory of those difficult early attempts at communication. Then a rather more attractive thought drifted into his mind. If Winnie and Joyce disappeared, he would have space and budget enough to get a real personal assistant: someone who would ease his workload, rather than add intolerable burdens to it. And he could redesign the furniture in the office and surmount the great shame he presently bore of being a feng shui master with a shockingly badly organized workplace. That, surely, would boost his spirits, not to mention his income. O let Winnie and Joyce be a wol! With that delicious thought bringing a guilty smile to his lips, he turned his attention back to his work.

Slowing his breathing, the feng shui master gathered his scattered thoughts around him and refocused his attention on the masterpiece on which he had been working for several years: a volume he hoped would be his first major work published in English. The handwritten journal was ragged and dog-eared, but remained his proudest possession. Two hundred pages of anecdotes and quotations, it was already more than one and a half inches thick. Yet there was still a great deal to do.

To get back to work, he first had to clear himself of all distracting notions. It shouldn't be difficult. The room was quiet. The clock on the wall didn't work (something he would never allow to happen at the premises of a client, a stopped timepiece being an intolerably negative feng shui omen). The air conditioner hummed and clanked distressingly loudly, but after four years it had stopped being an obtrusive sound. The water cooler normally dripped—but it had been turned off, since the office manager had not refilled it for two weeks. Perfect peace and stillness descended.

The thoughts of his favorite sage, Mo Ti, started to flow into Wong's head. It was as if he could hear the quiet but clear voice of the great thinker over the chasm of two and half millennia. For a few glorious moments, the only sound in the room was the scratch of Wong's pen on the paper.

Which was the moment Winnie Lim chose to arrive.

"*Aiyeeaah,*" she screeched in her rasping voice, pushing the door so hard that it bounced against the wall and returned back to slam against her still-outstretched palm. There was a splintering sound and a bright, gleaming crack appeared in the frosted glass.

"*Aiyeeaah!*" said Winnie again. "GLASS BREAKING. Cheap glass. I SUE YOU."

"I sue you for coming to work late," rejoined Wong.

"I sue you for always putting me in bad mood."

"You can't sue for that."

"Can. I get American boyfriend. American can sue for ANYTHING."

Wong considered this for a moment and then decided that it was true. He lapsed into defeated silence as Winnie threw her handbag onto her chair and then disappeared for her first job of each day: to spend five minutes in the toilet checking her makeup—a redundant task, since she spent most of the day reapplying it in various styles. She slammed the door again on the way out. The empty water cooler rattled. Wong closed his journal and slipped it into his drawer. He was unlikely to get any more writing done this morning.

When the office administrator returned to the room, Wong decided that he had to at least attempt to take command of the situation.

"I am ver' busy today," he said. "Plenty work. You must do all the letters, postings, filings, phone callings. I must do urgent work on my book. Nearly finish," he lied.

She froze and turned her head toward him, fixing him with an icy glare. She said nothing. Determined to tighten his grasp on the initiative with which he was grappling, Wong sat stiffly upright and glared back at her. He decided he would write her a detailed list of instructions to make sure she actually achieved some useful work today. The staring contest continued for a few seconds, and then Winnie, bored, sat down and started busying herself at her desk.

The feng shui master watched uncomfortably over the top of a piece of paper. He pretended to concentrate on reading a letter for a while, his irritation preventing him from actually taking in any words.

The phone rang. And rang again. And continued to ring.

"Pick it up," Winnie barked. "I'm busy." He glanced over and noticed she was applying tiny, sticky-backed images of Canto-pop singers onto vermilion and cerise fingernails.

He picked up the handset. "Hello?"

"Good morning. Who is speaking?" said a voice.

"You are speaking," replied the geomancer, who had grown up without modern appliances and had never mastered the intricacies of telephone etiquette.

"Is it Mr. Wong? I thought you had a secretary. When I call before."

"She is busy. Putting pictures of music people on her fingers."

"Oh," said the caller.

"Who are you?" The voice seemed familiar.

"I am Mrs. Tsai-Leibler."

"Oh. Mrs. Tsai-Leibler. How are you? You are okay? Better now? Very shocking, what happen on Saturday. Okay now?"

"Okay. Can I talk now, is it okay?"

"Okay. What do you want to talk about?"

"The fire. On Saturday. I know who did it. I know for sure."

"Ah, Mrs. Tsai-Leibler, very interesting. But I think better you not tell me. Better you tell police. Fire is very serious. Very criminal. Very police matter. Not for me. I am only feng shui master."

The woman on the phone sighed. "Mr. Wong, I need to talk to somebody. Can I talk to you in Cantonese?"

"Hai-ah," he replied.

"Ho," she said, switching into their vernacular. "Then we can understand each other better. Mr. Wong, the person who tried to kill me and my family on Saturday also tried to kill you. This matter involves you, too. You are involved. You cannot avoid it."

"Yes, yes, true, true. But still, I repeat, arson is a criminal matter for the police to investigate. You have a suspect, you should tell the police. Not me."

"I have told the police," she said, a tone of despair in her voice. "They weren't interested."

"No, no, I am sure they will be very interested."

"I'm telling you they weren't interested."

"Why not? Some problem?"

"Well, you could say that. The man who tried to kill us was a man named Joseph Hardcastle Oath. He used to be one of my husband's patients."

"Oh good. If you know name of suspect, makes it easier to find. You know where he lives too?"

"Yes I do. In the deepest part of Hell. He died two years ago."

C. F. Wong wasn't sure how to reply. "Ah," he said. "Understand. Police don't like to investigate crimes committed by dead people."

Calida Tsai-Leibler talked to C. F. Wong for almost an hour. After a while, he realized that she was not going to get off the phone until he had agreed to commit himself to take some action to investigate her claim.

She was convinced that the ultimate target of the arson attack was not her husband or herself—but their six-year-old daughter Melody. "When this man Oath had a big fight with my husband, he was always bringing Melly into it. Oath had a son who was a patient of my husband," she explained. "This was a long time ago, almost three years, in Hong Kong. My divorce had just come through and Gibson and I had just got engaged. Melly was three. There was a problem with the anaesthetist. The man turned out to be a substance abuser—apparently this is quite common among anaesthetists. They spend all day with strange substances, so they cannot resist the temptation to try them out on themselves. Anyway, the anaesthetist gave Oath's son the wrong stuff. My husband was removing four of the child's teeth to insert a brace. The child never woke up. He died. It was a terrible, terrible thing."

Wong did not want to hear any of this. "But—"

"It was in all the newspapers. Oath started a malpractice lawsuit against my husband and the anaesthetist—whom my husband had recommended. But before the case came to court, the anaesthetist had died of a self-administered overdose of something. Oath had no one left to blame but my husband, who was blameless in the whole affair. He used to phone up and curse us—tell us to imagine how we would feel if our child had died. Melly was three. So innocent! Can you imagine cursing a three-year-old? Shortly after the hearing started, Oath died. His wife did not wish to continue the case. That, we thought, was the end of it. But I have long felt that a malevolent spirit has been wanting to cause harm to my poor child. The ghost of Mr. Oath. Now I'm convinced it's true."

She went on to explain how a series of bad omens had left her convinced that an evil presence was causing harm to the family. And then, to Wong's surprise, the tiny, mild woman became belligerent, threatening to get "powerful friends in Hong Kong" to come to Singapore to look after her family, if no one here would take any interest. "I can get humans dealt with," she said. "But I don't know anyone who can take out a ghost."

Wong listened patiently, knowing from experience that many clients or would-be clients simply wanted someone to whom to tell their problems. When she finally paused for breath, he tried to convince her that it was not the job of a feng shui master to deal with dead spirits. Some feng shui practitioners did not even believe in ghosts, he said. But he explained that he was in regular touch with a group of people—the investigative advisory committee of the Singapore Union of Industrial Mystics—that did include individuals who had an interest in such matters.

The conversation ended with Wong agreeing to put Mrs.

Tsai-Leibler in contact with Superintendent Gilbert Tan, a senior police officer who was likely to be more willing than his colleagues to take her complaints seriously. Tan acted as a liaison between the Singapore police and the local mystics. He also referred her to Madame Xu Chong Li, a Chinese fortune-teller who frequently dealt with paranormal events and who would be happy to discuss the case in detail.

"Mr. Tan is used to listening to unusual explanations for things," the geomancer explained. "I will give you his phone number now. After you talk to him, you call Madame Xu. She is very helpful. She will offer consultancy service on the matter at competitive price. Money back guarantee."

As he put down the phone, he was startled to find that Winnie Lim had marched over to his desk and was standing glaring at him. She handed him a piece of paper.

"Take," she said.

He was flustered for a moment, not knowing whether to look at the sheet of paper or Winnie's unsmiling face.

"I have to go out. Very busy. Here is list of things you do while I am out," Winnie said.

"Where do you go?"

"Out. Very busy."

"Oh."

"Number three and four on list very important. Much overdue. Don't forget."

"Number three-four," he repeated mechanically.

He was so astonished at her insolence that he sat frozen in his chair, unable to move. Winnie calmly picked up her handbag and strolled out of the room, humming a Jacky Cheung pop tune. Only when the sound of her footsteps tripping down the stairs faded did mobility return to his limbs.

"Aiyeeaah," he breathed, looking at the list of tasks she had left him. Number three was "Buy New Clock." Number four was "Order Water Refills."

In an old flat decorated with red and gold flock wallpaper in Bussorah Street, Kampong Glam, a mauve plastic telephone in a style fifteen years out of date jangled noisily. Dilip Kenneth Sinha snatched up the receiver.

"Ye-es?" he said, drawing out the word into a poised and elegant sentence.

"Hello?" said the caller.

"Ye-es?"

"Is that Dilip? It's me."

"Well of course. I knew it was you. I always know these things," he said grandly. "I knew you were going to call even before the phone rang, Madame Xu."

The caller gave a short, dismissive laugh. "Ha! No need to try to impress me with such skills, Dilip. You know there is no one more psychic in this town than I am."

Sinha smiled. "Maybe so. But I was merely giving my own powers a little exercise. Knowing who's on the telephone has been a specialty of mine since childhood."

This was evidently not the right thing to say. The telephone delivered the sound of a woman taking a deep breath and raising herself up to her full height, which he knew to be in the region of five feet. Madame Xu Chong Li apparently saw his assertion as a deliberate challenge to her own reputation as a person of peerless paranormal powers. She replied, with an icy edge to her voice: "I myself knew that I was going to speak to you on the telephone this morning *several hours* before I actually did."

"But that's because you decided to phone me," Dilip said.

She was unmoved by this argument. "And," she continued, her voice becoming increasingly severe, "out of all the four million people in this city, I knew that it would be you who would pick up the phone."

"Madame Xu. The other three million, nine hundred and ninety-nine thousand inhabitants of this blessed conurbation do not share my telephone—although sometimes I feel they do," he said, thinking back to the days before his younger daughter's wedding four months earlier.

"Are you making light of my well-documented paranormal abilities, Mr. Sinha?"

"Certainly not, Madam Xu. I am second to none in the fervency of my admiration for your celebrated powers, which I believe can only be accurately described by the use of words such as 'legendary.'"

"Mmm," she said, somewhat mollified.

"I was once told by my father that I picked up a ringing telephone at the age of fifteen months and said 'Hello Mama' even though there was no way of knowing who was calling. There were no little screens or caller-ID services in those days. I was very proud of this story and repeated it to many people over the years as proof of the early manifestation of my psychic powers. However, I stopped using this anecdote after I had my own first child. That was when I realized that 'Hello Mama' is what all fifteen-month-old children say. It is more or less the sum total of their vocabulary. These days I am only impressed if a baby points to a ringing telephone and says something like, 'A man named Terence L. Gunasekera is calling in an attempt to sell you shares in a vacuum cleaner company.'"

"Very amusing, D.K."

Pleasantries over, there was a brief silence as Dilip Sinha waited for her to continue. She said nothing.

"Always good to hear from you," he proceeded. "Even on a delightfully sunny Monday as this, you add a special touch of brightness to the day."

"Yes."

"Nice to have a chat."

"Yes."

Another silence.

Since she seemed to be waiting for him to continue, he asked: "Now what exactly did you wish to speak to me about, Madame Xu?"

"You've got this all wrong," she said. "I think it must be your age. I think you must be getting a bit Celine or something."

"Celine?"

"You know. Celine. When your mind goes."

"Clearly a fashionable new phrase which I have not yet encountered, or which has passed me by entirely. Anyway, proceed. What have I done wrong to deserve the accusation that I have become, as you so interestingly put it, Celine?"

"Well, you know. You are asking me what I have to speak to you about. In fact, you have something to talk to me about."

"I do? And what might that be?"

"Well I don't know. How would I know that? I am not a mind reader, Dilip Sinha. Or at least I haven't been for at least five years, except when any of my ex-husbands come round."

As a practitioner of many Ayervedic sciences and various types of Indian astrology, Dilip Sinha was used to dealing with irrational and even deeply disturbed people. But for some reason, he was finding it particularly difficult to follow Madame Xu's train of thought today.

"Let's start at the beginning," he said with the voice of a patient schoolteacher. "You phoned me. That is where this discussion started, is it not?" Surely she could not disagree with that?

"I disagree. It all started when an image of you intruded

itself into my mind much earlier this morning, while I was preparing myself for the day. I was not even properly dressed! I knew you wanted to talk to me about something, but what it was, I couldn't begin to guess. So I replied to your summons by phoning your number. I am relying on you to tell me."

"Ahh," said Sinha. "Now I understand. So neither of us knows what I want to talk with you about. That does make this conversation rather difficult."

There was another silence on the phone, but it was not a particularly uncomfortable one—the two had been friends for long enough to be able to spend time thinking silently while aurally linked to each other.

"But I have an idea," said Madam Xu. "I'm expecting a visitor today, but I've got a gap in my timetable tomorrow morning. Why don't I just pop into your flat for a cup of tea, say ten o'clock? By that time, you may have remembered what it was that you wanted to tell me."

"That sounds like a perfectly splendid idea. I'll have the kettle on. Darjeeling?"

"Of course. Afterward, we could take the bus to Fort Canning, and have a walk, like we did last week."

Dilip Sinha smiled as he put the phone down. She probably just needed a bit of company. At his age, he found the attention flattering—after all, he was sixty-two and she was just a spring chicken, somewhere in her mid-fifties. He went to the kitchen to make some tea for himself and settle to work on a knotty problem that had arrived on his lap earlier that day.

Sinha had nominally retired. But these days he found himself busier than ever. Now that he was no longer a Singapore civil servant, his hobbies had grown into a full and active second career. His first book, published four years earlier, had given him some fame among Singapore's large Indian community. Although he was ostensibly a specialist in Indian astrology, the book had been filled with tidbits on other philosophies, ranging from Ayervedic medicines to the importance of using ghee instead of butter when cooking curries. His second book, published a year ago, had been "positioned" by the publisher as *A Guide to New Age Secrets From India*, and had sold well to several of the communities in Singapore, being particularly popular among women from the United States. The initial excitement of that book launch culminated in Sinha's finding himself profiled in *The Straits Times* and being invited to give a talk at a Rotary Club.

He then found himself besieged by parents of Indian origin wanting advice on getting their children married off to the "right sort of people," a topic touched upon briefly in the last chapter of the book. This tiresome business came to a spectacular end when his own daughter jilted the pitifully dull Punjabi import-export man her parents had chosen for her, and married an up-and-coming Chinese veejay. Sinha had initially been angry, but was delighted by the subsequent event—his reputation as a marriage expert collapsed. He found himself happy enough to pay for the rebel daughter's wedding to her spiky-haired beau.

Since then, things had quieted down. But he still found himself consulted at regular intervals by people wanting insight into their destinies.

Yet the most curious request he had had for months had arrived that morning. A man named Amran Ismail had called him at eight that morning, and requested an urgent meeting. The man spoke politely with a curious accent—a mixture of east and west Malaysian English, sprinkled with Malay and Chinese slang. But he sounded intelligent and sincere. As Sinha moved the conversation around to detailing his consultancy fees, the man had explained that he, too, was a mystic, and wanted a no-fees exchange on professional grounds. Sinha had agreed to this.

Amran Ismail had turned up on the doorstep less than an hour later, and Sinha and he had sat down to a breakfast of freshly baked bread, homemade fig jam and fruit, liberally washed down with blackish oolong. The visitor was a tall man in his mid-thirties from East Malaysia. He had espresso skin, dark and rather pockmarked from an excess of chili oil, Sinha reckoned. His thick jet hair was slicked back with something like Brylcreem. High eyes and a flat nose suggested he had mixed Malay and Chinese blood. He had a stockiness about his shoulders which suggested great strength. He wore Western clothes, somewhat rumpled and without a tie, and carried a small black briefcase. Yet for all the power of his physique, he walked stiffly and with a slight stoop, like someone who regularly slept in a bed too small. He wore a goatee beard and had a small, oval hat on his head.

After they swapped small talk and started on the breakfast, it had been Sinha who turned the discussion to matters of work. "You said you too were a mystic of sorts?"

Ismail noisily swallowed a large piece of bread and then wiped his mouth with his hand before replying. "Am," he said, putting his head on one side. "I am a *bomoh*."

"Really? How interesting."

Ismail tilted his head. "I know what you are thinking. Cannot blame you-lah. Don't look like a *bomoh*. Don't speak like a *bomoh*. How can I be real thing?"

The old Indian astrologer raised his bushy white eyebrows and smiled. "People come in all shapes and sizes. But I admit, you are right. You don't look like the other *bomohs* I have seen."

"*Bomohs* are funny things, aren't they?" Ismail spluttered

with his mouth full. "Witch doctors. *Chee-sin* old men and women. Some, they dress in strange garments, so *cacat*. They have things around their necks—necklaces, icons, pendants, amulets. Bones. Bones they love. Bones of fish, bones of animals, bones of people. Not me. I prefer accessories from Dunhill shop in Orchard Road, ties by Hermes, nice cufflinks, like that."

"You are not the only one who doesn't wear bones. I have seen conservative *bomohs*."

"Of course-lah. In Kuala Lumpur sometimes you see. Now K. L. is all full of Ah Beng types, yummies or what is it? But even in K. L., working *bomohs* still are mostly old and crazy. Never they are young men in smart-smart business suit. Like me."

"I cannot disagree with you there."

Ismail leaned back in his chair, having apparently achieved satiety after eating an enormous amount of bread—at least a loaf, Sinha calculated.

Then the visitor thrust his cup out. "Give me one more tea and then I tell you a story, very interesting, very amazing, very *shiok*," he said. "One time I was dead."

Between slurps, Ismail explained how he had been a wild young man, and spent most of his youth screeching around a small town in Sabah on a moped. His father had worked as a log cutter and his mother was a canteen cook for the timber company for which her husband worked. He had three younger siblings: Nizam, twenty-six, Musa, seventeen, and Zahra, thirteen. "My poor, sweet, sick Zahra," he had said with a sad smile, clearly having a soft spot for his sister.

Ismail left school at eleven and worked as a laborer in Sarawak, but in his early twenties had decided to go back to his studies and learn a profession. He did well at night school back in Sabah and was soon on a course that would lead him to an accountancy qualification. At the age of twenty-five, he raised enough cash to buy a secondhand Japanese motorbike; he had been thrilled at the speed and freedom it gave him and the friends who clutched his waist as he turned corners at angles of forty-five degrees.

The joy had lasted exactly one week. Seven days after he had bought the bike, his father's logging truck pulled out in front of him and he had driven straight into it at seventy miles an hour, a girlfriend holding on to his waist. The bike had been destroyed instantly. And so had its driver and his passenger, according to the first witnesses on the scene. The twenty-two-year-old woman, who had flown over his head and hit the truck's cabin headfirst, was declared dead on arrival at the hospital.

Amran Ismail had been thrown into the tarpaulin sheet covering the logs the truck had been carrying. His heart had stopped beating, but a passing teacher who had learned cardiac pulmonary resuscitation on a first-aid course six days earlier had managed to restart it. Ismail had been sent into intensive care, where he stayed for ten days. He was then moved to a general ward for six weeks, after which he was sent home to his parents. There was talk of amputating his right leg.

His father wanted to hire nurses to look after him, but his mother had had different ideas. A woman of great religious conviction, she arranged for a local female *bomoh* to take charge of his recovery.

"It turns out to be very brilliant idea," said Ismail. "Old witch doctor-auntie she knows more about medicine than all the useless young *goondu* doctors and nurses that come out of Malaysian schools. She didn't have to go again-again-again to the clinic for buying pills, powders, medicine, all like that. When I had pain in my bad leg or my head, she would go into the forest and come out with some leaves that worked better than any doctor rubbish.

"My *mak* gave the *bomoh* a little bit of money and she look after me for six months over. My *pak* thought she was *chee-sin*. At first I was very much not happy. In the early days, when doctors tol' me maybe I cannot walk after, I want to die, I think all finish with me-lah. I told my *mak*: Do'wan' be a cripple. Let Allah take me now. The *bomoh,* so many potion she gave me. But I would not take. *Nothing* I would take. That stuff all *pantang*. Not believing in superstitious rubbish, you know."

His head slowly revolved to one side and then the other on his thick, mottled neck. "But the pain in my leg—very, very bad. Cannot even tell you! Sometimes I was all wet, turning around and around on the bed, feeling my life all draining away, like water down a drain, you know?"

Sinha nodded sympathetically. "I can imagine."

"So one day I decide, okay, I take. The *bomoh* potions. I feel better already. Wonderful dreams, it gave me. In the dreams can walk, even I can fly. And you know what happen? Do you know?"

"Er, you got better?"

Ismail looked reverently at a dirty string bracelet on his left wrist and then tapped his thigh. "Allahu Akbar, she pour the life back into my dead leg."

After six months, he had no interest in going back to his old life as a student of chartered public accountancy. "Now I wanted to be a *bomoh*. My *pak* was horrified, but my *mak*—like in most Malaysian families, she was real big boss—she like the idea. So I became new sort of *bomoh*."

His chest swelled out with pride. Clearly, he was reaching the climax of an oft-told tale.

"Six months more I spend training, reading, visiting other

bomohs in East Malaysia, like that. Then I set up *bomoh* office in Penang, small, just me, I everything one leg kick. I think I am first hi-tech *bomoh*. All usual *bomoh* skills I got: know which spells, which potions, which incense, which books to use. But my appointments I got by mobile phone." He tapped the Ericsson swinging from his belt.

"Web site, my own home page also got." He pulled out a business card and pointed to some tiny print on it. "My invoices are attachment to E-mails. Even you can E-mail question to me and get reply in real time-lah. WAP phone even. You look skeptical. Any problem?"

Sinha blinked, his concentration suddenly interrupted. "Hmm? Oh no, not skeptical, not at all." In truth, the Indian astrologer's main reaction was to be astonished to have met someone who told longer and more involved anecdotes than he did. He buttered another slice of bread and spoke slowly. "I am not skeptical. But I am surprised at the conclusion of your story. Surely the type of people who use *bomohs* wouldn't have E-mail addresses?"

Ismail gave a broad grin. "Of course-lah. Everybody think like that. But that make me one big hit. *Bomohs* belong to the poor, the working class, the people in shacks and villages in the jungles? Those old things are taken seriously by old people in old kampongs only, right? Fine for grandmother, but not for grandson, right?"

Sinha did not know whether the correct answer to this question was "right" or "wrong," so said nothing—which was the right response, since the question had been rhetorical.

The visitor continued: "Everybody think this. The truth much different. Many middle-class Malaysians have same beliefs as their grandfathers. Deep down everyone same-same. Also foreigners I had consulting me. Even they put me in new age bookshop." He raised his empty cup as if to toast himself. "I am a new age mystic-lah."

"I know the feeling," said Sinha, whose large breakfast had left him feeling in need of a mid-morning nap. He stifled a yawn. "It does seem to be that you have found a niche to claim as your very own." He raised his own cup to share the toast. "But tell me, what brings you here? What did you want to see me about?"

Ismail thumped the vessel on to the table and leaned forward. He put both elbows on the rattan placemat and looked down, suddenly serious.

"To thank Allah for giving me a new life, all my spare time I devote to make home for orphans. Small-to-medium only. Eighteen children I have, age eight to twenty. Before they were street boys. I pay for two nurses look after them. I get sponsor money from businesses, from the mosque, to buy rice, daal, *mee*. Hotels give me old food, old sheets, leftovers, like that. My sister Zahra, she is very sick. *Pak* and *mak* cannot look after her. I look after her, special nurse got for her only."

Sinha noticed that the speaker was wringing his large hands together as he spoke. Evidently he was under stress.

"Are you looking for financial . . . er . . . ?"

"Money I don't want. Professional advice only." Ismail slumped further forward and studied his hands, suddenly deeply serious. "I wan' give you to see a case which I think very amazing. Case of a young person at my home with big problem—bad fortune in her stars. Very bad, *soay* only. I don't know what to do. Expert advice myself I need on this matter."

"Of course, I'll be more than glad to review the case myself. I'm sure there will be occasions in the future when you can render me the same service—we all get stuck, sometimes. Would you like me to meet her, or examine her records? Is it your sister?"

"Thank you. You are very kind. You are a gentleman like people said. I am very, very thankful for you giving positive answer in this matter. But is not my sister. Client only. One more thing I mus' tell you. On this matter, I wan' cast-iron promise of confidentiality."

"Of course. All my cases, naturally, are confidential."

"No. Need specific promise for this case only. Here got—" He opened a briefcase and took out a plastic bag. There was something wet inside.

Sinha was surprised to see that it was a dead chicken.

"We use these things a lot," said Ismail. "Is the way of the school of *bomohs* I belong. Sorry about this. I know is a bit messy, but . . ."

He took the chicken out, and Sinha was distressed to see blood dripping from its neck on to his placemats.

"*Sei-lah!* Sorry," Ismail repeated. "Twitching a bit but is dead, more or less. I kill it on the doorstep just before I came in. Blood must be fresh, you see, when you make serious vows."

Sinha watched his Malaysian visitor close his eyes and start to enter a trance-like state to prepare the chicken for the ritual, and was surprised to discover that the man was silently weeping.

Two hours later, a gently reverberating doorbell rang in a flat in a well-maintained block in Chinatown's Sago Street.

The door was opened by a Chinese woman wearing so much jewelry that it sounded as if someone was wheeling a rack of bangles across the floor of a department store. "Come in, come in," she said. "You must be Mr. Ismail."

"Yes. And you are Madame Xu," the visitor replied. "Very nice to meet you. I am Amran Ismail, your servant."

Madame Xu's broad smile disappeared instantly as she noticed that her visitor was carrying a plastic bag in which something was jerking violently.

"What's that?" she asked. "Your lunch?"

He glanced down at the bag in his hand as if noticing it for the first time. "Yes," he replied. "Later, *inshallah*. A chicken. I get through a big number of chickens."

"Reminds me of Hong Kong," she said with distaste. "Dreadful place. Everyone comes out of the markets with their shopping bags twitching. Everything is sold alive in Hong Kong. Why don't you give your bag to the maid— she'll keep it in the kitchen for you—and then come and sit down and have a nice cup of tea. Darjeeling?"

"Yes, yes, very kind," said Mr. Ismail. "But first, I wan' use your toilet. Already today I drink one gallon of tea over."

He returned to the main room of the apartment a few minutes later to find Madame Xu in a room designed in a surprisingly austere manner for an owner so obviously enamoured of fussy accessories. The floor was dark brown parquet, unsoftened by either carpet or rug, and the furniture consisted of a black leather sofa set and an altar table and cabinet in old-fashioned Chinese rosewood design, with inlaid fittings in a matt-gray metal. There was no television set, but a set of shelves in matching rosewood contained several dozen tiny photographs in non-matching frames.

They swapped small talk for five minutes, before Ismail gave her an introduction to his background as a *bomoh*. Then, after another round of tea, he grandly announced that it was time to explain his mission. He became increasingly serious as he told Madame Xu the same story that he had recently shared with Dilip Sinha.

"All details one hundred percent confidential must keep," he said.

"Why naturally," replied Madame Xu. "Since you haven't told me anything about the client or the case, I can hardly broadcast it to the world."

"No, but I will reveal shocking details to you now. Top *top* secret, understand or not?"

"Yes, yes, yes," replied the fortune-teller impatiently.

"In my school of *bomohs*, need spilling of blood to make vow. For this reason I bring chicken only. First, I go into kitchen and get it."

"No need, no need," said Madame Xu. "I'll get the girl to bring it." She reached for a bell from a side table and rang it energetically. Then she shouted in an extraordinarily loud voice for a woman so petite: "Concepcion! Bring the visitor's chicken."

"Yes, Ma'am," came a shrieked reply.

Ismail waited tensely, suddenly uncomfortable without his chicken. It was clear that he was unwilling to say what he had to say without it. Vows had to be taken with full formalities.

They chatted further on topics of general interest, and then the visitor took pains to again impress on Madame Xu the seriousness of keeping details of the case he was about to reveal to her completely to herself. While speaking, he kept turning around and craning his neck to see if his fowl was being brought to him.

"Why not I just go and get it?" he said.

"It's coming now," said his host. "Concepcion? Where are you?" she screamed.

Two minutes later, a sullen pudding of a domestic helper plodded down the corridor, clutching a large platter containing the bird—roasted, drenched in soy sauce, sprinkled with garlic slices, and surrounded by pandan leaves. "Is ready, Ma'am," she said.

"Oh," said Amran Ismail. "You cook it?"

"Microwaves," said Madame Xu. "We bought one a month ago. Six hundred and fifty watts. Now Concepcion can do a small chicken in eleven minutes. Twenty-nine if you press 'Dual cook.'"

"Er, thank you." The *bomoh* took the dish from the servant's hands. "What to do," he mumbled, his thick brows knotted. He rather awkwardly performed his ritual with the dish of roasted chicken, sprinkling pungent warm gravy on his hands and the hands of his hostess.

Madame Xu politely accepted the gravy splashes on her hands but quickly wiped them away with paper tissues. Her real handkerchief, which was made of perfumed silk, she retained purely for the purposes of patting her face from time to time.

"Would you like Concepcion to carve it for you?"

"Er, no. Later I eat."

"Okay, dear boy. Tell me about your client with the big problem."

"Yes," he said. "It's time. I am running an orphanage just outside Kuala Lumpur, praise be to Allah for allowing me grace to do this. Mostly I help runaway kids—teenage boys. Girls also I help. Send to cousin-sister's house. She is a religious. Boys I hang out on streets very late to find. One night, there was big fight in a bar in K. L. Two men fighting over one woman, lost, no money, no family, no friends, no contacts, just *pokai*. I pick up both men, skinny *koochi* rats both, throw them out. *Kacang putih-lah*. Can do with my eyes close." He smiled at the memory. "I did not take the girl to my cousin-sister's house. The men—bloody *lembus*—maybe they find her there. So I hide her. Something tells me Allah has sent me to help her. She was Chinese. Her features were small. Not so beautiful maybe. A little bit only. Skinny, *papan*. But she had a big spirit. Very not shy, you know? Had big fire."

"That is what they used to say about me," Madame Xu said dreamily. " 'A certain fire about her.' A few years ago. Now tell me, who was she? How did she come to be lost in Kuala Lumpur? Was she a girl from the countryside?"

"This also I thought. But not so. I realize she is not local. Her skin was whitish yellow and her languages were English and Cantonese. Also I can speak. She is from Hong Kong. What for she is in Malaysia? She says she is on holiday. She says she is tourist. But she was not so good at telling lies. What tourist girl end up *pokai* in bar in K. L.? No. I tell her, what you think, I am bloody fool? I can guess. She was someone guilty of great crime in Hong Kong. She was hiding in Malaysia. She was . . . *on the run*." He weighted his words with melodrama enough for a Hindi movie.

"What was her name?" the fortune-teller asked suddenly.

"Clara."

She made a note in a diary. "A lovely name. Very literary."

"She stay in my boys' home outside K. L. for eight days over."

"Boys' home?"

"Sure. Hiding. Who will look for girl in religious boys' home? I put her in *baju kurung*. Big *kudung* over her head. People think she is staff, cook. Only then I had idea of looking at her birth charts. You see, she was one of my rescued orphan, not one of my client."

He suddenly stooped to the ground and pulled a messy pile of papers from his ragged bag. "But then I decide to do the cards anyway. One afternoon I read her fortune with the cards, with the bones, with the symbols, with the fire method, with the birds, with every method. I look at the lines on her hands. I look at her face. I look at the lines on the soles of her feet. I look at the color in her eyes. I look at the stripes on her fingernails."

He held up a piece of paper that turned out to be a photocopied image of a small hand.

"Results so shocking. First test say she will disappear. Death coming quick-quick. Second the same. Third saw bad, bad luck coming very soon also. You know how messages come by in this business, Madame Xu? Little hints, small-small hunches. This point a little this way, that point a little that way, you interpret this, you interpret that, stick it together, eventually you decide-ah? But this one is totally gone case."

"I've had cases like that," said Madame Xu, who hated to be bested by anyone. "People facing imminent death. Loads and loads of them. Half my clients."

He ignored her interjection. "Six days ago, I take her to old man who lives in small-small hilltop village south of Melaka: a very, very great man, with very, very great power. He is called Datuk Adzil Abu Hitam Noor. But the *bomohs* call him only the Great Bomoh. 'Usually people ask me to tell their fortunes,' the old man said. 'This woman no fortune. She will die on first moon, which will be in ten days. At tenth hour of the day.'"

Madame Xu stirred uncomfortably. "This all happened recently?" she asked.

Ismail nodded. "Six days ago I took her to the Great Bomoh. After, I got some big problems-lah. I tol' her everything. I did it because I want her to be careful. To stay with me. To stay away from danger."

"Let me guess: Clara ran away."

"Yes. *Teruk!* One day after already she *cabut*. She left a note. It says that if she is going to die, she is going to die happy only. She came to Singapore to stay with family member here. I came too. To find her."

"And did you?"

"Sure," he said proudly. "I found her. She is living quietly with auntie or something. I am staying in small-small hotel near. I visit her. I tol' her I was wrong. She is not going to die. All a mistake only."

"But this is not true."

He gave a deep sigh, expelling air that appeared to be filled with pain, and sat back in his chair. "Yes. I *goreng* only, bluff her, cheating. Probably she knows. If the Great Bomoh is correct, she will die very soon. On four days. At tenth hour."

"But you cannot make predictions with such accuracy, surely? Even I cannot, and I am famous for my psychic powers. Why only today someone described my powers as 'legendary.'"

"I cannot. But the Great Bomoh . . . and all other evidence—you must look at evidence, Madame Xu. This case very special." He sounded desperate and his voice had acquired a tremor. His head had shrunk into his shoulders. His story appeared to have terrified himself.

Silence descended as the two inhabitants of the room contemplated the facts. A green parakeet in the corner of the room, surprised by the sudden peacefulness, filled it with a squawk.

"Two things I want you give me," said Ismail.

"Please ask."

He thrust the papers at her. "I give you see her papers. Got print of her palms, her feet, birth charts, all my research material, like that. Got photograph of her. I wan' you look at everything, tell me I am right or wrong. Want you to use your own method. If you find out I'm all wrong, I will be happiest man in the world."

"And if you are right?"

He swallowed. "If I'm right, you must find a remedy

please, quickly. Must find a way to reverse her fortune. I come to you because I need to work with best people in our business only. I do'wan' her to die. She is only nineteen years old."

From the pile of papers he was offering her, Madame Xu picked up the print of a tiny female hand. She lifted it to her face and put on her reading glasses. Her eyes widened immediately. "It is extraordinary," she said. "The lifeline. It is so short. And it just stops."

Amran Ismail nodded. His eyes were wet and it looked as if he did not trust himself to speak.

"I don't really like doing readings from prints," she continued. "I would much rather meet Clara in the flesh."

"Maybe also can. Later." He spoke in a whisper.

"Hmmf." The fortune-teller switched spectacles and then held the print very close to her face. "Well, you know as well as I do, Mr. Ismail, palm readers almost never give a precise date of death by looking at the lines on a hand. It simply isn't done. It *cannot* be done. For technical and scientific reasons. And you probably also know that the lines on the hands change as people get older. Especially since this hand-print is one of a child of nineteen."

"Yah. Continue."

"Nevertheless . . . there is definitely trouble here. I see what you mean. Goodness me." She stared at the print in front of her with astonishment. "This is really amazing. I can see why you are worried. All three of the major lines are remarkably short. They all fade into little wispy endings long before they should. This is quite amazing."

The *bomoh* nodded slowly.

"She has no rascettes," the fortune-teller continued.

"I don't know this word. We do different type of palm reading in Sabah."

"Naturally you would. But mine is the classical system which has been used for centuries. The rest of you are entitled to your own systems, even if they are wrong. Now rascettes—you better write this down—is the technical term for the rings at the point where the wrist joins the hand. On the inner wrist. Each of these is supposed to indicate thirty years of life. Your client has virtually no rascettes. I have never seen anyone without rascettes before."

She lowered the piece of paper. "I'll take the case. It will take me several hours to do the job properly. And I really would like to meet the young lady in question. It is a very serious and disturbing case and I would like to help if I can. This will need a lot of expertise to resolve in a happy way. I can't guarantee that it is even possible."

Amran Ismail nodded again.

Madame Xu looked at his pained expression. "I am a good judge of people, Mr. Ismail," she said. "And I know that most of what you have told me is true."

He moved awkwardly, clearly uncomfortable under her gaze. "You mean what?"

"Most of what you have said is true. But you have left out one fact. One very important fact."

He said nothing.

She continued: "You desperately want to save this girl's life because she is one of the teenagers in your children's home, and has become your most interesting client. But there's another reason."

Amran Ismail stared at her but said nothing.

"You are in love with her," said Madame Xu.

The *bomoh* sniffed. His face crumpled up and his chin fell to his chest. His goatee trembled. He burst into tears.

"Yes," he said, in a tiny voice. "Yes, I am-lah."

The loud and tremulous wail that burst from the huge

man's throat shocked the parrot into silence and distracted Concepcion from her task of cleaning her beloved new microwave oven.

❖

C. F. Wong blinked at the doorway, which was lit in such a way that it was simultaneously painfully bright and far too dark to see anything. Clearly a miracle of modern engineering. Then he looked again at the small piece of paper in his hand. "Dan T.'s Inferno," it said. "Mohamed Sultan Road." He glared again at the neon sign over the doorway. There were flames around a mishmash of letters in an indecipherable font, but he could vaguely make out a "d" and a "t." This had to be it. But where was Joyce McQuinnie? He scanned the scene but could not see her anywhere. But then he *was* a long way away.

The geomancer was peering suspiciously at the nightclub from a safe distance on the other side of the road. The place was not just unwelcoming, but positively frightening. Not only did the harsh glare of the doorway force onlookers to squint but the entrance emitted deep, fearsome sounds that left him with serious concern for the safety of his eardrums. Who would want to approach such a forbidding scene? The whole building seemed to throb with low thuds that literally shook the ground—he could feel the movement from where he stood, a good sixteen yards away. He couldn't hear any music as such; just the relentless thump-thump-thump of a disco beat, the stuttering background sound that had become ubiquitous on television and in shops. At this intensity, it was like the heartbeat of a panicking buried monster.

Although he felt physically repelled by the scene, the geomancer noticed that it had the opposite effect on young people: there was a line of them outside the doorway and it steadily grew longer as he watched. The individuals lining up to enter were garishly dressed. One young—*creature* (he couldn't tell what sex it was)—was tottering slowly forward in the line on huge platform shoes, surmounted by stick-like legs, and a white-faced friend appeared to be dressed in an ankle-length robe like a monk from a black order. Behind them, a tall young person with pierced ears and a shaved head was laughing next to another creature of indeterminate sex wearing a gypsy scarf.

A flickering lamppost gave the street the look of an emergency scene. A slight breeze came from the east. There was a smell of frying fish in the air.

It was dark. He was tired and hungry. He wanted to go home.

There was a movement in the line that caught his eye. At the same time he heard his name being called: "C. F.! C. F.! Over here."

He scanned the line again. The creature with the stick-legs was waving at him. Could it be . . . ? Surely not. He narrowed his eyes, trying to focus on the figure. "C. F.! We're here," it said again.

It was his intern. He raised one hand in curt acknowledgment and set off across the road, his face grim, to join her.

"This is him, this is him," he heard her say to her friends as he approached.

The one wearing the robe said: "Cool. A real feng shooee man."

"Good evening," the feng shui master said.

"Hey!" said Joyce. "Thanks for coming?"

"Yo, Mr. Feng Shui Man?" said a small thing next to her who was apparently wearing only black undergarments.

Wong had read in *How's Tricks: Colloquial English II*

that sentences with rising tones signified questions in standard English, but he had long ago noticed that the majority of statements made by his young intern and her friends had rising tones.

"My familiars?" said Joyce. "Ling, Nike, Sammo, and Dibby?"

"Wotcher?" said a tall creature with short, vertical hair, nodding at Wong.

"Watch who?" Wong asked.

"No one," it replied, cheerfully. "Just wotcher?"

"I see," he said, not seeing.

As Joyce made perfunctory introductions, the line lurched forward about three feet.

"Dani's blown us off," she said. "Dani Mirpuri was gonna come?"

Wong was amazed to hear the name of a client. "Mrs. Mirpuri is coming?"

"Nah!" laughed Joyce. "Her daughter. Mrs. Mirpuri is *waaay* too old. She'd never get in."

"Oh," said Wong, who was considerably older than Mrs. Mirpuri.

" 'Scuse me, Mr. Wong. Which way should my bed point?" asked a creature behind him. "Should be east, right?"

"Well, I read that my bed should point north," said a thing next to it. "Which is right?"

"Yeah. Which is right?"

Wong looked from one over-made-up face to another. "Er . . ." He hated having to answer questions which treated his complex and arcane art as a list of rules. "East maybe is right for one person, north maybe is right for other person," he said. "Maybe both is right."

Joyce laughed again. "Ha! That doesn't solve their problem. They sleep in a bunk bed."

There was a general outbreak of giggling at this. Wong wasn't sure if they were laughing with him or at him, so he merely smiled nervously.

"Wot about married peeps?" said a tall thing with short spiky hair and dangly earrings. "They have to sleep in the same bed. What if the feng shui chart says they have to sleep in different directions?"

"Yeah?" said someone else.

"Sixty-nine," said the one in the undergarments.

This baffling reply caused the spiky-haired thing to howl with laughter and pretend to fall over clutching its stomach.

Wong did not know how to give any sort of answer other than a serious one. "Usually I tell married people to sleep with their heads to the north. From the north is winter. Also is sexuality."

"*Ooooh,*" giggled several creatures at this last word.

Wong shut his mouth tightly and looked away.

The line moved forward again and the group found themselves at the door.

The bouncer, a large man of Chinese origin wearing a badge that said "Commissionaire-in-Chief," peered at Wong with puzzlement. "Who's he?" he barked at Joyce, whom he apparently knew. The geomancer realized that he did not fit the image of the people who normally entered this club. He wondered whether he should retreat before he was humiliatingly refused entry.

"My banker," Joyce told him. "My ticket. My sugar daddy. He's loaded."

The bouncer looked Wong up and down. "Loaded?" he asked, suspiciously.

"Check out the clothes," said the young creature who had told Wong to watch someone. "Would he dress that slack if he wasn't?"

The bouncer looked at the feng shui man's shabby Chinese suit, threadbare shawl and well-worn shoes. He nodded. "Okay-okay," he said. He nodded his head sharply to one side, and barked to a Chinese woman with tea-colored hair at a table on the other side of the curtain: "In. Four."

As they entered the darkness, Wong turned with amazement to Joyce: "You tell him I am your father?"

"No," she laughed. "Sugar daddy. That's like a rich, old guy who likes to hang out with, er, younger people. We call 'em bankers or tickets."

"Complete bankers," said the small creature.

"When we're feeling polite," interjected spiky-head with a laugh.

"Ah," said Wong, thinking. "You mean—"

"*Haam-sup lo,*" put in the small creature in the underwear.

"I see," said the feng shui master again, shocked at being presented as a dirty old man.

He opened his mouth to ask a question, but at that moment they entered the main room of the nightclub and the loudest sounds he had ever heard caused him to clap his hands tightly to his ears as his eyes tried desperately to acclimatize themselves to an eerie, red-tinted darkness.

They threaded their way through packed, sweaty bodies. Wong desperately grabbed a scarf-like piece of material that hung from Joyce's shoulders so that he didn't lose her. His intern was so unrecognizable in her off-duty guise that he knew he would never locate her again in this place, even if he were standing next to her.

And the noise! How on earth could anyone think of this as a place to meet and chat with friends? "*Aiyeeaah,*" he said—or thought he said. The music was so loud that he couldn't hear the sounds coming out of his own mouth, let alone anyone else's. And surely music at this level would cause immediate and permanent deafness. How could these people stand it?

The noise momentarily took him back to an occasion when he was a teenager, helping his uncle unload shipments of rice from a tramp steamer at the docks in Guangzhou. He had been balancing precariously on the side of the ship, throwing sacks down to his uncle, when a cousin of his had mischievously sounded the ship's foghorn. The blast had been so loud that Wong had thought the world had ended. It had thrown him off balance, causing him to fall forward off the ship. He had landed half on his uncle and half on the pile of sacks beside him. The uncle cursed both young men, having cracked a rib. Wong had hurt his left hand, with which he had broken his fall, but had gone straight back to work to prevent his cousin getting into trouble. But that terrifying noise had been a single, deafening blast. In this bar, the noise was just as loud, yet it was continuous.

Suddenly he felt himself being manhandled into a small, dark room. The door shut behind them. The room was partially soundproofed, so it was suddenly possible to talk, although the thudding music outside continued to surge through the floor and walls.

"More quiet," he said. "Better."

"This is the karaoke room," said Joyce.

"We call it the snogging room," sniggered one of the creatures accompanying her.

"He won't know what that means," said another.

"Pashing," explained a third.

"Makin' out," translated a fourth.

"*Yee-yee yup-yup*," said a fifth.

"Oh," said Wong, none the wiser.

"But karaoke's *so* out these days. The room's good for like talking?" Joyce put in.

"Out there, you can hardly hear yourself fink," said someone.

"Yes," the feng shui master agreed.

"Wait here, please," Joyce continued. "I'll get him for you. Wanna drink?"

"Er, *ching cha*," said Wong. "*Bo leih.*"

Joyce looked nonplussed. "I don't think they have Chinese tea. I'll ask." She slipped out, a roar of drums surging into the room as she opened the door.

Wong slowly shook his head. How could a Chinese drinking venue full of Chinese customers in a Chinese city not have any tea? The new Singapore baffled and discomfited him.

The feng shui master had agreed to meet his intern at this bar because she said a denizen of the club scene had some useful information that would help Wong in one of his investigations. But what could any of these wild-eyed, androgynous young people have to do with his quiet world of offices and homes and floor plans? She fouled up his days often enough—why did she have to waste his evenings as well?

Joyce was thoughtful as she waited impatiently at the bar to order drinks. Although she was happy enough when she was spending time with the group of friends she had acquired in Singapore—all of whom were borrowed from her roommate Ling—Wong's presence in the nightclub had reminded her of how she spent most of her days feeling like an alien. She could achieve a reasonable degree of intimate communication within Ling's little teenage clique. But she knew that most of the people in the city that she was trying to call home were more like Wong: quiet, intense Chinese adults who drank absurdly watery tea, talked in incomprehensible *non sequiturs* and thought about business all the time.

Catching the bartender's eye, she barked out: "Do you have Chinese tea?"

"What? No," he shouted back.

She sighed. Sometimes it felt like everything here was a problem. But then she recalled that she had felt the same when she had lived in Hong Kong. She decided she was rootless—not just in Singapore, but on the planet as a whole.

Joyce assumed that her feeling of not being able to fit anywhere was a direct result of her having inherited the restless nature of her father, a property developer. Born in Brisbane, he had expanded his business to Sydney and then London, where he had married a regional television presenter from Nottingham. They had their first child, Molly, two years later. After another two-year gap, Joyce was born, first drawing breath at St. Luke's, London, a little under eighteen years ago. McQuinnie moved his wife and children to his home country to "Australianize" them.

"You want Long Island Iced Tea?" the bartender hollered. "That's tea."

"Is that like Chinese tea?"

"Yeah. A bit. Well, not really."

She chewed her thumbnail. What on earth should she order for her boss? What do old guys drink? She decided to ask the barman. "I wanna drink for an old guy. Chinese. But I think no alcohol."

The barman handed her a drinks list and she scanned the pages. She couldn't imagine Wong drinking beer, and didn't want to insult him by buying orange juice. She flipped to the cocktails page. *Between The Sheets? Orgasm?* She couldn't order drinks with names like that for her boss.

She had got the habit of hanging out in bars despite being underage from her time in Hong Kong, the first place where she had achieved a little independence. Her parents had divorced in Sydney when Joyce was nine. Her father won custody of Molly and Joyce—to the great surprise of lawyers and

Australian newspaper gossip columnists. The main reasons were that he told lies in court and their mother had not put up any sort of fight for them. She had decided that both girls were far more like their father than like her. She moved back to the UK and quickly found a new boyfriend, a producer who got her a job as a newsreader. Joyce and Molly had lived with their father for the next four years, mostly in New York.

Since the lawyers weren't looking, Martin McQuinnie was again never at home. Molly, on reaching the age of eighteen, had gone off to live with a boyfriend who worked in a five-star resort in Jamaica. Joyce had continued to follow her father around until he was persuaded that the constant moving was doing no good for her studies or her emotional stability. So he had sent her to live with an aunt of his in Hong Kong, which was reputed to have excellent international schools.

Asia had become her home. For a while, it had worked. Life at a school where each classmate had a different cultural background had been fun. There were plenty of young people as mixed up as she was. There was even a sociological term for them: Third Culture Kids. And she had quickly got into the habit of sneaking off to the bars of Lan Kwai Fong with friends who used makeup to make themselves look over eighteen.

But the time had passed too quickly. Now the exams were over and the good-bye parties were just memories. Suddenly she was out of the safe and cozy confines of the international school system and on the streets of the real world—and she felt more lost than ever.

Joyce had an idea. "Do you have *chendol?*" she asked.

The barman shook his head.

Wong wondered if the walls of the karaoke room were strong enough to prevent him suffering from permanent deafness. Suddenly the volume jumped as the door opened and Joyce reappeared.

"Sorry, no *ching cha*. I got you a virgin colada?"

He was alarmed at this. "No thank you. Not want bar girls."

"*No,*" she scolded. She put a tall drink surmounted with a cherry and a little umbrella into his hand. The glass was painfully cold and slippery and the contents smelt revoltingly sweet. He took a sip. It tasted like a dessert. The umbrella went up his nostril. He hurriedly put it down on a counter.

"The Iceman will be along in a minute." Joyce looked a little concerned. "C. F.," she said, slowly. "I have to tell you about something first."

The other young people stopped talking, suddenly aware that Joyce might be about to say something important.

"What?" Wong asked.

"It's a bit like hard to tune into what he is saying, know what I mean? He doesn't just, like, *say* things, you know, straight. He's a bit hard to understand?"

"Not like us," one of the creatures put in.

"No waaay," said another, shaking its head.

"Waaaay," said a third, nodding.

"Jammo Ice J. is a rap singer?" explained Joyce.

"Wrap sinner," Wong echoed, without comprehension.

"That means, like . . ." she trailed off, looking to her friends for inspiration.

"Like P. Diddy," said one of the creatures.

"He won't know P. Diddy," said another. "He's way too old. He'll only know *old* music."

"Oh yeah," said a creature. "Old music. Public Enemy? Grandmaster Flash?"

"I don't think he knows any of those groups," said Joyce. "He'll only know *really* old music."

"He doesn't know any of that stuff? That's amazing," said a creature, pity in its voice. "Run-DMC?"

One of the other young people had a stroke of inspiration. "A rap singer is like a poet."

"Yeah," said Joyce. "Like a poet."

"A poet," said Wong. "Like Po Chu-i?"

Joyce considered this for a moment. "Yeah," she decided at last. "Like Po Chu-i."

There was another stunning blast of sound as the door opened and a young man entered. He failed to shut the door behind him, which meant that his opening remarks were missed by everyone in the room. One of the creatures kicked the door shut, and the young man spoke again.

"Yo good peeps, is dis da guy?

"Dis da guy who is apple of ya eye?"

Wong stared. The man, who had forgotten to put his shirt on, was slowly throbbing. He apparently suffered from an extraordinarily powerful case of delirium tremens or St. Vitus' Dance. His shoulders moved up and down continuously. His head rocked back and forth. His hips swiveled from side to side, providing some counterpoint to the way his upper body was moving. The chains and bits of leather that draped his upper body swung from left to right and back again. He spoke in a gentle rhythm, his words keeping pace with the slick, feline current that was surging through his body.

"Is he sick?" Wong asked Joyce.

"As if," she whispered back, her eyes running over the young man's brown, muscular chest.

She made the introductions. "C. F., this is Jammo Ice J., rap singer. Jammo, this is C. F. Wong, feng shui master. Jammo's solo now, but he used to be the drummer in the Gropies?"

Wong wondered whether he should offer to shake the

entrant's hand. But as he moved forward, the young man raised his hand up in a gesture that appeared to ask him to halt where he was.

"Gimme five

"If you're alive,

"Slip me some skin

"If you're not too dim."

The feng shui master felt in his pocket for a five-dollar bill. Joyce realized what he was doing and grabbed his arm. "No," she hissed into his ear. "Not five dollars."

There was a slight impasse. Neither knew what to do next. Then Jammo shook Wong's hand.

"You like to do it the old style way;

"Dat's cool with me, if it makes your day."

"He's so cool," the geomancer heard one of the creatures say, its voice touched with awe.

"Totally," said another.

"Totally cool," added a third.

"*And* totally hot," agreed the fourth.

"I am Wong," said Wong. "You are . . . ?"

This was the cue for Jammo to go into one of his set pieces. He spun around on one foot, clapped his hands, and proclaimed:

"Da name is Jammo, da temperature's high.

"Ain't no one like me, for I am I.

"I'm da main man, let no one disagree,

"For only I have da real pedigree.

"I was born on da street, I raise' myself up,

"Climbin' da ladder to da very top.

"For da top of the pile is where I belong

"And getting up dair won't take very long,

"Cause I am da king and dair ain't no other,

"I won't make room for any other mother. Unh-unh."

He spun around again.

Joyce's creatures shrieked and clapped.

"Awesome," said one.

"Totally," agreed the others.

Wong was frozen to the spot. He didn't know what the young man was talking about. It had become clear that this visit had been a very bad idea. Nothing this young man could say could possibly impinge on any of his cases. He needed to escape, immediately.

Joyce, noting Wong's look of alarm, grabbed Jammo's arm. "Iceman, I want you to be serious for a moment. You know what you told me last night about the fire in that building on Orchard Road? Could you tell C. F. about it too, please?"

The young man looked at her.

"Jammo never say da same thing twice;

"You may not like it, but it's not very nice;

"I am da future, I cannot go back,

"I say what I say, and baby, dat's dat."

"You don't have to say it exactly like you said it last night. But just tell my boss the same story, please? Use any words you like."

Jammo thought for a moment. "Okay," he said.

"I was walkin' down da road jes' da other day,

"When somethin' kinda odd jes' happen my way.

"I saw a man walkin' out with a waving cat,

"Came strollin' out his shop, just like dat.

"He put it in his car and he drove right off,

"One hour later—"

Jammo paused, apparently unable to think of a rhyme for "off."

Then he snapped back into his speech:

"One hour later, out ran all da toffs,

"Coz da building, you see, it wuz on fire,

"Da flames dey rose up higher and higher.

"Was it because, I ask to myself,

"Da guy remove da cat from the shelf?"

He stopped and made a slinky flourish with his hands. The creatures applauded. Joyce looked at Wong. Wong did not move his head, but his eyes slowly moved to the right until they connected with Joyce's.

The young woman decided that she should interpret. "You see, C. F., what he is saying is this. He saw a guy coming out of a building with a waving cat. On Orchard Road. That means one of those feng shui cats, you know, gold ceramic with one paw in the air? And then, one hour later, the building catches fire. Maybe there was a connection?" She looked at him, her face open and hopeful.

Wong, to Joyce's obvious relief, appeared to take the suggestion seriously. His head tilted to one side—but just for a few seconds. Then he turned to face her: "Joyce, I tell you. Probably half the shops in Singapore have feng shui cat. New shops open, old shops close, every day. Every day, people bring feng shui cats into new shops or take them out of old shops. Every day there is a few fires somewhere in Singapore. Is nothing odd. Only coincidence."

"Oh," she said, disappointed. Her eyes fell. Suddenly she looked embarrassed and he noticed her cheeks redden. "I'm sorry. Are they really that common? I just thought—sorry, I think I just wasted your time. Never mind. Whatever. It's like nice to introduce you to my gang and like have a drink with you?"

"Yeah," said the gang in unison.

Wong involuntarily glanced down at his drink—which remained untouched on the counter beside him.

Jammo Ice J. was backing out.

"Time for me to go,

"It's da end of da show,

"So I'll say bye, and see ya nex' time,

"You come back and enjoy my witty rhymes."

There was another thundering blast of dance music as he opened the door and slipped out. Wong watched him with all the fascination of a biologist looking at a newly discovered species. Through the open door, he noticed that a young woman was staring at him, as if she had never seen anyone so strange or so old. She had streaked hair and a severely disapproving expression. She spun around and moved away. It made him feel uncomfortable. Truly, he was out of place in this bizarre, noisy world.

Joyce looked out of the doorway. "That girl was looking at you," she said to the geomancer. "I think you've pulled."

"Woowooo!" shrieked one of the creatures. "Who would have thought that Mr. Wong would be the first to pull tonight?"

"Pulled?" asked Wong.

"Clear the snoggin' room," said another creature.

Wong pushed the door shut.

"Don't tease him," Joyce ordered. "It's so mean."

She turned to her boss. "I hope it's been like interesting for you? Not many people your age, I mean like *grown-ups*, have hung out in Dan T.'s Inferno with rap singers? And everyone wants to meet Jammo Ice J. If he becomes famous you can tell all your friends you met him? They'll be ever so impressed, I promise."

"Hmm. I see what you mean," Wong said, his mind turning back to Jammo. "*Is* a poet. But not very much like Po Chu-i."

He raced for the door.

T
U
E
S
D
A
Y

NO SUCH THING AS GHOSTS

*T*HE WORLD *was melting into sweat. There was salt in his eyes. His hair was wet. And now he had entered his office to find that even the walls were perspiring. And something, somewhere, was ticking. From the corner of his eye he caught sight of a drip of condensation running from the picture rail down the spongy wallpaper to the floor. It was hot.*

"Stolen," explained Winnie Lim, without looking up from the gossip magazine she was reading.

The feng shui master, who was standing in the doorway, wondered for a moment what she was talking about—and then he glanced in the direction of the windows, where the air conditioner should have been. It was missing. Raw sunlight and furnace-like heat poured into the room from the missing pane where it had been. Not only had its absence turned his office into a sauna, but it had made the room unnaturally quiet without its brooding presence.

Joyce, who had entered the room a few steps behind her employer, wiped the sweat from her upper lip with her thumb and forefinger. "Geez," she said. "*Killer* heat. And what's with the water running down the walls? Leak upstairs?"

C. F. Wong was still looking at Winnie. "*Laang-hay-gei hai bindo?*"

She merely shrugged her shoulders without looking up, and turned the page of her magazine.

He repeated his question in English with a sterner tone of voice: "Air conditioner: where is it?"

"How do I know-lah?" Winnie said, irritated. "Stolen."

"When?"

She shrugged her shoulders again and looked at him crossly. "I come in, not here. This morning. Half hour ago, about."

"You call management? Police?"

"Too busy-lah! So much work, see?" She swept her hand over her desk to encompass the morning's mail—four unexciting envelopes and a small package, all of which appeared to have been issued by machine.

"Water on walls is humidity," Wong explained to Joyce. "Big problem in Singapore."

"Why doesn't the electricity short out?" Joyce asked, flipping on the light switch. There was a short, sharp fizzing noise as the overhead bulb flashed once and then went out.

"Because we do not turn the light on," he said, his eyes closed. Why did the gods hate him so?

"Oops. Sorry." The young woman, forgetting to flick the switch down again, walked over to the window to look for clues. Sticking her head out through the rusty hole in the window where the air conditioner had been, she looked down and gave a snort. "Hah! It's not been stolen. It's fallen out. It's down there. Look."

"*Aiyeeaah!* Very bad, very bad," said a worried Wong,

moving swiftly to her side at the window to have a look. He abruptly took her shoulders and pushed her to one side before putting his own head through the hole. He winced in real pain as he looked down. "Eeee," he squealed between almost-closed teeth. There was a distorted cube of metal on the concrete floor below. Pieces of twisted metal dangled out like ruptured organs. There was a blood-like puddle of dark liquid beneath the main casing. He breathed out noisily. "*Aiyeeaah*. Very bad."

"It's not so bad. It never worked particularly well. And so noisy. It'll be good to have a new one."

"No! Very bad that it falls down. Very illegal in Singapore for air conditioner to fall down. Big trouble. Jail, maybe." He turned his eyes to look at Winnie. "For relevant office manager."

Winnie ignored the implicit threat and pretended to busy herself with the envelopes on her desk. "Aiyeeaah," she said, staring at the letter she had just opened. "Someone write you letter in computer language. Cannot read-lah."

"Give to Joyce. She can read," said Wong, wiping the humidity from his desk with a tissue from Winnie's box.

"Sure," said Joyce. "Hand it over. But first I have to ask you a question. What does *aiyeeaah* mean?"

Winnie tilted her head to one side, thinking. There was silence for thirteen seconds. "Cannot translate. No word in English. Only in Chinese and Indian."

"So what is *aiyeeaah* in Indian?"

"*Aiyoh*," said the Singaporean girl.

"But what does it actually mean?"

"*Aiyoh* means *aiyeeaah*. *Aiyeeaah* means *aiyoh*."

"Thanks."

Winnie flung the letter in Joyce's direction with the grace

of a toddler doing ballet. It landed on a cabinet on the wrong side of the room, where it balanced for a moment before falling neatly into a wastepaper basket.

"I think leave it," said Wong. "Probably it belong there."

Joyce got out of her creaking seat and retrieved the letter. "Might be something important. You never know."

She looked at the single sheet of paper for a few seconds. "Nope. Gibberish."

"Not computer language?" asked Wong.

"Not any language. Computer garble. Or secret code perhaps," she added with a laugh.

She dropped the letter back into the bin, then threw herself ungracefully into her chair, where she sprawled back and fanned herself with an eighteenth-century Chinese molding she had picked from a shelf behind Wong. "Can you *believe* this heat?" she said.

The geomancer opened his writing book but didn't feel creative in this furnace. The lack of white noise from the air conditioner meant that the roar of traffic outside seemed extraordinarily loud. And Joyce, no doubt, would turn on her headphone thing which made irritating *tsik-tsika-tsik-tsika-tsik* drumming noises. How could one even think in such conditions?

"I go tea shop," he said, snapping his journal shut.

"I go HMV," Joyce said, imitating her boss's low, staccato voice.

"I go home," chanced Winnie.

"No!" snapped Wong to his administrator. "Phone someone. Get new air conditioner. Get old one taken away. Quick. Before police come. *Aiyeeaah.*"

Winnie glared at him.

Joyce followed him through the door.

The feng shui master was moving quickly toward the staircase, but stopped suddenly on the top step. Something half-remembered had momentarily halted him. But the memory of the ticking he had heard when he had first stepped into the room had gradually sunk from his conscious mind to his subconscious. He gave his head a quick shake to clear it, and then trotted quickly down the stairs. The offices were set away from the main traffic of the nearby financial district, but the continuous sound of traffic still filled the air with a rushing noise like a distant sea. The feng shui master stepped into the sun, blinking, and strode quickly to get into a patch of shade. It was equally hot outside, but somehow the heat was more bearable than it was in the office. The intern hurried after him. They had barely walked two dozen meters when they were stopped by a screech.

"Wooooong," came a high-pitched voice.

C. F. Wong spun to look behind him. He saw only Joyce, but the voice hadn't been hers.

"Wooooong," came a shriek again.

"It's Winnie," said Joyce, indicating the window above them by tipping her head back.

The geomancer lifted his eyes to see his office administrator leaning out of their fourth-floor window.

"The phone! Calling. Important," she screamed.

"You get it," he shouted, walking back until he was standing directly under her.

"You say what?"

"Get it for me."

"Okay. You wait," said Winnie, and disappeared.

Wong and McQuinnie stood on the pavement under the fourth-floor office window, looking up expectantly.

A few seconds later, Winnie reappeared—and threw a small object out of the window. The two people on the ground stepped aside as something small and dark fell to the ground and hit the pavement with a cracking sound. It bounced once, spun in the air for a second, and then fell into the gutter with a splintering sound.

"Oh dear," said Joyce, looking at the smashed office mobile phone.

"*Ji-seen*," said Wong, shaking his head. The feng shui master looked back up at Winnie. "Aiyeeah crazy woman you throw phone down, smash it, why? Expensive. Very much money, you don't know? You pay."

"Not me," screeched the woman. "You tell me get phone for you, I get it for you."

"I mean get *message* for me, not get phone."

"Next time you say what you mean-lah," she spat. "*Aiy-eeaah*."

"Who call?"

"Don't know." Her head disappeared inside and she pulled the window shut behind her.

Joyce dropped to one knee and picked up the phone. The main body was in one piece but the antenna had almost come off and two small pieces of the casing lay nearby. The LCD screen was cracked.

"Hello? Hello?" said a tiny voice. Amazingly, the phone was still working. "Must be Japanese," said Joyce, putting it to her ear. "Indestructible. Hi. You want C. F.? Hang on a tick. He's just here." She handed him the phone. The voice had seemed familiar, but she hadn't quite been able to place it.

He looked rather unnerved by the way a piece of the casing, almost detached, swung under the handset as he took it from her.

"Waai?"

Joyce wondered just what Winnie would have to do to lose her job—burn the office down, perhaps. The office administrator had made herself completely indispensable by dint of having spent four years creating a filing system that only she understood. No client file could be retrieved without her. Very little useful work could be done when she was away. Nor could she ever be replaced. It was a good trick, and one worth remembering, the young woman decided.

She looked over at Wong, hoping this would be news of an interesting new assignment. The work diary for the week was worryingly empty.

"You say what?" said Wong to the caller, switching into English.

He said nothing more for a minute or so, and then his face took on a very serious expression. "Kidnap? Very bad, very bad," he said, nodding slowly. *"Gung hai-la!"* he added. "Of course. We come right away. No?"

The feng shui master tended to hold handsets a few inches away from his ear, and the young woman could hear the voice of the caller, but not what she was saying.

"No?" said Wong. "Oh, tomorrow, okay. Morning, eight o'clock? No? Oh, haircut. Understand. Will come after one hour. No? Two to three hours? For purning. Oh, perming. Understand. After three hours. About lunchtime. Okay. Bye bye."

He lowered the phone. Joyce, who had more familiarity with such instruments than her employer, took it from his hand and pressed the end call button.

"I have important job to do," he said. "Girl is kidnap. Must find."

He walked off at a brisk pace toward Orchard Road.

"Where are we going?" asked Joyce, trotting behind him.

He turned around. "We? I thought you go to HMV?" he said, pronouncing the "V" as "wee."

"Naah. I was only joshing. If someone's been kidnapped, you're gonna need me, right?"

He didn't answer.

"So where are we going?" she repeated.

"Dim sum shop. Breakfast first."

"Isn't this rather urgent? Shouldn't we go and see the parents or something?"

"Mother busy today. Meet her tomorrow."

"Oh. Isn't that kinda strange?"

"Yes. Must eat and think." He quickened his pace as he raced down the road but failed to lose her.

Ten minutes later they had settled into their seats at the restaurant. The young woman turned up her nose at the menu. "It's all in Chinese."

"Very special place. Only for Chinese. Food very delicious," said Wong, licking his lips as he stabbed a dumpling from a basket of *har gow*.

"Do they have blueberry muffins?"

"Don't know. Ask."

Joyce waved to the waiter-*maître d'*, a fat man named Ooi, wearing a dirty vest and calf-length trousers. It wasn't difficult to catch his attention, since he was sitting reading a Chinese newspaper at a table less than a yard away from them.

The restaurant was tiny, and had been difficult to find. Wong had marched quickly down Telok Ayer Street, and then taken a succession of sharp turns that had led him into a dirty-looking alleyway somewhere off Amoy Street. He had finally come to a halt in front of the doorway of what seemed to be an inner-city residential building, with his assistant trailing twenty yards behind.

Wong had rung a doorbell. When they were let into the premises, Joyce saw that the restaurant was actually the living room of a tenement house. It appeared to be unlicensed, judging by the lack of any signage indicating that it was an authorized business. The geomancer had immediately been given several bamboo baskets of food—the proprietor obviously knew his tastes. But none of the greasy-looking dumplings enticed the young woman. The feng shui man was impatient to eat, but was evidently conscious that he should wait to see if his companion could find something she liked to eat. "You like *cha siu bau*? *Cha siu so?*" he had asked. *"Siu mai?"*

"I don't think so," she replied, giving him an apologetic wince.

Joyce dropped her chin into her hands. Another problem: A breakfast joint that didn't serve breakfast! What was she doing in this crazy place? Did her father know what he was doing sending her here? When she thought of him, her emotions wavered uncomfortably between anger and affection. She lived in a state of longing to see him—but spent much of her mental energy compiling lists of complaints to give him.

She recalled how her favorite teacher at Hong Kong Island International School, a kindly, stick-thin Welshman named Daffyd James, had told her father that she was an unexceptional achiever only because she had been disadvantaged by her unstable home life. "She's actually very bright. If you put a little time and attention to the matter of your daughter's progress, she could really thrive," Mr. James had told her father. "She needs a parent."

So Martin McQuinnie had hired one. He purchased a

week of the time of an educational consultant to visit his daughter and ask her questions about what she wanted to do. Since everything in Joyce's life had been transient, all ambition seemed pointless to her. She told the man—a retired university professor who was on the board of one of her father's companies—that she wanted to go out and do some practical work; grow trees or look after animals or something. Being a gardener greatly appealed to her.

Her father had agreed to give her a year off to taste the real world on condition that she applied to a good university. Her first choice of college was unwilling to give an unconditional place to a student with such a poor record. But it offered her a spot if she could submit one Grade A 10,000-word piece of completely original research on a topic from a list dreamed up in an idle moment by the dean. The final item was: "Feng Shui: Art, Science Or Quasi-Religion?" She chose it immediately, having become slightly acquainted with feng shui in Hong Kong.

On hearing this, her father recalled that one of his contractors in Singapore had a geomancer on retainer. A few strings were gently pulled. The feng shui diviner in question was given no choice in the matter. The retainer was increased slightly. Joyce found herself enrolled as an intern for the summer in the offices of C. F. Wong & Associates of Telok Ayer Street, Singapore.

Although she had been initially embarrassed to accept a post arranged by her father, she had found the assignments fascinating and Singapore fun—it was so much easier to be in a place where English was spoken than in Cantonese-dominated Hong Kong. And the jobs she had had, following C. F. Wong around factories and offices and homes, mostly of very rich people, proved far more interesting than her only previous experience of work: a school holiday internship doing filing in a tax consultant's office. At first, she had intended to stay at the feng shui consultancy for only the minimum time it would have taken to complete her essay project—and then spend the rest of her gap year traveling the world. She wanted to see Tibet and South America. But the job was turning out to be addictive. Her father had not realized that although Mr. Wong's principal retainer was paid by a property company, he had achieved a reputation as an expert at surveying other locations with negative "vibes": scenes of crime. From the moment Joyce spent an evening with the investigative advisory committee of the Union of Industrial Mystics and their police liaison officer, Superintendent Gilbert Tan, she was hooked.

While life in Singapore as assistant to a feng shui master was fun, there were little things that constantly threw her off balance. There were simply too many adjustments to be made. Without the protection provided by family apartments well stocked with servants, she found Singapore difficult. She didn't understand the customs. She couldn't eat the food. She often felt that she and her employer didn't speak the same language. The conventions were all wrong. And this was an obvious example: he seemed to have absolutely no idea that early-morning foods were meant to be different from lunch foods. Who in their right mind would eat dumplings and spicy fried noodles for breakfast?

She waved again at the man at the next table. He didn't get up but lowered his paper and raised his eyebrows to let Joyce know that she had his attention.

"Do you have any like *breakfasty* stuff? Like *eggs?*"

"*Har gow. Siu mai. Cha siu bau,*" said the man, pointing to the steaming baskets in front of her employer. The man pointed to his ear and opened his hand to show that he didn't understand English.

"No, I mean like real *breakfasty* stuff." She turned to Wong. "Can you tell him I want a blueberry muffin—and a cappuccino. Do they have cappuccino here?"

"Don't know. I think no. No cup of chino. Only Chinese tea. If you don't like dim sum, try fry noodles. Very good breakfast." He wrinkled his forehead, cross that she did not realize how privileged she was to be offered Ah-Ooi's exclusive cuisine.

"Oh pants." Joyce decided she would have breakfast later. "I'll wait. Never mind," she said to Ooi. She turned to her boss. "So someone's been kidnapped. That is like SO serious, isn't it? Shouldn't the mother call the police?"

"Cannot," mumbled Wong, struggling to deal with a prawn dumpling that had burst in his mouth and filled it with aromatic oil. "She think police do the kidnapping."

"Oh. Well, I suppose she shouldn't, then." The young woman was nonplussed for a moment. Then she looked up again. "But I thought Singapore police were pretty straight. The Superintendent. Gilbert Thing. They're all cleaner than clean, right?"

The feng shui master nodded, irritated at having to talk instead of eat. "Mother of kidnap victim very strange. I think you met her before. Mrs. Mirpuri."

"Dani's mother. Dani—you mean *Dani's* been kidnapped?" She was alarmed. "Danita Mirpuri?"

"Does she have any other daughter?"

"No."

"Then must be Danita Mirpuri."

"Geez. That's awful. She's my friend. Well, I've met her three or four times. She's really a friend of Nike's. She was supposed to come last night. Remember I told you that one of the gang hadn't turned up? To meet the Iceman? And she said she'd phone Nike on Sunday and she didn't. So she's like *really* missing. Geez. That's like *so* amazing. Wait till I tell the gang."

Wong, speaking in bursts between consuming large amounts of dim sum, explained that Mrs. Mirpuri believed her daughter had been snatched by persons unknown on her way home from a shopping trip on Sunday evening. A ransom note had been delivered to the family home the following morning. But the mother did not think the kidnapping was particularly serious. The crime may have been committed by a policeman friend of theirs, the mother had said. Danita had just announced her engagement and it might be some sort of jealousy problem.

"Gotcha," said Joyce, nodding sagely. "It's lurrve. That fits. If I know Dani Mirpuri."

"Lerv?" asked Wong, pausing with a chicken foot halfway to his mouth. "What means lerv?"

"Lurrve is a type of love. If you love your mum or your dog or *N'Sync, that's love. But if it's like so heavy, you know, a big deal, with like drama and, and, you know the sort of thing, you want to kill yourself or something—like something in a movie—then it's lurrve."

"I see."

Joyce smiled. "That is *so* Dani," she said. "I only met her a few times, but both times she went on and on about the guys who were after her. There was one guy called Roger. I remember that, because I remember telling her that I thought it was a dorky name. Can't remember what she said he did. And the other guy . . . there was a guy called Kinny she used to talk about. I think he was a policeman. Yes, that's right, the policeman."

Wong saw an opportunity to get a bit of peace and quiet so that he could enjoy his breakfast. "Idea," he said. "Why not this be your case? You can do main investigation. You know everybody. I can work on other case. House burning down case. Ridley Park. With Madame Xu."

"Really? Me do it? That would be like so cool."

"But you must be careful. Gather facts. Write down. Consider. Phone people."

Joyce was thrilled. "This has gotta be my case, if you think about it. I know all the suspects and the victim and everything. I bet I can work it out. A kidnapping! But this is like *so* incredible. Totally."

She pulled out the remains of the office cell phone and started dialing her friends, while Wong gratefully devoted himself to the meal. He angled his seat slightly to one side, so he would not have to look at her.

She had long, involved conversations with each of the members of her gang and several of their associates, making copious scribbled notes on pages of her Filofax. "He did what? And she's like . . . ? Yeah. Gotcha. When? But what was he like? No, not what he looked like. What was *he* like? Nice guy type, evil kidnapper type, you know, what?"

They left the restaurant after a while, and Joyce insisted on making a stop at Delifrance to have her own breakfast. Wong had an odd feeling that someone was watching them through the window—but when he turned to look, there was no one there.

As she wolfed down eggs and ham, she told her employer what she had learned. "There were basically three guys in Dani's life," she said. "Ram was a geeky Indian kid who his parents wanted her to marry. Quite rich. But he had a beard which turned her off. Real scratchy. She was also going with this policeman called Kinny Mak, who was like totally besotted with her, you know? Then there was this other guy called Charles Something who she met at a club and really hit it off with."

"Hit what off with?"

"Just *it*. It means, like, they were really in tune with each other."

"Karaoke?"

"No, they just met at Dan's. But Charles was like an investment banker or something like that. Pots of dosh. Or so he said. Nike reckons that she must've run off with him, because he was like the most exciting. But I dunno. If he had loadsa money, they wouldn't need to do any sort of kidnap-ransom scam, would they? I think it's more likely that she has run off with Kinny Mak. I mean, if he's a policeman, he wouldn't earn very much, so they would need to do some sort of scam to get some money out of her folks, right?"

"But a policeman would not do a kidnap, I think."

"Normally, yes. But what if it's lurrve? Lurrve makes people do strange things. That's why they call it lurrve."

Wong made a mental note to look that one up in his *Shorter Oxford* when he returned to the office.

❖

They sat on the top deck of the SBS bus, an odd couple, fascinated by each other, but without the slightest trace of romance. "I love traveling in the front seat of the top deck of the bus," said Madame Xu Chong Li. "One feels satisfyingly ahead of the crowd."

"Unfortunately that would also be true if the bus crashed and we were all flung headlong through the front window. We would take first place," Dilip Sinha replied.

"What a morbid mind you have. All that time last year spent helping the homicide squad, I suppose."

"Possibly."

"It's the view from here that's nice."

Just then, the bus pulled up right behind another, and some small boys sitting in the back seat of the vehicle in front pressed their noses against the glass, making faces at the couple.

"The view is ever changing," said Sinha.

They conversed in a genial, relaxed fashion, but would sometimes go for several minutes without even a glance at each other. Instead, their eyes crawled over the city streets, collecting data and filing it away for future use.

It wasn't until they had been a good twenty minutes into their journey to the Chettiar Temple at the junction of Tank Road and River Valley Road, next to Fort Canning Park, that Sinha realized something was wrong. Madame Xu was preoccupied. The gaps between the bits of small talk were a fraction longer than they should have been. She cut from topic to topic much more often than normal. And her right hand was twitching restlessly, as she played incessantly with a heavy ring on her index finger.

He turned and looked at her face. There was an extra wrinkle between her eyebrows, a heaviness around her mouth. He was suddenly convinced: she was harboring a worry that she had not shared with him. It was his duty as a friend, he decided, to see if there was anything he could do to help.

"Don't worry about it," he said. "It may never happen."

She turned to him in surprise. "You know?" she said, astonished.

"Of course I do. A man with my skills naturally has a sensitivity to disturbances such as the one that is currently causing you great concern. Worrying about something which may or may not happen is like paying rent on an apartment you may never need."

"But how do you know?"

"Let us just say: it came to me."

"That's remarkable." She was silent for a moment, apparently dealing with a new level of respect for her friend's psychic ability. She turned to look him in the eye before speaking again: "How much do you know?"

"Everything," he said, with an all-encompassing flourish of his large hands. "I have been your friend for many years, after all. You have no secrets from me. I hate to see you repressing your unhappiness."

The conversation stopped there for a pregnant pause. The bus continued on its way for another two minutes before they exchanged words again.

Madame Xu laughed. "Of course," she said. "Of course!"

Sinha looked at her with a smile. "Returning to your normal self?"

"I should have guessed," the fortune-teller said with breezy cheeriness. "When I swore to tell not a soul about it, I should have realized that my twin soul was an exception—had to be an exception."

"There can be no secrets between us."

"Exactly! How can two people who can read each other's minds have secrets between them? It's simply impossible. This is nothing to do with breaking pledges of secrecy. It is simply a fact of life for psychic people. Secrets cannot exist for us. He should know that. Being one himself."

Sinha made a grunt of agreement, but wondered if he was losing the thread of the conversation. He imagined that secrets must be an awful thing for a person like Madame Xu to deal with. With her way of uttering almost everything that floated through her mind, it would be difficult to keep one set of facts locked away.

The thought reminded him of the one secret he himself had promised to keep, the previous morning: the analysis he had shared of Ismail's client Clara—she with the shocking astrological chart that descended into immediate oblivion. His instinct had been to race to consult experts, to work as a team to find ways of reinterpreting or reversing this awful fate, to look for remedies that would save her.

But the Malaysian *bomoh* had been adamant. He had revealed her secrets to him demanding confidentiality unto death. Sinha had agreed to the conditions, and was ready to abide by them. Amran Ismail had said he needed to deal with the issue himself.

"Secrets are heavy things," Sinha said philosophically to his companion on the bus. "Because they exist to us, yet they do not exist to the people around us. Thus the burden of carrying them cannot be shared. The loneliness of the mission appears to amplify the weight of the burden."

"It's not being able to DO anything about it that makes it difficult for me," said Madame Xu. "As you know, I am no talker. I am a doer. Strong, silent type."

"Er, up to a point," Sinha said. "But you know, I feel exactly the same about the burdens I carry for clients and friends of clients. For how can one know about impending crises without acting upon them? Especially when the secret one is carrying is one with the gravest of repercussions for the person concerned."

Madame Xu's unexpected reaction to this statement was a broad smile. "You DO know. You really do," she trilled. "Well. How remarkable." She shook her head in happy amazement. "I have long known that you and I have a spiritual connection, but I never realized that it is really true that we can have no secrets between us. Our ability to read each other's minds makes it quite impossible."

Sinha gazed at her.

"So what are we going to do about Clara?" said Madame Xu. "We have to do something."

Now it was Sinha's turn to be amazed. She knew! "You know about that?" he breathed.

"This is what we are talking about, is it not?" she asked.

"Er, yes. It is. It is." Sinha put one hand on her shoulder. "Let's get this straight. A Malaysian *bomoh* called Amran Ismail came to you, shared with you the details of a client for whom death is prophesied, and asked for you to confirm the prediction—is that what happened?"

"It is."

"And he made you swear not to tell another living soul about it, upon pain of death?"

"Correct."

"You swore on a chicken?"

"I did."

"Fresh blood on your wrists?"

"Gravy, really."

"Gravy? Curious. And your reading of the data of the young woman, whose name is Clara, confirms what his initial reading said: That she is going to die on a certain date in the very near future? Possibly even Friday this week?"

"Absolutely right. Dilip Sinha, your skills in mind reading are astonishing. You have absorbed the thing that has been on my mind all morning and you have every last detail correct. It is almost as if you were hiding under the table when Mr. Ismail visited my apartment yesterday afternoon." Her expression suddenly changed, and she turned a stern face to him. "You were not, I hope?"

"I was not," said Sinha. His mind was racing. Clearly, the *bomoh* wanted confirmation from more than one authoritative source about the impending doom of his client. Once he had checked the charts, and told him that he was on the right lines, the man had gone straight to Madame Xu for the same reassurance. "What were your conclusions about the prospects for Ms. Clara?"

"Something terrible is going to happen to her. On Friday. That's what the Great Bomoh told him. So precise. Too precise. And yet nothing I could find contradicted it. It really seems as if nothing can be done about it. Shame, isn't it? I mean, for a girl so young."

"Yes," he agreed. "A shame."

"Can we not put our heads together and get Wong in on this and come up with possible solutions to the problem?"

"You promised Mr. Ismail that you would not tell a soul about this."

"It's true. But I haven't told a soul about it. Your mind-reading powers extracted it from my mind. My mouth spilled no secrets. I am in the clear, as Inspector Tan would say."

"Superintendent."

"Yes, yes."

They traveled for another minute in silence.

"Her prospects are astonishingly bad, aren't they?" said Sinha.

"Yes," said Madame Xu. "Extraordinarily."

"Poor girl."

He smiled to himself as he walked into the dull, cracked-tile porch of an old commercial building on Perak Road. Now this was the sort of activity that made C. F. Wong happy. He had picked up his bag and taken a bus north over the Singapore River to find the offices of Mirpuri Import-Export and Sundry Goods Pte.

He had visited the Mirpuri home in a pleasant suburban street in Mount Faber Park several times. But he had never given the full feng shui treatment to the family business, which was spread over two floors of a rather run-down, mixed-use block on Perak Road, on the eastern edge of Little India. Of course, he hadn't officially been commissioned to do a reading of the premises, but he knew he could spend a few hours doing what he did best, and slip it on to an invoice that Mrs. Mirpuri would pay without reading.

Although Danita Mirpuri was officially Joyce's case, he had told her that he would have to do the feng shui examination until her skills had reached a higher level. A thought had struck him. If his intern could be trained to do a range of useful work independently, she wouldn't need to follow him around like a piece of gum on his shoe. Today, he would spend a few hours focusing on Danita Mirpuri's office. Then he would devote the following morning to doing a reading of her bedroom at home. If she continued missing, he would return to the family office the following afternoon and do the entire premises. This could, quite possibly, be stretched out to two full days' work, all charged at full rate time and a half, including the express service surcharge. He imagined that the so-called kidnapping—no doubt some sort of bizarre lovers' game in disguise—would come to an end within a day or two. It was thus logical to maximize billable income by doing as much as possible as quickly as possible.

A small, anemic elevator gave him a slow, rather claustrophobic ride to the sixteenth floor. There, it dropped him in an ill-lit corridor with three doors, none of which bore a name. Only by looking at small numbers on doorjambs could he work out which button to press.

The doorbell played "The Yellow Rose of Texas" in an irritating monotone. He was greeted and ushered into the musty, wood-paneled reception by a Chinese secretary, who then summoned her boss, Mohan Mirpuri, a stout man of fifty-three with white, slicked-back hair. Although Wong knew the family had been in Singapore for more than twenty years, the patriarch still spoke English with a pronounced north Indian accent.

"Mr. Wong! I am tinking it has been more than one year over since we saw you before. In the house," the businessman gushed.

"Yes. I think more than one year."

"Sooo sorry to be troubling you about my daughter but she is being a bit of a problem child from time to time, you know, ha ha?"

"Yes. So sorry your daughter missing. Hope is nothing serious."

"Not *very* serious," said Mirpuri. "Only kidnapping I think. By one of the boyfriends. But which one? This is the question we are asking ourselves."

"May I see the office?" Wong asked.

"You are very free to study the offices or our home, see if you can be picking up clues. Wark this way."

He took the geomancer down a dark corridor to a large, gloomy room with no door. It contained several desks and cabinets, all of which were piled high with dusty, yellowing papers.

"She has very big office," said Wong. "For very young woman."

"Oh, this isn't her office. This is *my* office," said Mirpuri. "I thought you make like to do my office farst? Business has not been so great recently. Also I have had a bad flu which I cannot shake off. So much snot you know. Very uncomfortable. I wonder if you can fix all that? Why do Danita's office when she is not even here? Seems pointless. Do mine now, and when she comes back, do hers. Can do?"

"Can."

Wong spent an hour gathering basic details of the office. The premises as a whole had a dragon hill to the northeast. The charts revealed that the most favorable direction was the fourth sector, and the least favorable the ninth. It was a K'an building, with the door oriented to the north. For a more detailed examination, he needed the occupant's personal details, key dates of his life history and job description, the date the building was built and the company moved in, and he needed an understanding of what each cabinet or desk in the room contained. He asked the import-export man more than two dozen questions, and then sent him out of the room so that he could think in peace. The geomancer sketched out various charts, all covered with scribbled writing in tiny Chinese characters.

When he had covered nine sheets with writing and diagrams, Mirpuri reappeared in the doorway. "How are you going? Come to any interesting conclusions?" he asked.

"Many," said Wong. "There is much you can do to make your fortune better."

Mirpuri produced a magazine. "Let me show you something. I got this from a friend. It's a catalog of feng shui stuff from Hong Kong. Mail order. I was thinking, I could get a cat at the entrance, and then a hanging money sword over that side, pointing to the room where we process the orders, and then a pair of door gods for the entrance, plus this thing called a seven fortunes bowl . . ."

"No need," said the geomancer. "Trinkets no need."

Mirpuri looked suddenly deflated. "Really? I thought I would be doing very, very good thing to get some objects scattered around the place, and perhaps a fish tank at the front entrance. Fish tanks are good, right? You think goldfish or tropical?"

Wong shook his head. "Hong Kong feng shui is too much superstition. Very silly. First job in feng shui is not to add things to room like this, already too much-much overcrowded. First job is to *clear* things. Not add things."

"Oh. I see," Mirpuri said. "What do I have to clear out of it?"

"I tell you. Lot of things. You sit down."

The businessman moved awkwardly around the desk to get into his large, padded leather seat. "Okay. I'm sitting. Now tell."

The geomancer looked around the room. Then he turned his gaze back on to his client. "Main problem with this office is dead energy. Too much dead energy. This kills your energy." Wong pointed to the piles of yellowing paper on the cabinets. "This pieces of paper. I think they are old, you don't use them now. You must get rid of them. Common problem in old offices, even some new offices. Dead energy makes"—he looked in his notebook for an English word he had written down—"leth-ar-gy."

Mirpuri moved his head diagonally from side to side three times to indicate qualified agreement. He had a guilty expression on his face, like a small boy caught with his hand in a cookie jar. "I am having spring clean from time to time. Things are piling up, you are knowing how it is."

Wong nodded. "Some people are file people. They file-file-file, put everything away in cabinet. Some people are pile people. They put on paper on top of another paper, pile-pile-pile."

"Which is better?"

"File people better than pile people. But throw-away people best of all." Wong picked up a sheet of paper from the top of a pile. It was a letter. "See this? Each paper contains what we call 'potential energy transaction.' Someone write you a letter. Or you write letter to someone. Or someone want you to buy something. Or phone them. Or send fax to them. Someone want to tell you something. They put some energy into paper. They put some effort into paper. If you read letter, do something about it, energy of letter-writer has become your energy. Turns into action. But if you take no action—if you just put paper on pile, energy dies. Then you get another paper. Add to pile. Then another. Then another. All these papers, you put on pile. Soon pile has hundreds of papers. You put into drawer. Drawer gets full. You make new pile on desk. Soon new pile has hundreds of papers. But each paper is a piece of dead energy."

"I see," said Mirpuri, tilting his head diagonally again. "I guess most of these sheets of paper are being pretty useless to me now. I just haven't got around to—"

"Piles of dead energy very bad. You come into office, you see big piles of old papers. Sucks out your energy. You feel tired, you feel dead energy too. You get leth-ar-gy."

"So I should be filing them aarl away in neat cabinets, like that?"

"No. Because then cabinets become full of dead energy. Best you throw away all old papers. Only legal ones, important ones, you can keep. The rest, out. Otherwise too much leth-ar-gy, spreads all over office."

Mr. Mirpuri nodded diagonally again. "Okay. This is making sense to me. Chuck out all the old piles of paper that are piling up everywhere. Fine. Do that farst. What else should I do?"

"Get smaller desk. This desk too big."

"But you don't understand. A senior executive is surely to

goodness having to have a big desk. I'm the chairman of this company. I need a big desk. No one will have any respect for me if I am not having the biggest desk, definitely. Also I have sundry items to put on desk."

"This desk too big for this size room. Looks wrong. Feels wrong. Cannot walk around it easily. Must change it."

"If you say so," said Mirpuri, reluctantly. "I brought it over from India you know. Carved out of a single piece of—"

"Business office is place of change. Or process. Everything that comes in must be processed. Must be changed. Then *ch'i* will flow. Also money will flow."

Mirpuri blinked at the word "money," a subject he evidently took very seriously.

"You also need new carpet," Wong continued. "And different chair. And change color of cabinets. And move partitions."

Mr. Mirpuri sighed. This was going to be more expensive than he had expected.

In a room with a view at police headquarters, Superintendent Gilbert Tan used his index finger to stab the telephone buttons with a great deal of unnecessary violence. It wasn't that he was angry—quite the contrary: he was a quiet, rather repressed man most of the time, and when he found himself in a state of happy excitement, he tended to express it with hurried, fidgety movements.

Impatiently tapping on his desk with one hand, he used the other to hold down the speakerphone button on his telephone. He heard the phone he was calling give three rings before it was answered by a female voice.

"Hello?"

Tan snatched up the handset.

"Winnie?"

"No, this is Joyce. D'you want Winnie? She's out."

"Hi, Joyce. How are you? Good, I hope? Actually, I want to speak to Mr. Wong. Superintendent Tan here."

"Oh, hi. He's out. On a case. There's this girl, someone I know, actually, who's been kidnapped, possibly, and, believe it or not, one of the suspects is actually a pol—" Joyce stopped abruptly. "Anyway, C. F.'s out."

"Hmm." The police officer wondered what to do. "He has got his cell phone with him, is it?"

"Er. He's not using it at the moment. There was an accident this morning with it. It fell out of a window, sort of. Can I take a message? We're expecting him back within an hour or so?"

"Okay. He referred a woman to me yesterday. A woman called Tsai-Leibler."

"Yes, I know. It was her whose house burned down in Ridley Park the other day?"

"That's right. Well, tell him that she came to see me this morning. Interesting case. But I have to tread carefully, because it is officially filed as an arson case, and I don't want to tread on anyone else's toes. You know, in the police business, turf is everything. Everyone has his own little area of responsibility."

"Ah-huh."

"Anyway, I had a long chat with her, and then I went around to see the husband just after lunch. Had a long talk with Dr. Leibler. Basically, it's an interesting case, and I think C. F. should take it on. It's quite unique."

"He didn't seem very keen on it yesterday. I think he wanted Madame Xu to do most of it."

"Dr. Leibler told me his partner—the other dentist—had tried a psychic. Two, I think. Didn't work. Won't try another. They need a different approach. Anyway, the most important thing is just to tell Wong that I've called a meeting of the committee tonight. At the night market at seven o'clock P.M. sharp. Our usual table at Ah-Fat's. I've already tried to call Madame Xu and Dilip Sinha. They seem to be out. And neither of them have answering machines or cell phones, damn them. But I've sent a courier around to each of their houses to drop a note telling them about the meeting. You can give him that message?"

"I'll tell him."

In his over-air-conditioned office, Tan picked up a pen and sucked on it. The story that he had heard from Dr. Gibson Leibler had been a real thriller, and he wanted to deliver it well. The police officer loved nothing better than a good, real-life drama. He often thought he should have been a reporter, or perhaps a lawyer. He had studied geology and quantity surveying at university but had put most of his emotional energy into the student drama club productions, for which he had written several well-received plays.

But that had been many years ago. Tan had performed various odd jobs in Kuala Lumpur and Singapore before joining the police force at the age of twenty-seven and had risen in the ranks very quickly, largely, he believed, because of his excellent verbal and presentation skills. He suspected he was too lazy to ever be the perfect detective. But no one could beat him when it came to delivering a slick-sounding summary of an investigation-in-progress to his superiors.

And his willingness to take offbeat assignments—no one else had wanted to liaise with the Singapore Union of Industrial Mystics—had several times led him to steal a march on colleagues who restricted themselves to more traditional types of police work. So what if the others laughed at him? Patience enough to listen to seemingly irrational allegations—

such as the one about the ghost arsonist—gave him a side-entrance into some intriguing and satisfying cases. And this, he was convinced, was going to be another.

❖

Wong returned to Telok Ayer Street to find that Joyce had a message for him, and Winnie Lim had fled. Gone to negotiate with the landlord for a replacement air conditioner, the geomancer hoped.

Joyce raised her hand to get his attention. "That police guy called? Mr. Tan?"

"Oh. What did he say?"

"He's called a meeting of the committee tonight."

"Ah. About the dentist?"

"Yep. The dentist's wife went to see him this morning? Then he went to see the dentist. He said it was a very interesting case. He said it was hard for him to take on the case himself, but he thinks you should. He said, 'Turf is everything.'"

"Tough is everything."

"Not tough. Turf. Squares of grass."

"Oh. Turf is everything."

"Yeah. Like, little flat squares of grass."

Deciding that he had already lost the thread of this particular conversation, the feng shui master thought it wise to drop it. He sat down heavily in his creaking, lopsided chair and patted the sweat from his face with a folded tissue. "Ho yiht," he complained to himself. "Now where is paper?"

"Newspaper?" asked Joyce.

"No. Paper in envelope this morning. Strange message. You see, I find out from Mr. Mirpuri that his daughter, she used to do secretarial work for father and mother. It was she who used to send checks to me. That means she knows my address. Letter from her maybe."

"I threw it away," said the young woman. She leaned over to look at the wastepaper bin. "Gone. Winnie must have emptied it."

Wong found this hard to believe for several reasons. First, it smacked of efficiency, a quality completely alien to his office administrator. Second, the timing was out. One would empty a bin at the end of a workday, not at the beginning.

"Mrs. Tong?" suggested Joyce.

He nodded. "Mrs. Tong. You call her please. She like you. Don't know why."

Joyce dialed the number for the building's caretaker's office. "Hello? Mrs. Tong? It's Joyce. From upstairs. Fourth floor. Yeah. Hi. You okay? Cool. Did you like come in to our office this morning and empty the bins? What? Yeah. The A.C.? Oh. Yeah, air conditioner; that's right, it's just like *gone*. Weird, truly. Yeah. Okay."

She lowered the handset. "Winnie called her up here to show her the hole in the window where the air conditioner used to be. Mrs. Tong is baffled as to how the thing could just fall out of the window. She says we have to clear it up because she can't touch anything outside the building 'cause of her contract."

"But where is letter?"

"Yeah, I'm coming to that. She was carrying a sack of rubbish, so she emptied our cans while she was in here. So I guess that bit of paper is gone forever."

"You go find, please."

Her face fell. "I was hoping you wouldn't say that."

"You go find," he barked.

Fifteen minutes later, Joyce was back in the office, having recovered the missing note. She hadn't enjoyed the job, since the can had contained several day-old meals. The last five of the fifteen minutes had been spent washing and re-washing her hands. "Yeeuuch," she said. "I stink of yesterday's fried noodles."

"*Kelinga mee,*" said Wong, who prided himself on the accuracy of his nose.

They both peered at the note.

Jr;[@@@@ O
Br nrrm lofms[[rf/ O
, om s fstl tpp, om s nio;fomh eoyj
{ptyihirdr.=dyu;e g;ppts yjtrr pt gpit ,omiyrd gtp,
Jplorn Dytrry/ Gomf ,r/ Ithrmy@@@ Fsmo/

"It looks like the sort of gibberish which comes out when your printer has gone wrong," she said. "But it's written with a typewriter. I don't think it could be from Dani. Must be from an old person. Who uses typewriters these days? I guess it could be a code. Did Dani ever write to you in code?"

"No," said Wong. "Danita Mirpuri study typing in secretary school. Usually write very neat. Not like other secretaries who do not go to school, type very bad." He frowned in the direction of Winnie's desk.

"Maybe it's in code," said Joyce, excitedly. "I bet I could break the code. Let me study it for a while. I could probably set up a computer program to do it."

Wong, who was forever looking for activities that would keep Joyce out of his hair, grunted his approval and picked his journal out of the desk.

She made a photocopy of the letter by running it through the fax machine, and then sat staring at it, a pencil between her teeth. "Unless it's Enigma or something, codes are usually pretty easy to break. You just add one to each letter in the alphabet or take one off or something."

She wrote out the alphabet twice on separate sheets of paper, and set them against each other in a variety of positions, in an attempt to make a key which would crack the code.

After a few minutes, the young woman decided to share her findings with her boss, who sat at his desk, unlistening. "It starts off with *j* and *r*. If you add one to the first letter, and take one from the second letter, you get *Is*. That's a word. Although it's an odd word to start a sentence with. But I don't know what to do with the punctuation stuff that's in the middle of the word."

She champed her teeth on the pencil. "But there's one thing I do know. This is something to do with the Internet. There's an 'at' symbol. This must be some sort of E-mail address. Also there's slashes. That's very computer-ish."

She started scribbling again. "I remember in Sherlock Holmes, it said you should start off by looking at the two- and three-letter words. Because, you see, two-letter words have to be *of* or *in* or *to* or something like that. If you can guess those, you can work backward and work out all the rest. Now the two-letter words in this sentence are *Jr, om* and *pt*."

She spent half an hour trying various permutations of letters to break the code, but got no further. "This sucks. None of the usual code-breaking methods work on this," she sighed. "It isn't a displaced alphabet thing. And the two- and three-letter words don't seem to follow any obvious pattern. I think it's just rubbish." She pushed the scribble-covered sheets away from her in a display of rejection. "Think I'll work on *my* case instead."

Picking up the phone, she started dialing her friends again, to ask questions about Danita Mirpuri and her boyfriends. After ten minutes of gossip, Joyce had a big grin on her face. She phoned two more people. "This is so perfect," she trilled in Wong's direction between calls. "I can spend ages on the phone asking my friends about who's seeing who—and it still counts as work."

Wong had also spent time staring at the piece of paper and had also failed to solve the puzzle. He had quickly given up trying and had decided to spend some time working on his book. The problem with the coded message had brought to mind a classic story about Zhu Gumin and the issues of communication and non-communication. Where had he read that? Was it in the *Zhinang*, the masterpiece written by Ming Dynasty scholar Feng Menglong? He decided to write it down from memory. He could check the facts afterward.

In ancient times lived a man named Tang Sheng. He considered himself a very wise man. He had heard that the sage Zhu Gumin had great power with words.
He invited Zhu Gumin into his house. Tang Sheng said: "I was told that you can use words in a clever way. You can even lure a stranger out of his house. But I think you could never get me out of my house."
Zhu Gumin said: "It is winter. It is very cold outside. I would rather use my skill to lure a person into a house. I could describe the warmth and comfort of a house in such a way that they cannot resist. They must come in even if they want to stay outside."
"Let us try it," said Tang Sheng. He stepped out into the cold garden. "Now use your words to lure me inside."
But Zhu Gumin said nothing.
Tang Sheng again asked him to use his power with words.

Zhu Gumin again said nothing.
Tang Sheng decided to go into the house. But the door was
locked.

Listening to what a man says accomplishes nothing. Listening to what he means is better. But most useful of all, Blade of Grass, is to listen to what you yourself mean when you ask a question.

(Some Gleanings of Oriental Wisdom
by C. F. Wong, part 344)

If he could work out what Dani Mirpuri had meant to do by writing him a message in code, assuming it was from her, he could take a guess at what it said. But where to begin?

Joyce and Wong had arrived half an hour late for the meeting of the committee, but found Sinha and Madame Xu unperturbed by their tardiness. The two old friends had clearly been engrossed in an intense private conversation. Further, the person doing the briefing—Superintendent Gilbert Tan of the Singapore police—had not arrived.

Food was ordered, and had quickly started to arrive on the table. The theme of the meal—set by Sinha—was *Nasi Melayu*, traditional Malay food. The smell of freshly grated coconut pervaded the market.

Joyce had noticed that coconut milk was used in sauces for savory dishes, as well as in cakes, desserts and even drinks. It was a pleasing odor—but the same could not be said for the other smell that dominated the night market: the sharp, bitter taste that she had learned came from dried shrimp paste. She avoided those dishes, and took tiny portions of the multi-colored dishes that had other flavors: lemon grass, ginger, shallots, garlic, and something that Madame Xu described as *kaffir* lime leaf. She carefully avoided the reddish curry dishes such as *assam pedas* and *lontong*, which she knew were full of hot chili powder.

But Dilip usually ordered something milder for her: *nasi goreng*, served with a sweet coconut milk, palm syrup and a jelly drink called *chendol*. Yet she found that her tongue was gradually becoming accustomed to Malay food. Beef *rendang*, which she had found suspiciously dark and pungent the first time, now seemed to her to be a tasty and acceptable substitute for the steak on which she had been raised in Australia and New York.

"Ha-ha! I choose my moment to arrive perfectly, is it?" Tan asked in a broad Singaporean accent, arriving suddenly out of the darkness and patting Sinha heavily on the back. The astrologer coughed on a peanut he had eaten. This caused the law enforcement agent to thump the old man with even more strength, until his spluttered protestations caused him to stop.

After the small, pudgy officer had expressed his apologies for being late, he pulled up a stool, sat down between Madame Xu and Joyce McQuinnie, and rolled up his sleeves. He picked up each dish and sniffed it, savoring the strong flavors, and then began to eat.

Dusk had fallen quickly, leaving them squinting in the sharp glare of the food stalls' strip lighting.

"There's no such thing as ghosts," said Joyce firmly, in a tone that brooked no arguments.

"Are you very sure of that, little plum blossom?" asked Madame Xu.

"Yep. My friend Seth does channelling, you know? He has a direct contact with Vega, who knows all things because she-he is part of the like, Life Force you know?"

"Go on," the fortune-teller continued warily. "Explain to us why your friend Seth says there are no such things as ghosts."

"Well, Seth was channelling in the early hours of the morning after an all-night rave, and he calls up Vega and he's like, 'Vega, tell us about the spirit world on earth.'"

Joyce looked at each face in turn, happy to have caught the attention of a group of people all of whom were three or four times her age. "And she-he, I mean Vega, is like, 'No, there's no such thing as ghosts, it's all just mumbo-jumbo.' And Seth's like, 'Wow. So all these ghostbusters and people are just wasting their time?' And Vega's like, 'Totally.'"

Breathless, she folded her arms.

C. F. Wong closed his eyes. He must have committed very great sins in a previous life.

Madame Xu looked vaguely disappointed. "Be that as it may, my dear, Vega's esteemed opinion may not directly affect our assignment tonight." Sitting bolt upright on her stool as usual, the fortune-teller placed one liver-spotted hand on top of the other and put both on her lap, as calm and motionless as a Buddha. "Inspector Tan has got a real-life ghost story for us tonight, and I for one am willing to make up my mind on its believability or otherwise only after full examination of all aspects of it."

"Superintendent," corrected Sinha.

"If you are waiting for me, do not wait. I am ready." C. F. Wong packed the journal in which he had been scribbling into his briefcase and slid it beneath the table, where he held it firmly between his old and rather sagging black shoes.

It was a windy night, and a fresh southeasterly breeze was blowing the day's humidity away. There was little cloud cover, and the cold light of the stars appeared to be contributing to an unusual but welcome coolness in the air.

Joyce was immediately regretting her outburst of skepticism. It was probably not the right thing to say at the month's first official meeting of the investigative advisory committee of the Singapore Union of Industrial Mystics, where all of one's fellow diners were people who seemed to spend more than half their day dealing with unseen things. And it wasn't just the company that made it the wrong thing to say, either; it was the surroundings. The entire night market at this late hour seemed to take on a paranormal atmosphere. Much of the lighting came from hanging strings of bulbs swinging in the breeze, or from the headlights of passing cars. This meant that all the shadows were constantly moving, shuffling and swaying back and forth at various speeds, or sprinting across the field as if running away from the vehicles that gave them birth. This gave the diner the impression that there were a thousand unseen creatures creeping around his or her peripheral vision.

Then of course there were the market's steam spirits, which would rise from each wok, as if the stoves were all direct openings into hell. The wind was blowing smoke from Ah-Fat's wok in their direction, so every few minutes a child-sized wraith carrying powerful odors of *tauhu goreng* would drift across the table.

Dilip Sinha snatched a fried shrimp from a platter and popped it into his mouth. "I am all ears, Superintendent Tan. Please proceed with your story about ghosts. I, for one, not only believe in ghosts but commune with them regularly, finding them more real than many people."

Tan, they all knew, had a very high estimation of himself as a raconteur. So he took the storytelling part of his job extremely seriously. After chewing his food carefully and wiping his lips with a sheet of tissue paper from the box in the middle of the table, he calmed himself, and seemed to be waiting for the correct moment to begin. He looked in turn at the face of each of his listeners. He picked his teeth with a toothpick, extracting a shred of beef. He put it back into his mouth.

Then he leaned back into his chair, having decided that at last the moment had come for him to tell his tale. He spoke slowly, carefully articulating each word.

"Helluva strange, this tale. As you will see. The case involves the room of a dentist in a modern office block in Singapore. I think you can picture the type of establishment. A tall building on Orchard Road near the junction with Clemenceau Avenue, offering a range of shops and services, with a small suite on the fifth floor shared by two dentists, a Dr. Liew Yok Tse and a Dr. Gibson Leibler. Dr. Liew had been practicing for many years in a rather run-down office on Mosque Street, and a year ago he had met Dr. Leibler, a newcomer to Singapore, who was anxious to set up his own practice. Dr. Leibler was of American origin, but had been living in Hong Kong for some years. He had married a Hong Kong woman a couple of years ago and now considered himself an honorary Asian. He was looking for an office, and Dr. Liew suggested they book one for the two of them and share expenses. This way they could get a better location, and could provide cover for each other on holidays. The two of them decided that their cultural differences might be a good selling point, as the joint practice would not be labeled 'Chinese' or 'Western' but would attract all comers.

"Dr. Liew found a place. The receptionist they had hired, Amanda Luk, had a good eye for colors and organized decorators for it. They moved in some three months ago. Now, Dr. Liew, of course, had many more regular customers than the newcomer, but Dr. Leibler was quite social, as was his wife, and they started introducing clients to the practice."

"When does the ghost appear?" asked Joyce, who was already bored with the story.

"Coming, dear. Have patience. One Saturday afternoon, about three weeks ago, Gibson Leibler was in his office, putting on his jacket. He had seen several clients that morning and through the lunch period, but had kept the afternoon free. The time was about two o'clock. He changed into his sports jacket and then slipped out of the door, and was standing in the waiting room, fishing in his jacket pocket for the keys, when he heard a sound from Dr. Liew's room. It was the pained grunt of a male patient. He said it sounded like the noise of someone moaning with some metal contraption holding his mouth open. This was followed by a few more yelps.

"These are not abnormal sounds in a dental office, of course—but are not expected in an empty one. Dr. Leibler had thought he was alone in the office—Dr. Liew usually left at lunchtime on a Saturday to go and play golf. The American realized that his colleague must be working still. He knocked on the door, planning to tell Dr. Liew that he was leaving, and he, Dr. Liew, should lock up when finished with his patient.

"There was no answer. Dr. Leibler knocked again. Still no reaction. He called out: 'Y.T.?' But there was silence from the room. Dr. Leibler thought about opening the door but then stopped himself. Why disturb the man? He decided that Liew would have the sense to check to see if he, Dr. Leibler, was there when he finished, and would lock the premises. Dr. Leibler picked up his bag and left."

"I can guess what is coming," said Sinha, rubbing his hands together with excitement at a good story. "Is it a ghost patient? Someone who was root-canalled to death in the chair, perhaps, and now will groan and clutch his jaw forever and ever?"

"Shhh," said Joyce, who had become interested, anticipating something similar. "I love ghost stories. Especially real ones."

"You must wait and see what the mystery is," said Gilbert Tan. "And as for the answer to it, well, you must provide that yourselves. This story is missing an ending."

"Excuse me, do continue," said the Indian astrologer.

"Dr. Leibler thought no more about this trivial incident until a few days later, when he was leaving the office late, and was again surprised to hear sounds coming from Dr. Liew's room. This time he was quite sure that Dr. Liew had left—the man had said good-bye to him at least half an hour ago.

"Again, Dr. Leibler tapped on his colleague's door, and received silence in reply. After knocking again, and calling out his friend's name, the dentist slowly opened the door. 'Dr. Liew? You in here?' He opened the door to see . . ."

The police officer stopped and looked at his audience. There was rapt attention. Sinha and McQuinnie were leaning forward, listening intently. Wong, as usual when listening to a story, had his eyes closed and head tilted back. Madame Xu was staring into the middle distance over their heads. Superintendent Tan was delighted by the suspense he had created.

"A ghost?" ventured Joyce.

"Nothing!" said the police officer, unable to resist a grin. "There was nothing there. The room was empty. No dentist, no patient. Nothing. The following morning—"

"Hang on," said Joyce. "There was no one there, but was the sound still there? Was the groaning still going?"

"I do believe it was. But our hero felt uncomfortable and did not enter the room to investigate further. He said it sent shivers down his spine. He left. Any other questions?"

"No, go on."

"The next morning, Dr. Leibler mentions it to his friend and colleague. 'Strange thing, but sometimes I think it sounds as if you are in the room, but there's no one there.' He had expected Liew to disregard the observation, but he didn't. The Singaporean says: 'Helluva strange you say that. Sometimes I hear groaning, you know, and I think: What's wrong? I haven't even got my hands near the guy's mouth. I'm over by the sink doing a rinse of some tool. Then I realize that the sound is not coming from my patient. There must be some strange thing where the sound comes from your room into mine.'

" 'You mean some sort of acoustic phenomenon?' Dr. Leibler asks.

" 'Yes, it must be your patient I can hear, not mine,' Dr. Liew says.

"Dr. Leibler realizes that this cannot be the case. He says: 'Yes, but I could hear someone when there were no patients on the premises at all. Neither in your room or mine. Pretty strange, no?'

"Just then, the other staff, Cheng Lai Kuen and Amanda Luk, arrive, and in the bustle of morning preparations, the conversation is forgotten. The whole subject disappears until a few days later when Dr. Liew calls Dr. Leibler at home one night. 'I need to use your office. I have an urgent case this evening, and there is some problem with my room. My client is here now.'

" 'Why of course, go right ahead. You can get in?'

" 'Yes, the spare keys are there where Amanda hides them.'

" 'My room is your room,' says the American.

" 'I'll call you later,' says the Singaporean.

"Some forty-five minutes later, Dr. Leibler has just finished a post-meal slug of eau-de-vie, when Dr. Liew calls. 'Was it okay? Did you find everything you need?' the American asks.

" 'Fine. Just a cosmetic job. It was Mrs. Poon, you know, the New Zealand consul-general's wife? Chipped a tooth, going on a trip tomorrow, needed a quick cover-up.'

" 'No problem,' says Dr. Leibler. 'Now, tell me, what was the problem with your office? You said you couldn't use it. Is it the electricity again? I've had this flickering light for ages.'

"Liew Yok Tse is initially reluctant to say what the problem is. Then he decides to take the bull by the horns. 'Gibson,' he says. 'I think you will think that I am crazy, but let me tell you what I really think. My room is haunted. There is a ghost in it. Someone is there, groaning, like a patient, when really there is no one there. I went in there to prepare, and I heard the sound. I checked in your office, there was no one. Then my client arrived, and I decided to call you and use your room instead. There is a ghost, and it is in my room.'

" 'Nonsense,' says his friend. 'It is an acoustic problem, like you said before. Just a sound coming from somewhere else.'

" 'But where? Your office was empty.'

" 'Maybe another dentist somewhere else in the building, and the sound travels?'

" 'No,' says Liew. 'Directly above us is some sort of boutique, and below, the whole floor is a restaurant. I don't think it is coming from next door. And the sound. You should hear it. It sounds so close. Like you can touch it, him, the person. Someone IN my room.'

" 'The voice: what does it say?' asks Leibler.

" 'He—it—just groans. It sounds like a bad patient of a bad dentist, when you haven't given any anesthetic.' "

Gilbert Tan scanned the faces of his listeners. "Now are you with me so far?"

Joyce nodded. Sinha slowly bowed his head.

"Good. Well, the two dentists decide to meet half an hour earlier at the office in the morning to check out the problem. At eight the next morning, they carefully examine Dr. Liew's office. Nothing strange, nothing remotely out of the ordinary there. In the cool light of morning, the problem seems ridiculous, and they decide to forget it. Dr. Liew laughs and says he would be a fool to take such ridiculous fears seriously. 'It was probably a cat,' he says. 'You know how human they sound when they are on heat? Probably in the air vents of the building or outside.'

"He laughs off the problem, but Dr. Leibler soon realized that he hadn't really forgotten about it. Dr. Liew had lost his cheerfulness. He used to sing under his breath, old Hokkien love songs, but no longer. When small items went missing, Liew would look very uncomfortable until Cheung Lai Kuen—that was the name of his dental technician, remember?—would find them, innocently misplaced under a newspaper or a jacket. The person who suffered most from all this was Lai Kuen. You see, she had to deal with an unhappy and jittery boss, and she too was unhappy most of the time, being a rather nervous soul.

"Gibson Leibler eventually decided to tell his wife Cady

Tsai-Leibler about it. She immediately decided that she knew who the ghost was. Soon after she got engaged to her husband-to-be, he got caught up in a malpractice lawsuit with a former patient of his, a man named Joseph Oath."

Wong's eyes opened briefly, then closed again.

"Oath's child had been improperly anesthetized for an operation, and had never regained consciousness. The anaesthetist concerned had afterward died of an overdose, and Oath's fury had been redirected at the dentist. The hearing, when it finally came to court, was slated to last for two weeks. But halfway through the first week, Oath died suddenly. The case was adjourned. His widow decided not to proceed with the case. But the damage had been done. Dr. Leibler, his reputation shot, decided to leave Hong Kong and move to Singapore. That's where the story ends—until a few weeks ago, when some spirit—possibly the ghost of Joseph Oath—started appearing in the office and upsetting everything. Mrs. Tsai-Leibler believes that the ghost followed her husband home to their new apartment in Ridley Park at the weekend and set fire to it. From her point of view, the most important thing to do is get rid of the wandering, unhappy spirit."

Superintendent Tan turned and looked directly at Wong. "Dr. Liew arranged for a Buddhist priest to come to the premises and chant for an hour on Friday last week. But it had no effect at all. He had a pair of psychics in, too. They were no use. So now they are at their wits' end. I told the dentists that I would pop in tomorrow morning with a couple of officers to see if there was any funny business going on. You know, anyone hidden in the ceiling panels or dangling outside the window or anything like that. But Dr. Liew also wants a feng shui man to come and cleanse the surgery. He now thinks that is the only way to solve the problem."

Wong nodded slowly, then turned to Joyce. "What do you call a person who exercises?"

"What?" Joyce was taken aback by the question. "I dunno. A fitness freak?"

"No, exercises the ghosts."

"Oh. An exorcist."

"Yes." Wong turned to Superintendent Tan. "You want an excer-cist. Not a feng shui man. He can get the ghost out."

"I thought about that, but I decided no," said the police officer. "There's no one I know here who does that sort of thing except old Father Fan, you know, Fan Yin Sze, and I wouldn't want to inflict him upon anyone."

"But you cannot get a feng shui *sifu* to do the job of an excerciser. It is too different."

"Maybe so," said Tan. "But the Buddhist priest Dr. Liew used, a gentleman named Brother Q, whom I believe Madame Xu knows, is a top man in that field. As I say, he had no effect."

Madame Xu nodded. "If Brother Q cannot get rid of the ghost, then clearly it is resistant to the efforts of normal operations against paranormal infestations. I think a feng shui reading may be an interesting way of attacking the problem from a different angle."

Wong was adamant. "No. Cannot. I already have difficult assignment this week. Busy today, all day tomorrow, maybe next day also. Confidential one. Also, I don't believe in ghost. Don't want to take this assignment."

"It's not his cup of tea," said Joyce.

Wong started to lower the cup of *bo leih* he had just raised to his lips and blinked at her.

"No, I don't mean that's not your cup of tea," said the young woman.

Superintendent Tan leaned over and put his small, fat hand on the back of the geomancer's thin, wrinkled one. "I know you don't want to take this case, but you will."

Dilip Sinha laughed and clapped his hands together. "There you have a fine example of emotional blackmail, which is what I believe they call this. You don't want to do it, but he knows you will do it for the sake of your old friendship with the Super."

"No," said the police officer. "That's not the reason why I know he'll take it. When I tell him what the dentists have offered to pay, he will take it. Dentists *yau cheen*. Plenty rich."

Wong suddenly looked interested and lowered his cup. "Tell."

By the time the meeting came to a close with a platter of *pulut durian*, *ondeh-ondeh*, *kueh kosuree* and other coconut-flavored Malay sweetmeats, Wong had agreed to go to the dental office in Orchard Road the following afternoon. Superintendent Tan left the table to hurry home to his family.

As the gathering broke up, Wong quietly told Joyce that he wanted to spend the following morning doing a feng shui reading of the home of Danita Mirpuri, after which he would meet the missing girl's mother, who was due to finish her appointment with the hairdresser at lunchtime.

"You also have some work. You please tonight write down everything you have found out about this girl, especially about her boyfriends," he told the intern. "Put it on my desk tomorrow morning. Then you can take day off. Go to HMV."

"Sounds like you have some homework to do tonight, Plum Blossom," said Madame Xu. "Just like in school. Better hurry home and have a quiet night."

"Home? I'm *so* not going home," said Joyce. "I'm going out. I'll see if I can find out anything about Danita from the club. That's where her friends hang out. I'll also see if I can find out anything more about your girlfriend, C. F."

Madame Xu and Dilip Sinha suddenly spun their heads to stare at Wong. "Your *girlfriend*?" said Madame Xu.

The feng shui master was speechless.

"He came to the disco with us last night," said Joyce. "And he was the first to pull."

"Pull what?" asked Sinha.

"Don't ask," said Wong, furious.

Joyce pulled out a mirror and a black lipstick to ready herself for another late night at Dan T.'s Inferno.

W
E
D
N
E
S
D
A
Y

LIFE IS NOT A MINISERIES

A S PLANNED, C. F. Wong began his day at the Mirpuri house in Mount Faber. He already had diagrams of the family home on file in the office. (Winnie had miraculously managed to find them at the bottom of an unmarked cardboard box.) So on this visit he focused particularly on the young woman's bedroom, which was a malodorous pile of clothes, magazines and used tissues. He also spent some time with her aunt, compiling a list of key dates in the young woman's life. The only other family member at home was Dani's brother Karim, but Wong was told by the servants that the young man had had a very late night hanging out with some dissolute, drunken Westerners, and wasn't expected to wake before noon.

The house was of the Tui orientation, with its main door facing west. Dani's room was in the northeast of the home, facing a large tree growing in a neighbor's garden. Despite the tree, Wong reckoned that it was basically a good location for a young woman to grow up, although there were certain problems with the room—one being that it had an excess of water energy. It was painted baby blue and pink, it contained a fish tank, and the pipes for the whole block ran up the outside wall near the window, providing periodic gurgling noises. This was not a good combination for a restful location, especially considering that the occupant was a wood person, born under the sign of the fire horse.

Nevertheless, the problems were all fixable. The analysis was relatively easy, and he had soon run out of ways to look busy.

As usual with relatively wealthy people, the problem was one of overabundance. They always expected him to suggest a list of things to add to the house—a statuette of a horse here, a pile of stones there, a sprinkling of salt by a window. But the house was not ready for items to be added to it. There were already far too many things in the dwelling place. It was a jumbled mess of energies and influences. Looking around Danita's room, it appeared to him that there was barely a single item in it that was necessary or had a real function. The books were leftovers from her childhood, the desk computer did not work, the collection of dolls of the world was dusty and neglected.

People did not understand the importance of destruction, he decided. There must be as much destruction as acquisition in a person's life. Otherwise the result was stagnation, accumulation, and eventually a clogging up of energy flows by dead items. And this deadness immediately transferred itself to the spirit of the person living in the cluttered home. To him, it seemed so obvious. How was it that people never noticed the immediate improvement in their inner being that followed a session of throwing things away?

Or was it something to do with Singapore society, where acquisition was treated as an end in itself, more important than happiness or contentment? Ideally, a person should have slightly more destruction in his or her life than acquisition. That way, a person would gradually change the balance of their existence from material to spiritual as they aged. They would thus end their lives gloriously unencumbered. But this concept was impossible to sell to people for whom shopping was entertainment. To most clients, feng shui meant nothing more than the addition of a fish tank in a hall or the hanging of a golden ornament by a door.

He left a detailed list of instructions with a servant. There had been no further contact from the kidnapper, and Danita, to Wong's delight, remained missing.

He arrived back at his sweltering office in Telok Ayer Street mid-morning to find Winnie Lim in a state of great excitement. She had bad news for him. "Landlord he says you must pay for new air conditioner because you threw old one out of the window."

"But I did not throw it out of the window. It fell out by itself."

"Still you must pay, he say. Air conditioners do not fall out of window by themselves, he say."

"This one did."

"Still you must pay."

"This is not right."

"Never mind. He is boss. This is his building. You must buy new air conditioner."

"Will not."

"You want us all to die of heat, is it?"

The geomancer, who had just sat down, suddenly rose to his feet, fired with anger. "You write to landlord. Tell him we have lawyers. Tell him we will not pay rent. You write now. Official letter. Use letterhead."

"Silly to fight. We die first of heat before you get any money from him."

But despite her protests, she started to type out a letter to the landlord.

Wong sat down again, and then noticed that Joyce's desk was empty. "Where's Joyce?"

"Don't know. Missing."

It was almost eleven o'clock. Hangovered, thought Wong. She went to the bar again last night. Or was it hanged over? Over-hanged, perhaps? Or just hung?

He decided to sit at Joyce's desk, because it received a little more of the breeze from the window, and do some writing in his journal. The pleasures of having spent two undisturbed hours doing feng shui readings that morning had left him feeling calm and creative.

The phone rang.

"Phone!" Winnie barked.

The geomancer picked up the handset. It was Superintendent Tan phoning from the Liew and Leibler dental office. He had spent several hours there and wanted to brief Wong on the case. The dentists had explained that the ghost seemed to have no regular schedule, but could appear at any time of the day or night. Each time it appeared, it kept up a murmuring wail that came and went for an hour or so before disappearing.

"Although I normally am helluva skeptical about ghost stories, I find this one really intriguing," he said. "There are so many separate witnesses: both dentists, the assistants, even the patients and a cleaning woman." He had arranged for an officer to compile a list of instances where the spirit had allegedly been heard, seen, felt, smelt or perceived in any way. "I'll fax it to you. But as I say, there doesn't seem to be any pattern to it."

The police officer also faxed floor plans of the office and a list of birth dates and birth places of staff. The geomancer tucked away his journal and devoted the next couple of hours to drawing up *lo shu* charts for the dentists, their assistants, their new business, and the office building itself. But he told the police chief that he would have to wait until the afternoon when he would actually visit the premises before he could come to any firm conclusions.

"A dentist office very difficult," Wong told Tan. "Almost as bad as a kitchen. You see, the rooms are small. But there is always much metal. There is always water. There are always cutting machines. There is fear. There is pain. There is money. All in a small space. All these things have very great effect on *ch'i* energy. Dentist office one of the most concentrated places of emotion, understand or not?"

Wong asked for Dr. Liew Yok Tse to be put on the line, and told him that he did not want to design or undertake a full cleansing process until he had personally experienced the disruption introduced by the unseen visitor. "I must listen to the ghost," he said. "Then I can make the room so that he does not come anymore, *ming-mm-ming-baak?*"

"Understand," said the dentist, sounding tired and unhappy.

Lowering the handset, the geomancer was amazed to find that his office administrator had actually finished a task assigned to her. Unlike most of the jobs she was supposed to do, the replacing of the air conditioner impinged directly on her personal comfort—and therefore qualified as something she was willing to do something about.

Winnie held up the letter she had typed. "Finish," she said.

At that moment, the office door crashed open. Joyce McQuinnie staggered in, moving awkwardly like an old woman robbed of her walker.

"Morning," she croaked in a low, damaged voice.

"Los' your voice?" asked Wong.

"Had a late night. Hoarse."

"Horse?"

"Yeah."

Wong said: "Never mind horse. Got a job for you. Please to proofread this letter. Winnie wrote letter." He expected Joyce to be amazed at evidence that Ms. Lim had actually done some secretarial work, but the young woman seemed to be too ill to comprehend the miracle that had taken place.

"Can you please do it, C. F.?" she asked. "I'm so like *bleeeeeaagh*. People my age should not be allowed to drink. Oh yeah, that's right, we're not." She fell into her chair, slumped backward and covered her face with Winnie's gossip newspaper.

"Okay. Give." He was annoyed. Did Mr. Pun really expect him to function normally if he had to spend all his time babysitting a teenager? The geomancer snatched Winnie's typewritten sheet. He began reading it with the usual pained expression that accompanied all examinations of Ms. Lim's written work. But halfway through the letter, his eyes suddenly widened. "Wah!" he said. *"Aiyeeaah."*

"What?" asked Winnie, proud of her endeavors, and peeved that he should make such a fuss. "Mistake? If you don't like, do it yourself."

"Mistake? This letter have plenty mistakes," said Wong. "But also have answer to a puzzle."

He pulled his chair across to Winnie's desk, and sat very close to her, much to her discomfort. He stared at her typewriter, and started scrawling on a piece of paper. Then he leaped to his feet and grabbed his bag.

"Where are you going?" Joyce groaned from under the classifieds.

"Out. To find kidnap victim."

"I'm coming."

"Why not you stay? Sleep?"

"It's my case, remember? Dear God," said the intern, attempting to move her aching bones.

As they left the building, Joyce insisted they go to a coffee shop so she could revive herself. "I feel like death warmed up," she said.

"Is that a type of cake?" he asked.

"No. Or actually, maybe it is."

After a large paper cup of something called caramel macchiato, the young woman began to revive. Then she ate a sausage roll and a double-chocolate muffin. "Vitamins S, C and G put me back on my feet," she said. "Sugar, caffeine and grease."

In between mouthfuls of what Wong thought was disgusting-looking food, she shared what she had discovered the previous night about Danita Mirpuri. She seemed impervious to the noise and bustle of the coffee shop. Wong found it rather uncomfortable. Why did it have soft low sofas, instead of stools or stiff wooden chairs like restaurants were supposed to have? The bitter smell of coffee made him feel nauseous—as did the revolting cow-milk smell coming from his assistant's drink.

Wong listened reluctantly. He thought it unlikely that she would give him any useful information, but there was always a chance that she had stumbled upon something that might help.

"Nike turned up? And so did his friend Sy. Sy dated her forever, like three weeks, so he knew like everything there was to know about her. And Dani's brother Karim spent the evening with me and my hangers?

"Danita was quite the social animal," Joyce said. "She had several boyfriends, whom she played off against each other. One named Ram was heir to a middle-sized retail fortune. But he was a little crazy. At first the parents were quite fond of him. But they were eventually persuaded that the question marks over his sanity might not compensate fully for the fact that he would bring cash to their daughter."

The mother had reluctantly asked policeman Kinny Mak for some advice about getting rid of the suitor. The policeman met Danita several times, and then he too fell in love with her.

"It was all like such a mess, totally," Joyce said, trying to drink and yawn at the same time. As she spoke, she lowered her drink and held her tired head in both hands as if it had suddenly become far too heavy for her neck to support. "Like her parents told her to choose one or the other? Initially they liked the crazy rich kid better. They thought he would fit better into their family—which was probably right, because they are all a bit crazy, the Mirpuris. Especially Karim. You should have seen what Karim did last night! He—but that's another story."

She suddenly looked away and bit her lip, distracted by her memory of the previous night.

Wong looked at her crossly. "Karim is sick this morning. They said he went out with wild friends. They think it is your fault."

"As if. He's the wild one. Not me. He—"

"Talk more about Danita, please, not her brother."

"Yeah, yeah. Okay. Anyway, the family was a bit greedy. They reckoned that a policeman in Singapore didn't do too badly if he was tipped to reach a senior rank?

"Dani had promised to make her final decision by the previous week," Joyce said. "When the time came for her to announce it to the family, she stunned them by naming a third person—a male called Charles Winterbottom none of them had ever heard of. He worked as a stockbroker down-town. When her father told her that she could only select from the list of the two preapproved candidates, she threw a tantrum and ran off to stay with one of her girlfriends—or that was what she told people, anyway. Mak, the policeman, was incensed. He went off to find her. That's where the trail stopped for a couple of days. Dani was hiding with a girl-friend or something. She came home on Saturday night and everything seemed normal. And then on Sunday she disap-peared again.

"And then the news turned really bad," said Joyce. "On Monday. Like her mom got this note saying that Dani had been kidnapped and that we would never see her again unless she put one million Sing dollars into a package and leave it at a certain place at a certain time: the little park off Maxwell Road? Real cop-show stuff."

"So what did she do?" asked Wong.

"Nothing. She treated it as a joke. This is real life. She ignored it. But yesterday morning she got a call from a guy sounding angry? He said he had really kidnapped her and that she would come to harm if she didn't come up with the money? That's when she called us?"

Wong scribbled notes as she spoke. Joyce's version of the story had turned out more detailed than Mrs. Mirpuri's.

"But there's more," said Joyce. "It gets worse. I found out something amazing about another young woman in your life."

"Who?"

"Your girlfriend."

Wong's face became a mask of anger. "Please to stop say-ing this. I do not have girlfriend. I spend a long time last night to try to explain to Madame Xu—"

"Ha," Joyce laughed. "Did they tease you about that?

Sorry. Couldn't resist it. But the way the girl was looking at you, she did look interested in you. Hey, where are you going?"

Wong had risen to his feet. It had not been easy, since his bones were stiff and the seats in the coffee shop were like sponges. "Must go. I think Mrs. Mirpuri will be ready to meet me soon. You can stay."

"Wait," said Joyce. "I haven't finished yet. I haven't finished my muffin and I haven't finished my story. Sit down, please. This is really interesting, I promise you."

Wong reluctantly sat down again. "I do not pay you to eat," he said.

"I'm an intern. You don't pay me at all."

The feng shui man had no answer to this. "So what you. want to tell me?"

Joyce, speaking with a mouthful of chocolate sponge, said: "I got talking to the girl who was looking at you? Her name is Maddy. She's from Hong Kong. She said she's met you? She knows some of the same people I know in Hong Kong. She hung out at Insomnia and Le Jardin in Lan Kwai Fong just like me. She scored eight and a half on a ten-meter pike at a diving contest at my school pool. She knows this guy Lenny I used to know—before he got busted for drugs. I was friendly enough but I didn't pay her that much attention. I wanted to find out what people knew about Dani. I was working really hard all last night." She stopped for a moment. "Can I get expenses for what I spent at the club?"

"No."

"About two o'clock in the morning, I decide it's time to go home? I'm just saying good-bye to the gang, when this girl Maddy comes up and grabs my arm. She's like, 'Can I go with you? Can I talk to you?' It's a bit strange, but I'm like, 'Sure.' She says that I was so concerned about Dani being missing that I must be a nice person. She said she didn't have any friends and wanted a friend like me, who cared about whether she disappeared or not. It was a bit strange, what she was saying. Anyway, we're walking along and she steers me into one of those late-night noodle shops you get up on those roads past Kilimanjaro on Boat Quay, you know? I'm trying to make conversation, so I'm like, 'You got a boyfriend, then?' She's like, 'Yes. And he wants me to die.' Ever so casual."

"Young people, they get drunk, they say silly things. Is not real."

"Maybe. Maybe it was just the drink talking. But she told me she's got this boyfriend? Actually, fiancé. He's a lot older than she is, like ten years or something. I think she said he was like thirtysomething. Anyway, she told me she went to the cheap flophouse where he stays yesterday, and found he was out. She managed to get into the room—she didn't say how. She decides to wait for him. While she's there, to pass the time, she starts reading the papers and letters and stuff on his desk. The letters are boring stuff, invoices and things. But there are some papers tucked away. She finds that he has taken out an insurance policy on her life. She keeps reading. He has insured her life for like *two million ringgits*. Then she finds another insurance policy, also made out in her name. Then there's a third one. Basically, she finds that her fiancé has taken out loads of life insurance in her name. Like millions. I don't know what that is in real money, but I bet it's a lot."

"This is normal. People get married, they get insured."

"I don't think so. She said that there was no insurance coverage in *his* name. All of it was coverage for her, with him as the—as the—ben . . . ben . . .—you know what I mean."

"Yes," said Wong. "The benny-something. Know what you mean. Benny factor?"

Joyce wrinkled her brow. "It's on the tip of my tongue."

"What is?"

"Beneficiary."

"Beneficiary." Wong was pleased he knew the word. He must find a way to use it in his book.

"Yeah. Anyway, he's going to make an absolute fortune if she dies. And the most suspicious thing of all: he hasn't said one word about all this to her. It's his little secret. It's suspicious, isn't it? Go on, C. F., admit it. It is suspicious."

Wong stood up again. "Maybe so. But Joyce, I want you to remember one thing. We are not comic hero. We are not Superman. We do not save the world. We are not good guys. We are consultants. We are businessmen. When people pay us, we do things. At the moment, Mrs. Mirpuri will pay us rack rate plus fifty percent for express service. Dentist will pay us big money. I will make up outrageous big number for them. Already I have done some work for them. This will be good week for our finances. Very necessary to have good week from time to time. But this girl Maddy is not our assignment. We cannot help her. We are too busy. Must earn crusty bread, as the English say."

He marched angrily out of the coffee shop. "Always we waste time," he mumbled.

Joyce scooped up the remains of her breakfast and ran after him. "Wait," she said.

She caught up with him and swallowed the foamy dregs of her coffee before speaking again. "Listen, C. F., I was just coming to that. Maddy, the girl in the disco, *is* one of your clients, sort of. Her full name is Madeleine Tsai. She's the cousin of one of your clients. You know. She was in the apartment that nearly burned down with you in it on Saturday. Maybe the ghost wasn't trying to kill Mrs. Tsai-Thingy. Maybe the fiancé was trying to kill Maddy."

Wong stopped dead in his tracks.

❖

The office door crashed open. The crack in the glass lengthened.

"Hell-ooo!" said a cheery voice. "Mr. Wong?"

Madame Xu poked her head into the office. "Ah, Winnie, my dear. Is Mr. Wong at hand?"

Dilip Sinha appeared behind his friend. "Good afternoon, Winnie. How are you? We are here on a little surprise visit to your employer. Is he around?"

Winnie, who was in the middle of a lengthy private phone call in which she was trying to find out whether she could prosecute her employer for forcing her to work in a room without an air conditioner, sighed at the interruption. "Not here," she barked.

"He's not here," Madame Xu echoed, disappointed.

"Oh dear," said Sinha. 'Well, never mind. We'll see him later, I'm sure. Is he expected back shortly? Should we wait?"

"No," said Winnie.

The two visitors were stumped. They waited for Winnie to invite them in and offer them *ching cha* while she phoned around to find out where her boss was. They waited in vain.

"Well, what can we do?" Madame Xu sighed. "We can't enlist him in this battle to save this poor young lady if he is not here to be enlisted, can we? We'll just have to talk to him another time."

"We don't have a lot of time. The unfortunate girl may no longer be with us by Friday evening," Sinha said. "It's already Wednesday. Really, this case is the most troubling one I have had to deal with for many years."

"He must have gone out with Inspector Tan to deal with the ghost at the dentist. That did sound a fascinating case. Is he at the dentists', Winnie dear?"

"Don't know," snapped Winnie. "Talk later," she said into the phone, reluctantly ending her call.

Madame Xu decided to take control of the situation. She pulled Joyce's chair over to the corner of Winnie's desk and sat down heavily in it. "Listen, my dear," she said to the office administrator. "Can you give a message to Mr. Wong when he comes back? It's *very* important."

Winnie made no move to pick up a pen or paper.

"We need Mr. Wong to urgently find a remedy for a person of a certain birth date who is facing a major problem on a certain date which is very close. Do you understand?"

"Hmm."

"Can you deliver such a message?"

"Okay," Winnie barked, without attempting to hide her irritation. "Which person?"

"I can't tell you that."

"Which date?"

"I can't tell you that either."

"What problem?"

"I'm afraid that, too, is confidential." The older woman gave the secretary an apologetic smile. "I know it's all really very difficult, but you have to bear with me. I swore on some chicken gravy."

"Gravy?"

"So you see how serious it is."

Winnie's brows knitted themselves together to show her exasperation. "Don't understand."

Dilip Sinha cut in. "I think, my dear, if you would simply

124

tell him to contact us urgently on a matter of great importance, that would suffice. Where will we be, Chong Li?"

"Let's go back to my house. Yours always smells of curry."

"It does, I confess. One of the reasons I'm fond of it. We'll be at Madame Xu's house. Sago Street. Mr. Wong knows."

"We're going now," Madame Xu said, creakily rising to her feet. "You don't mind being left all your own in this office?"

"Yes," said Winnie, rolling her eyes to the ceiling. "Don't mind."

The pair left the office. As they walked down the stairs, Madame Xu said to Sinha: "Actually, I had this feeling that he wouldn't be there. I didn't want to say, but I had a strong premonition that he would be out."

"Odd, but so did I," said Sinha. "I knew it would be useless coming here."

"Well, why didn't you say so? You could have saved us a journey."

"Well, you didn't say so either."

"You didn't ask."

They bickered affectionately down four flights of stairs.

Wong, as usual when he was concentrating, retreated into his shell. After running out of information to deliver to him about her investigation into Danita's love life, Joyce asked him several times what he had discovered about the coded letter, but he said nothing, merely continuing to mumble to himself in Cantonese as he strode briskly through the crowded mid-morning streets. He made marks in a Singapore map-book as he walked.

"This way," he said out loud after jaywalking briskly across a road. "I think down here."

Joyce had expected him to lead her to a kidnapper's den. But instead they found themselves at the Hair Today Salon, a rather tacky beauty shop fronted with dark glass, its frontage liberally sprinkled with Christmas lights.

"Well, Mr. Wong, what do you think?" said a large, dark-skinned woman decked in a silk sari and heavy jewelery, who was waiting for him on a sofa at the entrance.

"I think we find her quite soon," said the geomancer, shaking her hand as they stepped out of the shop.

"No. What do you think of my hair I am asking," she snapped in a low alto.

"Ah, very nice, Mrs. Mirpuri," said Wong. "Very . . . black."

"Thank you," said Mrs. Mirpuri. "Now what were you saying about Danita? Have you found her? Is she with that awful policeman?"

"I don't know," the geomancer replied. "But I think she is *really* kidnap. Not run away."

Mrs. Mirpuri looked momentarily discomfited by this news. But the expression on her face was more one of irritation than distress. "Really kidnapped? You think so?"

"Yes. Not run away."

The woman looked into the middle distance. She appeared to be attempting to come to terms with this idea. She turned to Wong. "I don't know which is worse. To run away with unsuitable boy. Or to be really kidnapped. Both are equal bad news, no?"

Joyce was annoyed. "Of course it's worse to be kidnapped. I mean, they may hurt her or something."

"Who is this person?" Mrs. Mirpuri asked Wong.

"My assistant. Ms. McQuinnie."

"It's different in our culture," the Indian woman explained to the teenager. "In your tradition you girls just go with anyone you like and then switch every day. In our tradition we have this thing called marriage. We take relationships seriously. Much better."

"We have marriage too," snapped Joyce. "We invented marriage."

"No, you did not," snarled Mrs. Mirpuri. "That's ridiculous. We invented marriage."

"Rubbish," said Joyce.

"You invented divorce," Mrs. Mirpuri barked at Joyce.

The feng shui master held up his hands. "Please. Must hurry."

"Mr. Wong, tell your assistant that we invented marriage. Westerners hardly ever do it even now. Look at Madonna."

"She's married," said Joyce.

"Of course she isn't—"

"Truly, I don't know about any Donna," said Wong. "I do research first. Provide written answer at later date, is it okay?"

He started marching at a brisk pace along the road, pulling the older woman by the arm. "We go to find your daughter. On the way, please to tell me about policeman boyfriend and other boyfriends."

"Okay," said Mrs. Mirpuri. "But I warn you, Mr. Wong. It's a rather bizarre story, truth be told."

Mrs. Mirpuri repeated much of the story that Joyce had told Wong, about a wayward daughter who had been playing different boyfriends off against each other—and then, as the anger and passion and jealousy had mounted, had suddenly disappeared.

"We told her to choose one. We thought we liked the crazy rich one better, but then heard that the police officer had reasonable prospects. The stockbroker was useless—he was unemployed, and a bit of a conman, as all stockbrokers are. Anyway, I had this note on Monday morning from the kidnapper, and then a call yesterday morning. He said he had Danita and wanted money so they could run away and get married. He sounded crazy. I asked to speak to her, but he said that was not possible. I began to think that maybe this wasn't some silly lovers' thing, but something serious. So I phoned you."

"But you didn't want us to come yesterday. Why is it?"

"Yes. There were a couple of reasons for that. First, I thought I would leave it one more day, just to see if it all resolved itself. You never know with Danita. She's a silly girl. Second, I had a lot of things planned yesterday. I was scheduled to help my sister choose a trousseau for her daughter. This is a big event in Indian society. I couldn't just cancel that."

"And this morning? Why did you go and get your hair cut?" asked Wong.

"I was thinking, if this is a real kidnap, then I shall surely end up on television and in the *Straits Times*. And, Mr. Wong, I know this is not important for a man like you, but it is vital for a woman—your assistant might understand, although it is probably not the same for Westerners—but it is particularly true of a woman of a certain age, such as me—that she looks her best. I have not had my hair done for several weeks—"

"Was it the policeman's voice on the phone? Or the rich kid? Or the stockbroker?"

Mrs. Mirpuri's brows knitted. "Not exactly. It was a distorted voice. It sounded like a robot. He was speaking through some machine to change the tone of it. But I am assuming it was the policeman. He was always into drama, so he would have been the one to set up something like this."

She reached into her handbag. "I've been very efficient. I knew you would ask me about her boyfriends, so I have brought photographs of them all."

"Let me see," said Joyce.

"This is Ram Chulini, the rich kid. See that funny look in his eyes? A bit odd. And this is Mak Kin-Lei. Everybody calls him Kinny. He's the police officer. And this one, Winterbottom, is the stockbroker. He's tall, quite good-looking."

"I bet I can sort this out," said Joyce. "The first one's a dog. Forget him. I've met him. I went to a party with Danita and him ages ago. Maybe two weeks. Didn't rate him. This guy, Kinny, is all right. I'd give him a seven. I think I've seen him down at Dante's. I'm not sure. But this guy Charles— he's got weird eyes. And no chin. Only a five, or maybe less. I'd go for Kinny Mak. He'd make a good son-in-law."

"You think so?" Mrs. Mirpuri looked at Joyce, evidently trying to decide whether her opinion was worth anything.

"Sure. Not that I'm an expert on guys. But my sister is. If she were here, she could just look at those pictures and instantly tell you all about these guys, what their strange habits are, what's good or bad about them, all that kind of thing. She's really amazing."

Suddenly, the feng shui master came to a halt at a junction. "Your daughter is close here, I think. On this road. Joyce, I want you to go to that shop, pretend to buy something, have a look round. See if you can see one of the boyfriend. Mrs. Mirpuri please wait. She will come back here after one-two minutes. Or maybe not."

Joyce refused to move. "How do you know we're in the right place? Did you break the code? What did the message say?"

"No time for that now."

"I'm not moving until you tell me."

Employer and employee stared at each other.

"Okay, okay, I show you," said the feng shui master, backing down. "But I think you should hurry."

He carefully got out the note, which was folded in his pocket—and also the envelope in which it came, which he had found under Winnie's desk.

"Here is message." Joyce stared hard at it, giving it one more chance to give up its secret.

Mrs. Mirpuri reached into her bag and got out her reading glasses.

Jr;[@@@@ O
Br nrrm lofms[[rf/ O
, om s fstl tpp, om s nio;fomh eoyj
{ptyihirdr.=dyu;e g;ppts yjtrr pt gpit ,omiyrd gtp,
Jplorn Dytrry/ Gomf ,r/ Ithrmy@@@ Fsmo/

"Is not an alphabet code," said Wong. "Is not a code at all."

"What is it, then?" asked Joyce.

The feng shui man smiled. "Is bad typing."

"What?" This was Joyce. "What do you mean bad typing? It must be really bad typing—I mean, if you can't even read a single word of it."

Wong pointed to the first word. "If you type a letter but your fingers are on wrong buttons—one button too far right—then this is what happen. You want to press 'h' but you get the next letter, is 'j.' You want to press 'e,' but you get next letter, which is 'r.' You want to press 'l,' but you get next letter, which is dot-and-comma. And so forth and so fifth."

Joyce nodded slowly. "I get it. Someone typed it with their fingers in the wrong place on the keyboard."

"Correct," said Wong.

"But how did she end up with her fingers in the wrong place?"

"Is old typewriter. She is typing in the dark. Maybe some keys on edge are missing."

"I don't follow any of this," said Mrs. Mirpuri.

"Like we care," said Joyce, under her breath. To Wong, she added: "We need a typewriter keyboard to work out what it means."

"Already done," said the feng shui master. On the lower part of the sheet, he had scrawled out in scratchy handwriting the letters adjacent to the letters printed. He showed the translation to Joyce.

Help!!!! I've been kidnapped. I'm in a dark room in a building with Portuguese-style tile floors three or four minutes from Hokien Street. Find me. Urgent!!! Dani.

"The instructions are a bit vague," said Joyce. "How do we know we are in the right place? 'Dark room in a building with Portuguese-style tile floors.' Could be anywhere."

"She say 'dark room.' But I think she mean 'darkroom.' You know, photo-developing darkroom. In *any* room, there is a bit of light, you can see what you are typing. Even at night, with moonlight, you can type in the dark. But if she is in photo developing darkroom, there is no light. No light at all."

"I thought there was a red light."

He rolled his eyes. "In movies, there is red light. But in real darkroom, most of the time is just black. If you remove optional red lightbulb, then is black all the time."

"So you reckon she's in a photo studio, in a darkroom?"

"Most photo shop today have modern machine. No darkroom. Only old-style photo studio have old-style darkroom.

I check in Yellow Pages. I know this area a bit. Only a few shop like that. And only two shops in tile-floor building I think," said Wong. "This one and one on that street." He pointed to a junction half a mile up the road on the other side.

Joyce was suddenly excited. "Yay! Let me do this, chief," she said. "After all, it's my case. Let me go first. I've met some of the guys. I'll be able to spot the perp."

"Perp?"

"Perpetrator. Don't you watch crime shows?"

"Maybe dangerous," Mrs. Mirpuri said.

"Yes." Wong thought about this. Was the potential danger a good reason for him to go first or for him to let her go first? She was surely stronger and faster than he was. But then she was a female and a minor. What if she got shot or something? Maybe Mr. Pun would deduct something from his retainer. "Maybe we go together," he said eventually.

"I bet I'll be able to recognize the guy," she said.

The feng shui master and his assistant marched together into the shop. As they approached the counter, they saw the counter-staffer—a stocky, heavily obese man. He saw them and froze, his mouth dropping open.

"It's you!" said Joyce, dramatically.

"*Alamak!*" the man said and spun round to race through the door into the back room.

"Go out, call police, *fai-dee*," said Wong.

Joyce started digging in her pockets for what remained of the office cell phone.

Wong disappeared through the door after the fat man. There was the sound of a brief struggle—and the geomancer came hurtling back through the door. He fell heavily against the counter. "*Aiyeeaah!*" he said.

They could hear the sound of his assailant panting and

pushing aside boxes as he scrambled to escape through the rooms behind the shop.

"You all right?" asked Joyce, jumping nimbly over the counter to her boss's side.

"All right," said Wong, rubbing his upper arm. "Let him go. Police will catch. Not our job. We go find girl."

They went through the door into a suite of offices, untidy stock rooms and tiny studios, and eventually found an exit door that was still swinging. The shopkeeper had raced into a backyard and had disappeared from sight. Wong told Joyce that it was no use further giving chase.

So they searched the premises. The young woman soon found a locked darkroom, entered through the office by way of a blacked-out revolving door. Although the key was in the padlock, Wong waited for Joyce to search the premises and find a flashlight before they entered.

Inside they found a rather attractive young woman fast asleep on a bed she had fashioned out of dozens of packets of photographic paper. She had removed her sari to use as a sheet. There were boxes of chemicals, piles of old photographs and various other items of junk—including a battered old typewriter—in the corners of the room.

Wong clasped his hands together and looked smug.

"Mystery solved," said Joyce, speaking in a whisper so as not to wake Dani. "She must have typed out the note in pitch darkness." There was McDonald's fast food debris and two empty bottles of Diamond Black on the floor.

"Who was it? The man?" the feng shui master asked. "Which boyfriend?"

"I don't know."

"But when we enter the shop, you look at him and you say: 'It's you.'"

"Yeah."

"So you know who it is?"

Joyce frowned. "Not really. It's just—well, in movies and stuff, when they finally find the bad guy, they always say, 'It's you.' So I did."

The geomancer was confused. "Is it one of the people you see in the photographs?"

"No. It's nobody we know. It's a stranger. Probably some other boyfriend that she never got around to telling anyone about. Someone who turned nasty and decided to really kidnap her. I haven't the foggiest. Life is not a neat little detective mini-series, you know, C. F."

"Oh."

But despite her dismissive tone, Joyce felt oddly unsatisfied. Surely there should be some universal law which required the perp to be someone the investigators knew?

On the fourth floor of the building in Telok Ayer Street, the office door once again crashed open. The crack in the frosted glass lengthened further.

A lithe young Chinese woman with streaked hair entered the room. "Is Ms. Joyce here?"

"Aiyeeaah! Too many people today." Winnie Lim, who had restarted her interrupted phone conversation, peered at the entrant with distaste. "Joyce go out."

"Where is she?"

"Out."

"Did she say where she was going?"

"Don't know. Not listening. Too busy."

"When will she be back?"

"Don't know."

"Will she come back today?"

"Don't know."

"Has she got a cell phone?"

"Yes."

"What's the number? No, don't tell me: you don't know. Look, I really need to find her, talk to her about something really important. Is there any way you can help me? It's urgent."

Winnie Lim thought for a moment. A very short moment. "Don't know," she spat through half-closed teeth. "Come back later maybe. Or tomorrow maybe."

The young visitor looked around the room. Her eyes stopped on Joyce's desk. It was very obviously the desk of a teenage female, with a portable CD player in the center of the desk, and a single pink designer sports-shoe visible under the seat.

"My name's Maddy Tsai," she said. "I'm a friend of Joyce's. I've met Mr. Wong, too. Can I wait here for her?"

Winnie opened her mouth languidly, as if she was going to say, "Don't know," again, but closed it without saying anything. She shrugged her shoulders and went back to her phone conversation.

Maddy sat in Joyce's seat. It creaked and threatened to tip to one side. She looked around the office. It was shabby and dirty, and the air was hot and still. There appeared to be no air conditioner. But at least it was the room of a friend–something she desperately needed just now.

She looked at the CDs on the desk. Modern Western pop singers, pretty boys, some with little beards on their chins. They all had baggy clothes. They looked defiant. They looked as if they ruled the world. That's how it should be. Young people do rule the world. Old people are dying people. *It will be our world soon—if we live to inherit it.* The thought caused a feeling of white pain to sweep through her brain. How could she possibly be about to die? Her life had hardly begun.

Her reverie was interrupted by a crash as the door swung open again.

"NOW WHO?" shouted Winnie, her face showing astonishment at yet another interruption.

"Oh no," gasped Maddy.

A tall, broad-shouldered, dark-skinned man entered the room, a smile on his face. "So now? Why are you here, my dear? Visit a friend-lah?"

"You followed me." She spoke angrily.

"Maybe. Maybe not. Maybe I was passing only and saw you come into this building, is it?"

"You followed me. Can't you just leave me be for a while?"

"*Takboleh-lah.* Cannot-lah. I'm so much concerned about you, man. I've eaten more salt than you. This is good Malay saying. Have news for you. Come, come."

Amran Ismail moved menacingly into the center of the room.

Maddy glanced quickly around the room. Ismail was in front of the main door, but there was another door on the other side of the office. Did it lead anywhere?

Winnie Lim, apparently guessing what was going through her mind, shook her head. It led only to an internal room, a meditation room Wong used for afternoon naps.

"Stay away from me." Maddy Tsai sprang to her feet.

"I'm your only chance-lah," said Ismail. "Your only hope. Why you like to run from me? You need me. Without me you got nothing. You are dead. Really dead. I got some news. I found a place we can go. A place you can be safe. Listen to me, can or not-lah?"

They maneuvered around each other.

Suddenly, Ismail sprang forward, reaching for the young woman with his long arms. She ducked out of his grip and tried to scuttle under his left arm toward the door.

But he fell sideways and reached out, grabbing her ankle with his hand.

"Got you," he said, pulling her back.

"Let me go," she shouted, trying to wriggle out of his grip.

"Don't like that," he said, holding her tightly by the arms. "Now calm down."

They struggled for some time. He looked strong, but she was wiry and agile, and hard to keep hold of. "Get away from me," she shouted, wrenching one arm free.

"Come," he replied, grabbing her wrist with his free hand.

Both of them froze in their tracks as an enormous bellow filled the room.

"STOP THIS NOISE!" screamed Winnie Lim, standing up. "I AM TRYING TO GOSSIP ON PHONE. GET OUT, GET OUT, GET OUT OF MY OFFICE."

The struggling couple were so astonished by the extraordinary volume and sheer intensity of emotion that came out of the body of the tiny receptionist-like creature that they froze.

"GET OUT NOW," Winnie shrieked, pointing to the doorway. She stamped her size three feet.

Ismail momentarily loosened his grip.

Maddy wriggled free and ran out of the front door.

The *bomoh* chased after her.

Winnie was silent for a few seconds. Never could she remember a day when there had been such drama in her office. And from two complete strangers. How exhausting. She picked up the telephone and dialed a number to continue the conversation that had so often been so rudely inter-rupted. She said to her friend: "I think I need new job."

❖

The police took over the investigation at the photographic studio and Wong left an overexcited Mrs. Mirpuri and her yawning, bleary-eyed daughter with an inspector. Danita, excited at seeing Joyce, initially wanted to tell the whole story to her—but the police told the kidnapping victim that she should give a statement to them first. The two friends eventually agreed to part after Joyce promised to phone Danita later that day for a *major* gab session.

Mrs. Mirpuri, after giving her daughter a quick hug, was instantly on her cell phone summoning the television net-works, radio stations and newspapers to relate the story of how she had single-handedly rescued her daughter from an evil kidnapper. "Bring cameras," she said to everyone includ-ing the radio newsroom editor. "Bring cameras."

In a taxi on their way back across town, Joyce, who was also in a state of hyper-excitement, was struggling with questions. "There's lots of things I don't understand, C. F. How did Danita manage to get that letter delivered to our place?"

Wong nodded. "Is a mystery, truly. But I tell you what I think. She is kidnap on Sunday night, stuck in darkroom. She feel around, find photo paper, find old typewriter which is now junk—now everybody use electric typewriter or com-puter. She write 'help' message to me. Try to describe where she is. She type in dark, so her writing is all wrong, look like code. Some keys missing on edge of typewriter. Then she put letter in envelope. She write address on envelope with her hand, so is correct, even though she write in dark. Then she put envelope on floor of black-out revolving door. When fat man comes in and out, maybe to deliver food, drink, letter is moved, swept out into office area directly next to darkroom. She hope he himself finds it on floor next day or something, mails it."

"And he did?"

"I don't know what happen really. But maybe he find letter on the floor and mail it. Or maybe he has staff or assistant or family member who work with him. They think it is business letter. She wrote 'urgent' on it. Maybe even the kidnap man mail it himself. He think other staff member drop it."

Joyce grinned. "Totally amazing. Her gamble worked. Someone picked up the letter and mailed it—to us. She must have written it on Sunday. It got mailed some time Monday morning, I guess, which is why we got it yesterday."

"Correct."

The young woman shook her head. "Poor thing. Imagine being stuck in the dark for days. Must have been awful. No wonder her eyes are squinty. Poor Dani."

"Too bad," said Wong, agreeing. "Too, too bad."

The feng shui master saw a good opportunity for him to have a break from his assistant. He dropped her at Telok Ayer Street so that she could write a hefty invoice to Mrs. Mirpuri and then deliver it by hand. He also asked her to contact Calida Tsai-Leibler, to make discreet inquiries about Madeleine Tsai and what she saw as her imaginary murderous fiancé. He retained the taxi to take him to his appointment with Dr. Liew Yok Tse, for which he was already late.

"Off again? No peace for the wicked," said Joyce, waving good-bye from the pavement.

"No piece of what?" asked Wong. But the taxi whisked him away before she could answer.

He found the dental office in a nondescript tower on

Orchard Road without much difficulty and spent some time talking to each of the people who worked there. Superintendent Tan had gone. The ghost had not appeared all day, so staff were starting to lose the tension that had gripped them. But without exception, they remained morose and uncomfortable-looking. Both of the actual offices were almost fully booked with patients for the afternoon, so Wong took the opportunity to talk with individuals when they were free, and carry on with his floor plan analysis when they were busy. Once he had finished doing that, he took out his journal and spent some time working on new entries.

Dr. Gibson Leibler was noticeably more polite than he had been on Saturday, but still maintained a certain aloofness. Dr. Liew Yok Tse was friendlier. He was a tall, but rather underweight man with heavy bags under a pair of frog-like, hooded eyes. He appeared harassed and looked as if he carried the weight of the world on his shoulders.

The dentist told Wong that he had worked for a group practice for the first ten years of his life, before setting up his own firm four years ago in Chinatown. Then he had met Gibson Leibler a year ago and they had settled on a plan to run a joint operation in a more upmarket location.

The two dentists presently shared Dr. Liew's dental technician Cheung Lai Kuen, although an advertisement had been placed for a second full-time technician. In the meantime, the role of technician for Dr. Leibler was sometimes informally filled by Amanda Luk, who was really the receptionist—although she preferred to call herself "front office manager." She had had just enough training to be able to carry off the job of technician, although she seemed to dislike the task, preferring her desk.

She was a rather buxom Eurasian woman with hair dyed the color of copper wire, who had previously worked in the hotel business. She was attractive and dressed rather too well for her role, Wong thought, looking at the woman's elegant black dress. But then, that was a characteristic of Singapore's female workers generally.

Dr. Liew's technician was very different. Cheung Lai Kuen was a thin, bespectacled woman who tended to murmur under her breath, and walked stiffly around as if she had lower back pain. Wong had got the impression that she was rather resentful of the fact that her parents had been unable to send her to good schools. She seemed to think that she had the brains to have been a dentist, as opposed to a dental technician.

The time inevitably came when all staff had been called to deal with patients, and Wong had to busy himself with his readings. The building had its back to the waterfront and faced a hill, and thus was an unusual feng shui configuration known as "sitting empty, facing solid." But the general picture was good. The water star was located in the east, and the east of the building faced the water, which was highly auspicious.

"When we find this, we say, 'The water star falls in the water,'" Wong said to Dr. Gibson Leibler during a gap between two patients. "Good sign."

Dr. Leibler, for the first time, gave the feng shui master a polite nod and half a smile.

On the whole, the intangible forces were good for both rooms, although the reception desk was ill-situated, Wong decided. The front surface was unhappily facing northeast, and he decided that when he next visited the office, he would hang an ornament—six copper coins with prowling tigers—over it. Despite his general dislike of superstition and the use of trinkets, he knew that physical reminders of non-visible energy often served a good purpose if used judiciously. He also realized that three out of the four people in the office—

Gibson Leibler being the exception—would probably take comfort in physical items designed to ward off evil.

There was a small number of other negative factors revealed by a study of the floor plans. A temporary *shar* of five was found on the northeast side of the suite of offices, toward the back of Dr. Leibler's room, and a *shar* of two at the entrance to the office. These were calculated on a monthly basis, and would fade with the next moon, the geomancer calculated. But for now, there were likely to be more repeats of the bad phenomena. "Never mind," he told Amanda Luk, who had emerged from one of the labs to make reminder calls to two patients who tended to miss appointments. "I can deal with it."

The feng shui master knew he could make the superstitious Cheung Lai Kuen happy by preparing a symbolic Cup from the Heavenly Pond to counteract the forces emanating from the Three Curses Position. He prepared several other feng shui items, but these he wanted to keep back until the problem reoccurred.

After finishing these operations, Wong quickly got bored. After the excitement of the arrest at the photographic studio at lunchtime, the late afternoon passed slowly. There was almost nothing he could do except sit in the waiting room, as if he were a phantom patient who waited quietly but whose name was never called. He decided to while away a few hours writing in his journal about the brilliance of the sages. The human atmosphere in the premises felt very uncomfortable, and he found himself drawn to the subject of deception.

Cao Wei, a great leader of Weizhou, was at a social engagement with other army generals.

Just then, a messenger arrived on horseback. He had bad news.
"Some of your men have defected. They have joined the
enemy," the messenger said.
"Oh dear," said Cao Wei. And then he smiled very slowly.
The messenger rode back to the battlefields and told every-
one what Cao Wei had said. He also told them that the
leader had smiled very slowly.
The enemy leader, hearing this, decided that the new men he
had got were spies. He picked them out and had them all
executed.

The smile of a child comes from the heart. But never forget,
Blade of Grass: no one knows where the smile of an adult
comes from.

(Some Gleanings of Oriental Wisdom
by C. F. Wong, part 345)

❖

Joyce phoned Wong at the dental office at 3:11 P.M., to say
that she had delivered the invoice to Mrs. Mirpuri, and was
now heading home to change before going out to Dan T.'s
Inferno for the happy hour session which began at five
o'clock. She said that Mrs. Mirpuri had banned Danita from
going out that night, but had allowed the two friends to
spend an hour talking on the phone.

Joyce said all her attempts to get in contact with Calida
Tsai-Leibler to ask about her cousin Maddy had come to
nothing. Mrs. Tsai-Leibler had gone to a secret location to
protect her child from the murderous ghost, a domestic
helper had explained.

"I so don't need another late night," the young woman told Wong on the phone. "But I do want to talk to Maddy again. I think there might be another case there that I can solve. I seem to be doing pretty well this week."

"Yes, yes, you try to solve more cases, very good for me," Wong replied. "Do my work for me. Then I can just do invoices, collect money."

Wong was pleased to get some writing done, although he felt a little uncomfortable in the waiting room. The earlier part of the day had been a little too dramatic for him, and he was annoyed to discover several nasty bruises on his arms he had got from his encounter with Danita Mirpuri's kidnapper. He decided that the best thing for him was to be home putting traditional Chinese ointments on his aching limbs, not sitting on the uncomfortably soft benches of a dentist's waiting room. He wondered if Dr. Liew might have some Pak Fa Yeow in the office. But would it be wrong to ask a modern doctor for traditional white flower oil medicine? Would he be laughed at? Worse, would he be charged proper consultation fees? Better not ask.

Still, at least it was cool and air-conditioned. He suddenly realized that he could probably get more work done on his journal here than he would in his un-airconditioned office over the next few days. He pulled the large volume out of his bag and started working on it again. Now what theme should he consider? Still deception. The sages, both greater and lesser, often used a type of deception to solve problems and advance themselves, he mused.

During the period of the Five Dynasties (907-960) the King of Zhao was a man named Li Decheng. He came from the

Southern Tang Dynasty in Jiangxi.

A mystic came to him and told him that he could spot great-ness in a person with a single glance.

The king was intrigued by this claim. So he arranged a test for the mystic. He dressed his wife, a woman of great class and breeding, in the costume of the court dancers. Then he put her into a group of court dancers, so that she looked no different from them.

When all was ready, he summoned the visiting mystic.

"Which of these ladies is my wife?" the King asked.

"It is obvious," said the mystic. "It is the one with a glowing golden cloud over her head."

The women tried not to move. But at the same time they strained to see what was over the Queen's head. They saw nothing.

But it was easy for the mystic to correctly identify the Queen.

Blade of Grass: If you cannot see something with your own eyes, arrange to see it with someone else's eyes.

(Some Gleanings of Oriental Wisdom
by C. F. Wong, part 346)

At 4:01 P.M., there was a scream. Wong dropped his journal and leaped to his feet. Receptionist Cheung Lai Kuen ran out of Dr. Liew's office and almost crashed into the feng shui master. With a yelp, she ran out of the premises and stood with her fists to her mouth in the elevator lobby. She was almost immediately followed by a large blonde woman in a pale blue apron with a metal device in her mouth. "Ak-grr-kr-warrr,"

she said and then also ran out of the office in the direction of the elevator.

Dr. Liew appeared.

"Stupid patient. She's run off without her shoes or jacket."

"And with a mouth extension clamped between her jaws," said Dr. Leibler, who had been watching from the doorway of his room. "She's going to have a tough time explaining that to her family."

"*Mutyeh si?*" Wong asked.

"The ghost is inside. It's in the room." Dr. Liew spoke calmly and factually, but there was a noticeable tremor in his voice.

Wong marched toward the door of the room and stopped. He saw nothing inside. Carefully, he leaned the upper half of his body through the doorway. The drama all became too much for Amanda Luk, who also scampered outside to stand with Lai Kuen in the corridor. "I can feel it. It's in there. It's horrible," she said. A shiver of horror ran through her body.

"You should have heard the sound it made. It was right next to me," said Lai Kuen, starting to cry.

Wong stepped right into the room. Dr. Liew remained at the door, peering in.

There was no one in the room. That was immediately evident. It was a small space dominated by the dental chair, and there was simply nowhere anyone could hide. He glanced under the chair. Nothing. Cabinets lined the walls on one side, but they were shallow. It was difficult to imagine that anyone could hide inside them.

The room was silent except for a general hum. He realized that there were two buzzing sounds—one coming from a tiny air-conditioning vent in the ceiling, and another coming from a small machine on the ground: a fridge, or sterilizing unit of some kind, he ventured.

The geomancer looked around the room. "There's nothing. It's—" He stopped abruptly.

There was the unmistakable sound of a male voice. It gave a pained, gently vocalized sigh. "Ahhhh. Owwww." It apparently came from an invisible person sitting in the dentist's chair.

"Can you hear him?" asked Dr. Liew.

"Can," whispered Wong, his eyes suddenly wide. "He's there." He stood in front of the chair, and heard the sound repeated, coming from roughly where a person's head would be. It really did seem to be a ghost patient. The geomancer's jaw dropped.

Dr. Liew started to back away toward the door. "Come out. We must leave this place." He turned around and stepped out.

Dr. Leibler marched into the room. He had a studied expression of detachment on his face, but his nervousness revealed itself in the distance he kept from the center of the room, where Wong stood in front of the chair. "Where is this alleged spirit?" he asked with studied carelessness.

"In the chair," said the feng shui master. "There." He pointed to the spot where the thing's face would be.

"Owwww!" said the voice, which appeared to be male. It had a constricted quality—unmistakably the sound of a person moaning with a dental tool placed in his mouth. It followed this with a long, low whimper.

Dr. Leibler gulped, despite himself. "I can hear it," he whispered. "It is like a patient. Like I said."

Wong walked slowly around the chair, pointing his *lo pan* at it.

"What is that?" asked the American dentist. "Can it detect the ghost?"

"No. Only a compass. I want to see if the ghost affects the direction of compass. No effect I think."

After circling the chair, Wong lowered the compass and stood straight, staring at the chair, and twirling the long hairs on his chin.

"I want to try something," the geomancer said. "How do I make the chair go down?"

Dr. Leibler pointed to a control panel jutting out to the right of the chair. "There. Press that top one."

The feng shui master leaned over and pressed the button that tilted the chair back, and then pulled the lever next to it. With a noisy hiss, the chair dropped almost sixteen inches. It was a modern chair, which tilted back a full 95 degrees, leaving the patient's head slightly lower than his feet.

Dr. Leibler stepped over, and locked the chair into its new position and the two of them stood and waited. A minute of silence passed.

"Come, let's all go," said Dr. Liew, who was watching from the doorway. "This is making me feel helluva uncomfortable."

"No," said Wong. "You can go. I want to see something. I want to see the sound is coming from where."

There it was again. The sound of an unhappy patient, giving a low, moaning croak. This time it wasn't from the chair, which had been dropped to its lowest point, but from the air in the middle of the room, above it. "Interesting. I move the chair. But has no effect. Sound stays there, in the air. Ghost patient has his ghost chair. Or ghost can fly."

Dr. Leibler, with a sharp intake of breath, spun on his heel and marched briskly to the door. "Weird," he said. "Seriously weird."

Wong followed more slowly, and strolled into the waiting room, where he picked up his bag. He pulled out a small vase in the shape of an altar and a bag of candles.

"These will look after me. You can go," said Wong. "You give me a key to lock up. I will stay."

T
H
U
R
S
D
A
Y

GHOSTS CAN'T GET ANY DEADER

THURSDAY DAWNED cool and damp. C. F. Wong woke early, his thoughts distracted and confused after his encounter with whatever-it-was in the dental office the previous afternoon—an exchange which had lasted for more than an hour. He had gone home with a headache and slept badly. He was not surprised to find himself suddenly wide awake in the dark.

Noticing through his curtainless windows that the dawn had yet to even think about breaking, he decided that he would go to work immediately to take advantage of the coolness of the morning. He left his tiny apartment in Chinatown's Pagoda Street at 5:44 A.M. And was at the door of his office ten minutes later. He entered the dark suite of rooms and was pleased to find the temperature pleasant for the first time in forty-eight hours. The vestiges of a pre-dawn breeze were gently blowing through the space in the window where the air conditioner used to be. The night was almost silent. The murmur of traffic, which formed a constant background during the day, had disappeared. In its place was a very low, undulating hum from the distant main thorough-fare, interrupted only by the occasional rattle of an early-morning delivery van carrying newspapers or *char siu bau*.

Wong sat down in his chair and pulled out his journal. He would be able to do several hours work before it became insufferably hot and he would have to retreat to Ah-Ooi's Noodles, perhaps even producing several new gleanings for his chapter on the ingenious problem-solving methods of the great sages. He set to work.

The Emperor of Qi was a man named Jin Gong. One day he found that his stablehand had accidentally caused the death of his favorite horse.

"My favorite horse is dead? The stablehand responsible shall also be put to death," the ruler said. "Kill him immediately."

But a wise sage named Yan Zi interrupted.

"O mighty Emperor," said Yan Zi. "You are right in all that you do. But you have said in the past that a man must die knowing exactly what crime he has committed."

The Emperor agreed.

A court was assembled. The stablehand was placed in the dock.

Yan Zi read out the charges. "You will be marked in history for doing three bad things," he said to the stablehand.

"Three bad things?" asked the emperor.

"Three bad things?" said the stablehand.

Yan Zi related the three sins to the man in the dock. "One: You killed the Emperor's favorite horse. Two: You caused the Emperor to kill a human being in return for the death of an animal. Three: You spoiled the reputation of the Emperor, who had previously been known as a wise and

*kind ruler. For these reasons, you must die," said Yan Zi.
"No," said the Emperor. "I forgive him."*

In a dispute, Blade of Grass, let time intervene. Only when anger has dissipated will there be room for wisdom to enter.

*(Some Gleanings of Oriental Wisdom
by C. F. Wong, part 347)*

He smiled, proud of his use of the words "intervene" and "dissipated." He flicked through his dictionary, looking for more long terms to use.

Wong had been working for almost half an hour when he started to feel oddly distracted. He had gradually started to sense, at first only in his subconscious, that he was not alone. Before the thought penetrated fully into his conscious mind, he continued to write for several minutes. Then something made him look up. Had there been a tiny movement in the room, some motion glimpsed from the outermost edge of his vision? Or had there been a sound, a noise so low that it was barely audible to a person concentrating on something else? He glanced around. The only light came from his desk lamp, so the rest of the room remained filled with deep shadows. He pricked up his ears. He identified no sound except the faraway whispers of vehicles speeding along Orchard Road. If there was no motion and no sound in the office, what had he detected? Was there some sort of presence in the room?

Ji-seen, he scolded himself. He had spent so many hours last night thinking about the ghost that he was now starting to think he could detect spirits all around him. Ridiculous! He turned his attention back to his writing.

❖

Two thousand and five hundred years ago, a child was born who was already old. His hair was white and his brain was filled with wisdom. He was called Lao Tzu, which means The Old Child.

The Old Child lived fifty-four years before Confucius. He was a great sage. But he refused to write down any of his thoughts. He believed that writing words down killed them.

At the end of his life, when the Old Child had become an old man, he rode on a water buffalo to retire in a faraway kingdom.

But the lowly keeper of the gate refused to let him in. "Write something for me and that will be the price of your entrance," he said.

The Old Child sat at a table and wrote 5000 characters. The result was the Tao-Te-Ching, *which is one of the greatest classics of ancient wisdom.*

Blade of Grass, every person thinks other people are like themselves. Lao Tzu, The Old Child, was a great sage. But he believed that every man could journey through ideas as he did. But the poor gatekeeper knew something that Lao Tzu did not. Most men cannot share the journey of a great sage without a guidebook.

(Some Gleanings of Oriental Wi . . .

He froze. This time, he knew he had heard a sound. It was unmistakable. It was a tiny, low moan made by a human voice. It was similar to the sound in the dentists' office, except it was made by a closed mouth. And it was right here in this office. An involuntary shiver ran down his spine. Had the thing in the dentists' office left its haunt and decided to follow him around? Or had yesterday's experience made him suddenly more attuned to the existence of supernatural spirits? Had a ghost been occupying his office for some time?

He couldn't write one more word. He had to investigate. Lowering his pen, he grabbed a tiny ceremonial sword, faintly ashamed to be using such a device as a talisman to ward off evil spirits in which he didn't really believe. He started to walk carefully around the room.

"Unnh . . ."

The husky groan appeared to come from the meditation room. He approached it carefully and looked through the glass window. It was empty. He listened at the door. He heard a third gently voiced moan. It was in there.

The geomancer opened the door with infinite care and carefully moved his head inside.

Something white moved in the shadows. A ghastly pale face with angry red eyes materialized suddenly before him.

"Aiyeeaah!" he gasped, dropping his talisman.

A replica of an old-fashioned phone, inlaid with *cloisonné* and mother-of-pearl, trilled prettily three times. Bejeweled fingers picked up the handset.

"Yes?"

"Madame Xu?"

"Yes?"

"Good morning, Chong Li. I hope you slept well. It's me."

"That's right. I knew that it was you, Dilip Sinha. Even before I picked up the phone."

"I knew it was me, too. We seem to be in general agreement on that point. That's a good start."

"I suppose it is."

"Now listen, my dear. I could hardly sleep at all last night. I don't know why, but this week my spirit can't seem to settle at all. I'm sleeping badly. So many worries. Last night, I kept thinking about that unfortunate young couple. The girl, only a mere slip of a thing at eighteen or nineteen or whatever she is, and her heartbroken boyfriend . . ."

"Fiancé, actually."

"That's right. Well, what struck me most painfully last night was the sheer impossibility of anyone doing anything about this except us. I mean, think about it. If young Ismail takes her to the police and tells them to lock her in their strongest cell for safety, they will think he is mad, and lock him up instead. If he goes to doctors, they will tell him that there is nothing wrong with her, and they will be correct. Medically speaking, there *is* nothing wrong with her. She's young and fit."

"He could go to the government. There must be a department to deal with this sort of thing. Underage death."

"I don't think so. If he goes to any sort of higher authority—government officials, or academics, or judges or what have you, they will merely think that this is a load of mystical tomfoolery. And perhaps some of it is—I mean, some of Ismail's stuff, like the chicken blood and the soles of the feet stuff—it all seems frankly irrational. But our own readings, which we ourselves trust and know to be reliable, confirm so much of what he has said. So we have to take his fears seriously and act upon them. It is clear to me that we are the only people who are going to listen to this problem, and also the only people who are going to be able to do anything about it. We are running out of time."

"But what can we do?"

Sinha sighed. "That's just it. I don't know. I've been struggling with it. I mean, each of us has, in his or her armory of mystic techniques, certain remedies for ill fortune. I spent several hours last night going through my books looking for the right remedies for this situation."

"I spent several hours last night doing the same thing."

"Of course you did. That is because you and I are deeply concerned about this. But I am not confident that we can solve the problem. The remedies seem so . . . inadequate, somehow. Last night, I got my friend Arun Subramaniam, who is a tarot card reader, to read the cards of poor Clara. He doesn't like to do what he calls 'remote readings' without the subject present, but he agreed to do one for me. He turned up the card of death at all significant points. Of course, as you know, in tarot readings the death card does turn up regularly and is often interpreted to mean things other than death. But even Arun was shocked at the regularity at which it turned up in the readings for this particular young woman—and how negative the other cards were, too."

"Dilip! It sounds to me as if you broke your vow to not tell anyone else about the case."

"I didn't tell him what it was about. I told him as little as I could. I didn't tell him the name of the girl. I just gave him the basic details he needed to know to do the reading. But anyway, this final confirmation of doom led me to another thought: the pillars of destiny."

"Ah. Mr. Wong."

"That's right. We must have another try to get C. F. Wong involved with this. He can read the earthly pillars and heavenly what-is-its for Clara for tomorrow and Saturday, assuming she might be at various destinations. It strikes me that he, if he has all the information at hand, may be able to specify a *location* where she may be likely to be safe. I think the only thing that can save her is a combination of our arts. Putting her in a safe place would seem to me to be a perfect start."

Madame Xu assented with a genteel grunt. "Hmm. Yes. It would be very nice to have C. F. involved in this. We did try yesterday."

"Also, he has an uncanny knack of looking at things from curious angles and seeing solutions where the rest of us see nothing. It has happened several times. Remember the murder in the hotel kitchen where there was no murder weapon?"

"Yes, I do. You're right. Let's try to see him again this morning. He might be at the dentists', trying to exorcise the ghost."

"Not this early. The dental office wouldn't even be open. I phoned him at home, there was no one there. I also tried his office. You know he often goes to the office at the crack of dawn. But no answer there, either. He must be on the road somewhere. Anyway, I propose we call a Code Red lunch meeting of the committee."

"Code Red! We haven't done that for a long time. Two meetings of the committee in one week would be unusual."

"You're right. But this is an emergency. It's Thursday already. Clara may be dead by the end of tomorrow. It's a more urgent business than the ghost that Wong is dealing with. The ghost, after all, is already dead. It can't get any deader. Whereas our young lady can."

"True. And if we don't do something for poor Clara, we may have another ghost on our hands by tomorrow night," said Madame Xu.

Sinha was twirling the phone cord in his hand. "Odd that C. F. is neither at home nor at his office. I wonder where he can be?"

"Geez. You Singaporeans eat all the time. That's all you do: eat, eat, eat. It seems you can't talk or meet or do anything without eating." Joyce held her head in her hands. She stared at the empty dishes in front of her. She didn't dare even look at the stuff Wong was eating. Just the knowledge that it was there, glistening with pork fat, was enough to make her feel sick.

"I bet I look like death warmed up," she said, her voice a low croak.

"A cake?"

"No. I was just saying that I must look terrible."

"Yes. You look terrible."

"Thanks."

"Is okay."

She noticed that there was a mirror in the corner of the room by the door and she made a mental note to look the other way when she passed it. She knew full well that she would be starting this new day looking absolutely hideous and did not want to be reminded of it. She could feel that her eyes were half-closed, bloodshot and puffy, and she knew her face had gone limp. Her hair shot out in all directions. Her midnight blue makeup, she realized, would be smudged in broken circles around her eyes, and her dark maroon lip gloss would probably have vanished, although bits of black lip liner may still be in place.

"You are hanged-over," Wong said sternly.

"A bit," she agreed. "But I didn't really drink that much? It's just staying up so late that did it. Third night in a row. But it was an interesting night. I've found out loads of interesting things to tell you."

"Tell," he sighed, knowing that she would, whether he was interested or not.

"I will. When the guy brings me some water. My throat really hurts."

A bottle of mineral water eventually appeared and Joyce drank nearly all of it.

"Feel better?" said Wong, not unsympathetically, when she lowered the bottle. "Now want some food?" He offered her the last piece of something shiny and glutinous.

"No, thank you," she said, quickly looking away.

He wolfed it down greedily with his mouth open. Joyce screwed up her painful eyes and concentrated on imparting information. "I'll tell you what happened last night. In the end, I went home to change first. Then I went out to happy hour. My first stop was Wong San's on Mohamed Sultan. I know Maddy often starts her evenings there. But no sign of her. So I go on to Dan T.'s Inferno. She's not there, but there are loadsa people I know there, and it's early, so we hang out there for a while. Then, about eleven o'clock, we all traipse down to Pop Cat in Chinatown. No sign of her there. But we ask around, and there's like another of her friends there waiting for her. A girl called Ally, who met her on her first night in Singapore, a few days ago? This girl says that she'd been waiting an hour for her. Ally had assumed that Maddy had decided to stay home tonight. Now I had Calida Tsai-Thing's phone number in my bag, so I called the number. Mrs. Thing's away, as you know, so the domestic helper answers it. The helper's like, 'Maddy hasn't been home all day' and she reckoned that she must be down in one of the nightclubs. So basically she's missing. Oh thank you," she said as Ah-Ooi brought a second bottle of mineral water for her.

"Anyway, so we all go down to Kilimanjaro about one, where she likes to get a snack. None of the guys at Kilimanjaro's have seen her. So we go back to Dan T.'s, and then to Blue Cow and then to The Mitre and then to someplace that Karim knows. By this time, it's about three o'clock in the morning. She's nowhere. She's definitely missing. I wondered about phoning the police. But then I thought they'd laugh at us. Besides, I'm officially too young to be in these bars anyway, so I didn't really want to talk to the cops?"

"Maybe she went to different restaurant. Maybe she go and see boyfriend. Maybe she go to movie."

"As if. She's like obsessed with herself. Always tense. Utterly. Can't relax. Can't see her going to a movie. And her boyfriend: she thinks he wants to kill her. I told you. Before. She's hardly going to want to go and hang out with him—not by choice, anyway. Something's wrong. I'm sure of it. Really."

"Too bad," said Wong.

Joyce let out a long, slow yawn before continuing. "So anyway, by the time we'd finished like scouring the whole of Singapore, it's past four o'clock in the morning. I decide I'm not going to trek all the way home, only to have one or two hours of sleep and then trek all the way back to the office. So I decided to come here and start my day's work early. But by the time I got there, I was so tired, I decided to have a little lie down in your nap room—"

"—the meditation room."

"Yeah. So I just went in there. Must have fallen fast asleep. Until you woke me up, prowling around in the dark. Scared me stiff."

"Yes," said Wong.

She finished half the second bottle of mineral water and the color started to return to her cheeks. The sun was rising and the day outside was becoming bright. "I'm feeling a bit better," she said. "But I still can't eat this stuff. Do you think any other restaurants will be open now?"

"Not many," said the geomancer, looking at his watch. "Ah-Chow's on Smith Street may be open now."

"No, I mean Western food. I can't eat dim sum and noodles for breakfast. I need pancakes. Or eggs and bacon. I need a nice cup of tea with lots of sugar."

"I think there is twenty-four-hour McDonald's on Orchard Road."

"That'll have to do. Let's go. By the way, what happened to you yesterday at the dentists'."

"I found the ghost."

"You *found* the ghost?" Joyce jerked upright. "Tell me tell me tell me. What happened?"

"I heard it. Was in the chair."

"That is *so* cool. Did you exorcise it?"

"No. Maybe today."

She rose to her feet. "What was it like? Could you see anything? No, tell me at McDonald's. This mineral water is not doing it for me. Maybe a Diet Coke is what I really need."

"I think not good for you."

"You're right. Rots the teeth. Never mind. We're going to the dentists' later this morning, aren't we?"

"I am going to the dentist," Wong corrected her. "You go home and change clothes and wash face. You look terrible."

Wong arrived at the Liew and Leibler dental office on Orchard Road just after nine o'clock to find the door to the offices shut. Cheung Lai Kuen was sitting on the waiting room sofa, weeping. Dr. Liew was holding her hands and comforting her. Dr. Leibler was on the telephone. "I'm sorry, Mrs. Tam," he was saying. "All appointments are being canceled today, including urgent operations. You will not be charged anything, of course. If you want advice on an alternative location for emergency treatment, we can advise you. If it's not an emergency, someone from this office will call you shortly to make a new appointment. It'll be next week. We're shut for the rest of the week. No, I'm sorry, I can't record a new appointment just now." He put the phone down.

Dr. Liew spoke to Wong without looking up. "I'm sorry, Mr. Wong. We don't need you anymore. The investigation is being transferred to the police. We will pay your bill in full."

"Thank you."

Wong looked at Gibson Leibler and noticed that his face was ashen. There was a heaviness in the muscles under his eyes.

"Some problem . . . ?"

"You could say that," the surgeon said. "Anyway, good-bye." Clearly, no further information was going to be forthcoming.

Wong nodded politely at him and started to back out. "I send invoice later," he said.

Which was when the chubby figure of Superintendent Gilbert Tan came out of the surgery. "Wong. Thank goodness you're here. I need you to sit down and tell me everything that happened last night."

Leibler bridled. "Surely we don't need a feng shui man for this? Hasn't this all got rather too serious for that sort of thing?"

"We need him more than ever," said the Superintendent. "The Singaporean police are peerless in most things but have a poor record of catching ghosts."

"What happened after we left last night?" Dr. Liew asked, suddenly becoming interested in Wong's presence.

"First, what happen this morning?" asked Wong.

Superintendent Tan took his arm and pulled him into Dr.

Liew's office. He shut the door behind them. He turned around and Wong noticed that he had donned his most serious expression. "I'm sorry to report that one of the members of this office, Ms. Amanda Luk, was found dead in her bed this morning."

"Dead. Oh dear," said the feng shui man. "What . . . ?"

"Did she die of? Come on, Wong, you are joking, is it? You know I'm not allowed to say anything like that until after the autopsy-lah."

"Yes. I know. But also I know you tell me anyway usually."

"Yes, yes," said Tan. "Well, don't tell the world, and definitely don't tell any press, but I do have some interesting initial observations. I understand from the officer who was in charge of the investigation that there were no surface wounds on the body of any sort. There were no obvious, outward signs of poisoning—you know, swollen tongue, odd-colored pupils, that sort of thing. But of course, that doesn't mean anything. She could have been poisoned."

"And . . . ?"

"What do you mean, 'and'?"

"What do you think? How she died?"

The police officer rubbed the tip of his nose with his forefinger. "I don't know. If we wanted to be melodramatic, we could point out that she had an expression of terror on her face. Maybe our ghost followed her home and scared her to death. I don't know. But that's a bit airy-fairy for a nice tough policeman like me. I am going to subscribe to the poisoning theory or perhaps a heart attack until the coroner tells me something different."

There was a knock on the door.

"Come," said Tan.

The two dentists entered the room. "We'd like to know what happened last night in this office," said Liew.

"We're entitled to know," said Leibler. "We're paying him."

The police officer looked at Wong. "Sure. Do tell. I too, would like to know. I'll ask you to do a proper statement later, but my curiosity is killing me. Let's just pretend this isn't happening. A detailed, but unofficial version, please."

"The ghost continue moaning, on-off, on-off, for a long time," said Wong. "Poor ghost. Very unhappy. One hour over. One hour and a quarter nearly. Moan-moan-moan. Then he goes. I did some more measurements. Then I left the office too. Go home. Went to bed early."

"The ghost usually stays about that long," said Dr. Liew. "Where do ghosts go when they go?"

"What's the relevance of the length of time?" asked Dr. Leibler.

"I don't know," said Wong. "Tell me, is there a dentist operation that takes one hour and fourteen minute? That was how long he stayed."

Dr. Liew rubbed his chin. "Well . . . not really. I mean, most people need a combination of treatments. Most individual treatments can be done within the hour, but it would not be unusual to do a treatment that could stretch to that long. A complex crown, for instance. Or the removal of several wisdom teeth in a single operation. Or an operation that needed a short period of anesthesia."

"Remove several teeth? Like to make room to insert brace for child?" Wong looked at Dr. Leibler as he said this.

"This whole idea of using a feng shui man to solve this is ridiculous," Gibson Leibler snapped. "A woman is dead. I can hardly believe . . ."

"Very sad," said Wong.

"We all need a break," said Dr. Liew, slowly sitting down in the dental chair. "A few days off. Maybe we shouldn't open at all next week. Just have a break. Get over the shock of what happened to Amanda. Poor girl. It is unimaginable."

"Yes." The geomancer moved to the table in the waiting room and unfolded a fresh floor map of the premises he had drawn the previous night, this time with every possible influence scratched on in tiny Chinese characters.

"I think a holiday is good idea. I want one also. And when you open again, many changes must be made," he explained. "There has to be some important movements of things. First I want to ask a question. Dr. Leibler, would you work in this room? Dr. Liew change to that room? Is it okay?"

"You want us to swap offices?" asked Dr. Leibler. "What would that do?"

"It would be better," said Wong.

"Wouldn't it just mean that he gets stuck with the ghost?" asked Dr. Liew. "No, don't answer this. I don't think I can bear to discuss offices when such a terrible thing has happened to one of our staff. Gibson, can you handle this?"

"I'll handle it," said the American.

Dr. Liew walked like a broken man across the waiting room and slumped into a chair.

"Okay. Mr. Feng Shui Man, what good would swapping rooms do?"

"I think *he* would have not so much trouble."

Wong explained that Dr. Liew had moved diametrically north from his previous office, which, this year, meant that he had moved in the direction of five. But Dr. Liew was forty-two years old, which meant that his personal *lo shu* number was also five. This was bad enough as a clash. But he had then taken the rooms on the northeast side of the office suite, causing a massive negative *shar* to descend.

Dr. Leibler, on the other hand, was thirty-four, and his *lo shu* number was four. He had moved in a southerly direction to this office, in the direction of two, and he had taken the room on the northwest side of the premises. "This is also bad," said Wong. "For this is a year of two and you should not move in the same direction as the number of the year."

"So we both have bad offices?" said Dr. Leibler. "Are you saying that neither of us can work here, and we should both move? This is simply not helpful or practical advice." He was clearly irritated.

"No, you are misunderstanding. You have different square numbers and your offices have different influences. If you move into Dr. Liew's room, it will be better for you. If he moves into your room, it will not be perfect for him, but it will be better than it is now. He will be moving away from his *shar* and into a neutral number, three. We can add some positive effects. Both of you will be happier."

"And the ghost or whatever it is will stop?" asked Dr. Leibler.

"No. I think the move I suggest will not stop the ghost."

"Then what's the point?"

"I'm not moving." This was Cheung Lai Kuen, who was standing in the doorway. "I'm not going to work in any of these rooms. Not after Amanda . . . I'm not going to work in this building anymore. I think we should leave and get a new office or close that office down completely and just use it as a storeroom or something. And after Amanda spent all that time redecorating the place." She burst into tears again.

Dr. Leibler repeated his comment. "What's the point of switching offices if it doesn't solve the problem? I don't mind moving in there—it's all the same to me. I mean, to be honest, I don't really believe in ghosts, and I don't really believe in this feng shui stuff, with all due respect. I mean, I don't know what it was we heard in there—some bizarre phenomenon of some kind, I don't honestly know what the explanation is. But I don't want that noise scaring my patients. After what happened to Ms. Luk—I think Ms. Cheung is right. We should move out of this whole building."

Superintendent Tan, who had been eavesdropping, said: "Are there other alternatives? You said there were a few things they could do."

Wong said: "The move I am suggesting would be good for both dentists. As for getting rid of the ghost, I can do that too, but it requires a different operation at a different time."

"What do you mean?" This was Gibson Leibler.

"I will return when the ghost does. I will be back on Monday. Ghost also. He will be here at seven o'clock evening."

"How do you know?"

"He came on Monday at nine morning, Tuesday at six evening, yesterday at four afternoon. So he will come next Monday at seven. I am sure. He will be here for one hour over. I will come with some different equipment. I will get rid of the ghost forever."

"Are you sure about that?" asked Superintendent Tan.

"No," said Wong. "But I try."

The feng shui master and his assistant had raced to a restaurant in Chinatown for lunch with the other committee members. They had had a Code Red invitation—which indicated an urgent assignment for the Union.

"My turn to choose," said Dilip Sinha. "And I want Szechuan."

"You always want something spicy. What about Little Plum Blossom? She will burn her tongue," said Madame Xu.

"I can eat hot stuff. I ate a whole jalapeño chili once,"

said Joyce, deciding to omit the fact that she had spent at least twenty minutes on the toilet the next morning, and had been unable to sit down for a further ten.

The Szechuan food was delicious. It had that aromatic sweetness of the best Cantonese cuisine but had a spicy bite to it that was reminiscent of Thai curries.

The table talk was dominated by Joyce's breathless report about how she—with a little help from Mr. Wong—had solved her kidnapping case the day before. Madame Xu and Dilip Sinha listened and grunted politely at all the right moments, but seemed preoccupied.

Yet despite the upbeat atmosphere, Joyce began to feel increasingly guilty as the meal drew to an end. There had been an air of finality about the discussion, as if a big mountain had been climbed, and now it was time for a celebratory break. But at the back of her mind, Joyce had become deeply worried about Maddy—about whom she had a bad feeling. Something was seriously wrong. She had reached a dead end in her personal search for her newest friend. She needed her boss to take on the case—even though there was no official commission and no deposit had been paid. How could she ask him for help?

Her concern turned to alarm when Wong suddenly rose to his feet and said: "*Waah!* Too much work this week already. One big assignment cracked. Another half done. Now time for holiday." He started to move away.

"C. F.," she called.

"What?"

"Er. Where are you going?"

"Over there. See Mrs. Leong, second table? She is travel agent. I am going to ask her book ticket for me. I go to *heung ha.*"

"When? You mean soon? Like next week?"

"Tonight."

"C. F., can I talk to you about something, first? I think it would be great if you would help—"

"No," he snapped. "Too much helping already. Now is time for holiday."

Joyce was surprised to see that Madame Xu and Sinha also looked agitated. "Sit down for a minute more, C. F.," said Sinha. "There's something else. We didn't summon this special Code Red meeting of the committee just to have a nice lunch and hear about Joyce's kidnap thing, impressive though it was. There's a case that Chong Li and I would like to talk to you ab –"

"No, sorry," said Wong. "No more cases. Maybe next week. Really, is holiday time now. Just for two-three days. Back in action next week. Monday." He set off across the crowded open-air market to catch Mrs. Leong.

Joyce slumped back in her stool. What could she do now? "Where is he going?" she asked Madame Xu. "Where is Heungha?"

"He said he wanted to go to his 'heung ha'—that means his ancestral home. He wants to go back to Guangdong province in China," she replied. "The town of Baiwan."

"Oh." Disappointed, Joyce felt helpless. She sat there, staring into space for a while. Oh well, I tried, she said to herself. Sorry, Maddy, I really tried.

She wondered for a moment whether there was anything else she could do. But by that time, Wong had disappeared into the crowd.

So Joyce did what she always did when she felt down—reached into her bag for a musical pick-me-up. She found her minidisc player and untangled the earphones. Then she pulled out a copy of *Elle* magazine and started flicking through it. Soon, she was lost in her own little world—and she only half noticed that Madame Xu and Dilip Sinha had quickly begun a very serious and earnest conversation about something.

It was only when the first track was over and there were a few seconds of silence before the next track began did she catch what Sinha was saying.

"– tell him that this unfortunate Hong Kong girl urgently needs our help. She's facing an imminent death. We have to do something. He'll understand."

The opening chords of the next track started thumping in Joyce's ears. She turned the volume down so she could eavesdrop further.

"She's Cantonese, like he is. He'll want to postpone his holiday to help when he hears about her case," Madame Xu said.

"If we both ask him together, and refuse to take no for an answer, I'm sure he'll see sense," said Sinha. "You have a way of persuading men to do what you want, I'm sure."

"I don't know what you mean."

It sounded like they were talking about Maddy. "What're you guys talking about?" Joyce asked, yanking the earphones out.

Madame Xu's brow wrinkled. "It pains me to say this, but I am afraid I'm not able to tell you. Dilip and I are discussing a client that we have in common."

Sinha interjected in his best "kindly-grandfather" voice: "Of course we consider you a full honorary member of the investigative advisory committee of the Union of Industrial Mystics, my dear. But the particular case we are discussing at the moment is not advisory committee business, but a private affair, and highly confidential."

"That's cool," replied Joyce. "I understand. It's just that —" She paused, unsure how to continue. "It's just that—well, it may be that I know more about young Hong Kong women facing imminent death than you might think."

This statement produced an unexpectedly dramatic response from both Madame Xu and Dilip Sinha. They both turned sharply to stare at her, and then looked at each other before turning their gazes to her again.

"What exactly do you mean by that?" Madame Xu asked.

"Yes. What exactly do you mean? Are you talking about a *particular* young Hong Kong woman?" Sinha asked.

Joyce nodded solemnly.

"Who is facing an imminent end?" Sinha added.

Joyce nodded again.

Sinha turned to Madame Xu. "Extraordinary. What we thought were individual consultations with the two of us must really have been widespread discussions with every mystic in town."

"And even their junior assistants," added Madame Xu, her pin-thin pencilled eyebrows arching a full inch upward.

"Remarkable."

There was silence as this point was carefully considered.

"I didn't know you guys knew about her," said Joyce. "I really didn't. How did you find out? I guess the urgent question is where is she? Where has she disappeared to?"

Sinha frowned. "Disappeared? I have heard nothing about that. She is staying with an aunt in an apartment in town while waiting for her fiancé to deal with some, er, other pressing matters, right? For the fact is, that she is quite unwell—seriously unwell, as I imagine you know."

"She's sick?"

"Not sick. But in very real physical danger. As I presume you know. But tell me: What makes you think she has disappeared?"

"Because I was up practically all night searching for her.

Her domestic helper thought she was out clubbing. Her friends at the clubs thought she was at home. She's vanished. I phoned around again this morning and no one has seen her. She's not been home. I'm really worried about her. Maddy's so worried about just staying alive at the moment. I mean, when she disappears like this—"

"Who's Maddy?"

"The Hong Kong girl. Madeleine Tsai."

"Oh. Perhaps we are talking about different young women. We were thinking of a young lady named Clara."

"Oh."

"I don't know, though." Sinha was intrigued. "Tell us about your Maddy."

"She's a little smaller than me; dark hair streaked with brown and gold; boyfriend called Ismail who is seriously weird—he comes from Malaysia and is into all this *bomoh* stuff; she went to Hong Kong International School for a while. She's small but strong-looking. She was in the school swimming team when she was thirteen—"

Sinha held up his hand, signaling her to pause. "It is the same girl. Definitely. Perhaps Madeleine is Clara's middle name or something. Now listen carefully, girls. We've got to get C. F. interested in this case. We can't do it ourselves. We need to work together on this one."

The three of them huddled around the Chinese teapot and plotted.

This was the plan. As soon as Wong returned to the table, Madame Xu was going to coerce him to sit down next to her. He would be too gentlemanly to refuse. They would then corner him and refuse to allow him to leave the table until he had agreed to take on the girl's case. Sinha, with his easy gift of eloquence in English, would present an impassioned plea for him to put all his energy into extricating

Clara/Madeleine from the dire straits in which she found herself. Madame Xu would present a similar plea in Cantonese if necessary. Joyce, meanwhile, would head over and intercept Mrs. Leong, who would be told that Mr. Wong wanted to cancel the travel plans he had just made because an urgent assignment had just come up.

"Here he comes," said Sinha, as Wong reappeared, strolling between the tables. "Off you go, Joyce."

"Go for it, guys," the young woman said, passing the geomancer and racing to find Mrs. Leong's table.

She quickly located a round table two dozen yards away, where a bespectacled Singaporean woman was discussing tariffs and surcharges with a large group of middle-aged people in business suits: A group of mostly female travel agents having a social lunch, she decided.

"Excuse me, Mrs. Leong?"

"Yes?"

"I'm Joyce McQuinnie. I work with C. F. Wong. I think I've spoken to you on the phone before."

"You're right," said the travel agent. "C. F. seems to have a secretary who is permanently unavailable to answer the phone, so my calls are always answered by you or him."

"Well, he just asked you to book a ticket for him?"

"Yes, a Dragonair flight to Guangdong, for tonight or tomorrow. I promised I'd do it as soon as I got back to the office. I told him I couldn't guarantee him a seat at such short notice. But I can try."

"Well, I've just been sent over to tell you that he probably won't need the ticket after all. Something came up."

"But he just asked me for the ticket a few minutes ago. A few *seconds*."

"Something just came up, while he was talking to you."

The travel agent looked at her suspiciously. Joyce decided

that she was sounding rather vague and had better deliver enough details to make her story sound authentic. "It's something very urgent. You see, there's this Hong Kong girl called Madeleine Tsai who has gone missing with her Malaysian boyfriend and we need—I mean, C. F. needs to find them urgently. Like today and tomorrow. This week, anyway. So there's no hope of him taking a holiday for at least a couple of days until—"

"Did you say Madeleine Tsai?"

Joyce looked around. The question had come from a small, rotund Malay woman with thick glasses sitting directly opposite Susan Leong.

"Does she travel with a gentleman called Ismail?" the woman continued.

"Yes," said Joyce. "How did you—? I mean, do you know them?"

"I booked a pair of tickets for them yesterday. The guy bought them. Paid cash. But those were the two names on the booking, Amran Ismail and Madeleine Tsai. He wanted the tickets issued right away."

"Where are they going?"

"Where have they gone, you mean. They're not in Singapore anymore. They left on the evening flight to Sydney last night."

"Oh. Thank you."

Joyce headed back across the crowded restaurant slowly, much in thought. Had they lost the battle to find Maddy and help her? What should they do now? As she approached their table, she noticed that the other plotters had succeeded in pinning Wong down. She eavesdropped on them from behind. The geomancer slouched on a stool as he was assailed from both sides with demands that he abandon his silly idea of having a holiday until a missing young woman was found and relocated to a safe spot, and her appointment with death postponed for at least fifty years.

She wondered whether the news she would bring—that Madeleine and her fiancé were no longer in Singapore—would make their mission unnecessary. Wong was hardly going to let himself be persuaded to go flying around the world to save someone he didn't know, and who wasn't paying him.

But then she decided to wait until the discussion was over. One thing at a time. It would just be adding a needless complication if she immediately announced that the person they wanted to find was lost not in Singapore but in Sydney. She dawdled for ten minutes, listening in from a few yards away.

Joyce found herself becoming increasingly amazed, as Madame Xu and Dilip Sinha told Wong an extraordinary story that she had not heard: about how every type of predictive mystical art available in Malaysia and Singapore had confirmed and reconfirmed that Madeleine (whom they referred to as Clara) was facing an unspecified but near-term death, and would almost definitely have expired by the end of the following day. Wong had seemed highly skeptical at first, but appeared to become more and more interested as details flowed. When Sinha opened his bag and took out the paperwork he had on Clara/Madeleine, Wong quickly started flicking through it.

"Unusual," he said. "Very unusual. Never seen case like this. Of course, is impossible to predict time of death precisely like this. Very silly and impossible."

"Exactly my initial reaction," said Sinha. "But look at the facts."

"It seems strange, but all signals point to this week," said Madame Xu. "For her to expire."

Joyce quietly rejoined the table and made her own contribution. "She's a really, really nice girl. She doesn't deserve to die. You understand what's going on, don't you, C. F.? The insurance thing that I told you about?"

The geomancer looked up and nodded. "Understand," he said. "This man Ismail, he finds that girl is due to die on a certain day. The stars say which day. Then he gets engaged to her and takes out big life insurance on her: millions of ringgit. But he is nervous or something, so he goes to other *bomohs*, other fortune-tellers, who confirm that prediction is correct. Like you two."

"How do you know he's bought life insurance on her?" asked Sinha, surprised.

"Actually, I delivered that piece of information," Joyce declared, smugly. "That Ismail guy has taken out like at least three separate insurance polices on her life. I found out from Maddy—er, Clara."

"I can't believe that," said Madame Xu, genuinely shocked. "He can't be doing all this for money. I thought he was such a nice young man. And so in love with her."

"In love with her insurance policies," said Joyce. "She found the documents hidden in his room."

"If it's true . . . what a cad," said Madame Xu.

"The bounder," said Dilip Sinha.

The geomancer pulled at the hairs on his chin. "So he is going to wait for her to die of natural causes, as predicted, very soon or even tomorrow, and then collect the money: clever plan," said Wong. "Very clever. He gets rich. But no murder committed."

He shuffled the papers into a neat pile and then pushed them back toward Sinha.

"What are you doing?" said the Indian astrologer.

"Holiday," said Wong. "I told you."

"You can't go on holiday. We have to save this unfortunate girl."

"Yes," Joyce added. "She's my friend."

"A gentleman known as the Great Bomoh said that she would die by the end of tomorrow—by five o'clock. My own work confirms that she will be dead very soon, as does the work of many lesser mystics," said Madame Xu. "If you go on holiday, by the time you get back, it will all be over."

"This is not the normal business of a feng shui master," said Wong. "We do not interfere with predictions of other people. Some predictions are right, some are wrong. Even if it is right, we do not try to stop death. The gods give life, the gods give death. It is not for us to change anything. We cannot change anything."

"Wong, for pity's sake, please just read through the birth charts and at least look at her earthy pillars of destiny for us," said Sinha. "That's something none of us know how to do. So we can advise them on where to go to maximize their safety tomorrow, during the danger hours."

"Okay, Dilip," said Wong. "But then I go on holiday. Already booked. Mrs. Leong is getting me a ticket to my *heung ha* to leave tonight. On Dragonair."

Joyce's head retreated into her shoulders with guilt.

Wong spent the following half-hour carefully going through all the papers, and scribbling on charts and diagrams. He also read the notes provided by Amran Ismail and listened to accounts of meetings from both Madame Xu and Dilip Sinha. Joyce sat at a distance, watching all this, and shooting up prayers that Wong would take the case seriously.

After his tenth cup of *bo-leih* tea, Wong pushed back the papers and his cup. He'd finished his studies. "You are right," he said. "If these dates are correct, the client enters very negative phase tomorrow. Her earthly branch is fire and it is interrupted by a powerful influence of metal and water tomorrow afternoon. Very negative."

"Enough to kill her?" This was Joyce.

"Feng shui does not show that. It only shows positive and negative. Not facts and details. What we do know is that tomorrow is very negative. But when we put it together with other findings . . ."

"Then . . . ?"

"Then it looks very bad. And certainly when you add findings of other mystics, it looks worse and worse."

"So you believe it? She really is due to like actually *die* tomorrow?"

He thought for a moment. "Probably," he said. "But it is not as bad as it could be. It is what I might say, only 95 percent bad."

Madame Xu interrupted. "Not as bad as it could be? What's good about it?"

"Location is not the worst," said Wong. "Look at this chart here. Stars are unfavorable. But not the worst. Now if she was locate elsewhere, could be much worse."

"What do you mean located elsewhere?"

"If she was in southern hemisphere. Like South America. Or Australia. Then death might even be 100 percent certain. My opinion only."

"Australia?" Joyce yelped. "Excuse me. I have something to say."

❖

Joyce settled back in her airline seat and clipped on her seat belt. The plane's engines started to roar as the aircraft taxied down the runway. She was filled with pride. That afternoon, she had performed a miracle. She had done something way above and beyond the call of duty. She had managed to persuade C. F. Wong to abandon his holiday and pay cash—out of his own pocket—for two tickets to Sydney, the aim being to find a young woman who had not hired him and had made no promises to pay him anything at all. In short, she had achieved the impossible.

She recalled the look of amazement on the faces of Dilip Sinha and Madame Xu Chong Li as Wong had agreed to take on the case. And it was all because she had made a dramatic speech. It must have been a great speech. Unfortunately, she couldn't remember a word of it now. It had just burst out of her mouth in a great torrent of words. It didn't seem to make a lot of sense as she was saying it, but it seemed to have done the trick.

"Damn!" she said quietly out loud, as she realized that her minidisc had been sitting on the table in front of her at the table at Ah-Fat's. She could have easily taped her speech, had she thought of it.

"What?" said Wong, who thought he had been spoken to. He was in the next seat, fiddling with his seat belt, which was too long for his skeletal trunk.

"Nothing," said Joyce.

She realized that it was when she was detailing the rewards that would be his that he started to become convinced that maybe he should take the task. She recalled vaguely saying that she, Joyce, would be grateful to him for the rest of her life. But that probably hadn't been the deciding factor. Then there was her observation that the young woman in question, whose life he was sure to save, was highly intelligent and would be a worthy citizen of the world in future. That was also unlikely to have been a major contributor to changing his mind. No, the clincher would have been the line where she talked about Maddy's rich family.

There was Maddy's father, an ultra-rich and powerful Hong Kong businessman who owned more than a thousand properties in the city, and had six cars and a private cruiser. And there was her brother, also a major financial figure in his own right. Yes, that was the moment that Wong's head had tilted to one side and he had become interested.

He had briefly interrupted her, she now remembered, to get more details about her family. She had been unable to provide any except for the fact that she recalled Maddy saying that her father was a very big property developer and her brother had loads of staff and was one of the most powerful businessmen in Hong Kong. Joyce had decided it would be wise to leave out the fact that Maddy had told her she was estranged from her family.

Wong was fascinated. "Madeleine Tsai? Father is property developer?" he had echoed. "You mean Tsai Tze-ting? Is this Ms. Tsai the daughter of Tsai Tze-ting? Why nobody has told me this before? Why did not Mrs. Tsai-Leibler tell me this?"

Joyce had no idea what Maddy's father's name was, but she had thought it wise to nod. "Yeah," she said. "That must be the guy. Her dad and her brother are like really rich. It would be good to get some people like that to feel deeply, deeply grateful to you. That sort of gratitude is worth much more than a few dollars paid as a deposit."

There had been further discussion on these lines. Joyce, in truth, couldn't remember very much about what Maddy had said about her family. But she hoped that the details she had related to Wong had been more or less accurate.

She felt herself being pushed back into her seat by the G-force as the Cathay Pacific jet lifted its nose from the runway at Chek Lap Kok and soared into the night sky.

Two hours into the flight, Joyce grabbed Wong's arm. She had picked up a copy of the *Asian Wall Street Journal* and was flicking through it, trying to find something that would remind her of the name of Maddy's brother's company. She'd already gone through the *Financial Times* with no success. She had eventually found it on the fifteenth page she had scanned of the *Journal*. "Here it is," she said. "I think this is what Maddy's brother's company is called. I remember at the time thinking it was an odd name, because it was more numbers than letters."

She pointed to a headline on the page.

He peered at it. "What? What name do you mean?"

"There," she said. "401(k). That was the name of his company in Hong Kong."

She scanned the article. It seemed to be about tax laws in the United States. There was no reference to any Hong Kong firm.

"The article is not about his company, but his company has the same name as this tax thing: 401(k)," she said. "I'm sure of it."

"Strange," said Wong. "This 401(k) is name of tax law. Maybe he is tax consultant. So he name his company after tax law."

About five minutes later, Wong grabbed her wrist so hard that orange juice slopped out of the glass she was holding.

"Joyce. I have important question. The company of Maddy's brother. Maybe is not 401(k). Maybe is 14K. Can you remember?"

"Don't know. Hmm." She thought for a few moments. "Actually, it could be. It could be 14K. Why? Do you know anyone at that company?"

Wong breathed out very slowly. "There is a big group in Hong Kong called 14K. But is not a company. Is an, er, organization."

"That must be it," said Joyce.

Wong was silent for a few more minutes. Then he turned to her again. "Joyce, I have one more very important question. Very important. When Maddy talk about her brother, did she say 'brother' or did she say 'big brother?' Please remember carefully."

Joyce tilted her head up as she tried to recall a late-night conversation at Dan T.'s Inferno two nights earlier. "I think . . . she said . . . *big* brother, actually. Does it make a difference?"

Wong opened his mouth as if to breathe out again. But no breath came. He seemed to be in a state of shock. Joyce watched with astonishment as the geomancer appeared to physically sink into his airline seat. Both his head and body seemed to shrivel and he was pressing himself back, as if he wanted the economy-class seat to swallow him.

❖

In Ye County during the rule of Wei Wenhou, a witch had said that a beautiful girl-child should be sacrificed to the River God every year to ensure there would be no floods. Once a year, a girl was placed on a floating bed of reeds and pushed into the water to drown.

Families with daughters moved away and the town began to become deserted.

The new magistrate, Ximen Bao, wanted to help the village. He said he would attend the sacrifice.

The witch appeared and the rituals began.

"Stop," the magistrate said. "This girl is not beautiful enough. Find a fairer maid."

Ximen Bao ordered that the witch be thrown into the river to tell the River God that there was a delay.

The witch could not swim. When she failed to reappear,

Ximen Bao said: "Send her assistants to bring her back."
All the officials were thrown one by one into the river until those who were left declared that the River God no longer wanted to marry human girls.
The annual marriage ceremony was canceled and the town began to grow and prosper once more.

If you cannot push an enemy in the way you want him to go, Blade of Grass, push him in the direction in which he is already going. He will still fall over, which is the aim of the exercise.

(Some Gleanings of Oriental Wisdom
by C. F. Wong, part 350)

A PERFECT MURDER

ALTHOUGH THE double-layered hotel curtains stretched from floor to ceiling, morning light streamed into the room through a narrow gap that had been left when they had been clumsily yanked together late the previous night. Joyce woke up, blinking at the unaccustomed walls and alien furniture around her. A disconcerting period when she didn't realize where she was passed in seconds. This was Sydney. Madeleine was here, somewhere. She turned to the bedside table and noticed a red LED panel showing 7:58 A.M.

This was unusually early for her to be awake—she normally considered herself short-changed of sleep if her roommate woke her before nine o'clock. But today was different. There was no time to waste. Somewhere in this teeming city was the missing Ms. Tsai, and they had only a matter of hours in which to find her. Joyce's biggest worry was that Amran Ismail would be furious that the day would pass without Maddy being hurt or killed in some sort of accident—and then decide to make up for fate's shortcomings by taking practical steps himself.

Wong, surely, would already be up. She couldn't remember his room number, so she pressed the button on the phone marked "Operator." When a hotel staff member answered, Joyce found that her voice wasn't ready to speak yet—she coughed long and hard into her pillow before apologizing in a croak and asking to be put through to her traveling companion. The phone in Wong's room trilled but went unanswered. Clearly he had risen early and gone out on the job. Or perhaps he was in the hotel having breakfast downstairs somewhere. *I'm hungry too*, she thought.

Still exhausted after her succession of late nights, Joyce had great difficulty in pulling her bones out of the over-soft hotel bed. It was as if they had been glued to the sheets. Yanking herself free of the heavy coverlet, she slouched groggily to the window, pulled open the curtains and gazed at the city below her.

The glare hurt her eyes. But at the same time, the view triggered an involuntary intake of breath. She was thrilled to be reminded of what a magnificent city Sydney was. Clusters of tall buildings, standing shoulder-to-shoulder on the waterfront, crowded to get a glance at the ocean. Even at this hour, the harbor was a hive of activity, with powerboats and marine police vessels and working trawlers all crawling past and around each other in what seemed to be a well-rehearsed dance. Ferries whisked commuters across the bay and a small water-tours boat skimmed the coastline, readying itself to show tourists the sights.

Looking inland, Joyce marveled at the way the city itself seemed almost as full of motion as the water, despite the solidity of the stone and glass monoliths dominating the waterfront. Roads and expressways pumped energy around a network of concrete veins. And the pulse was not just throbbing at ground level. There were raised motorways, hovering helicopters and shimmering aircraft appearing and disappearing behind clouds. Between two skyscrapers, she noticed part of a monorail curling along a curved track. The pavements would soon be thick with crowds, pouring out of cars, buses, taxis, trains, boats and aircraft. How on earth were they going to find one young Chinese woman? It wouldn't be easy.

She headed to the shower for a blast of water to wake her up.

❖

At last: There was the hotel again. C. F. Wong had risen too early to make calls, so he had gone out for a walk to get a feel for the environment. He had quickly got lost—it was rather embarrassing for a feng shui master to have such a poor sense of direction. But he had grown up in a place where you could always see the sky. In low-slung cities, slow-moving clouds act as useful direction markers for hours on end. But in modern skyscraper cities of crowded canyons, there was nothing from which to get one's bearings. He had never been a good map reader, so these days had got into the habit of guiding himself around with his south-pointing *lo pan*. After leaving the hotel, he had walked for twenty minutes in what he thought was a triangular route, but had ended up in a totally unfamiliar quarter.

He decided to sit on a small wall and use the opportunity to study the map of Sydney he had picked up at reception. Although tourist maps tended to omit important things, such as contours and mountains, they usually included watercourses, viewing towers, cable cars and so on, which provided him with a basic overview of a city's feng shui.

Water meandering gently between east and west to the

south of a key location was always the most favorable situation. But it was clear from the map that the *ch'i* in this city had pooled to the south of the river. North of the waters, there were relatively few items marked as being of interest to tourists. South of the channel, the map was covered with tiny symbols identifying key landmarks. Evidently Sydney was a yang city south of the estuary and a yin city to the north.

Then there was a network of major roads, a bridge, a tunnel below the harbor and a sizeable railway operation. He reckoned he could easily spend a couple of weeks examining the feng shui characteristics of the city. But no time for that now. They probably had only eight or nine hours in which to find Madeleine Tsai. He tried, without success, to fold up his hotel map. Then he crumpled it up in his pocket, and took a chance on a small road to his left as a possible route back to where he had started. To his surprise, it proved correct. He had turned one further corner and gratefully sighted the hotel again. Time to go back to his room and make some calls.

As he rose in the elevator, he shook his head with wonder at his own strange behavior. He had astonished himself, agreeing to go to Sydney on what appeared highly likely to be a wild goose chase. And to have allowed himself to be persuaded by his irritating intern, of all people! What hope did he have of finding two people in a place as large as Australia, without any clues as to their address or itinerary? Especially since at least one of the two people had no intention of allowing himself to be found. It all seemed a gamble with the longest possible odds.

But the news that Joyce had delivered of Madeleine Tsai's status as heiress to a business fortune could not be ignored. Her father Tsai Tze-ting had a fortune of legendary proportions and was once reputed to have given a million Hong

Kong dollars to a man who had recovered a hat he had left in a park. Wong believed that everybody got one golden opportunity in life—and this just might be it for him. There was a possibility that Joyce could be bringing him his chance to make enough money on which to retire. The gods were known to have an ironic sense of humor. It would have been just like them to use her to deliver a golden rice bowl to him.

But it was the practicalities that counted. No cash gift would be forthcoming unless he found the missing girl and made sure she got through this difficult period alive. Their best hope, Wong had immediately realized, was to find out exactly what had motivated Amran Ismail to go to Australia. It was simple logic: certain feng shui charts showed that Australia, and a few other more distant southerly places, were the worst possible locations for Madeleine Tsai's prospects on this date. Or, to see it from Ismail's point of view, Australia was the best possible location for him to fulfil his aim of seeing her suffer an untimely death and become eligible to collect his winnings from insurance companies.

But Ismail was a *bomoh*, not a geomancer. He would be highly unlikely to know the right feng shui lore about locations at specific times—the heavenly stems and earthly pillars of destiny. He must have consulted someone from the same school of feng shui as the one to which Wong himself belonged. This gave a limited number of options. If he limited himself to professional geomancers, he reckoned there were a total of nineteen people in Singapore who could have done the necessary calculations that would have prompted Ismail to head for Sydney.

Wong was carrying a list of these names. Before leaving Singapore the previous night, he had given a similar list to Dilip Sinha and Madame Xu.

He got back to his room at the hotel at 8:42 A.M. to find the message light blinking. There were two messages. One was from Joyce McQuinnie, informing him that she had woken up "really *really* early" and was ready for action. The other was from Dilip Sinha at 8:39 A.M.—5:39 A.M. in Singapore—asking him to return the call as soon as possible.

He quickly dialed Sinha's number.

"Sinha? Is me."

"Ah, Wong. Good to hear your voice. How was the journey? Comfortable, I hope? I am always amazed at what a long journey it is from Singapore to Australia. One thinks of Australia as being just below this part of East Asia. But—"

"Never mind," snapped Wong impatiently. "Did you phone all those feng shui men last night?"

"Indeed I did. Not all of them were in, but we were diligent. We made careful notes of those who were in to take our calls, those who only received recorded messages— goodness, how I hate talking to a tape recorder, it's so discomfiting—and those who were not contactable, but would need repeat calls—"

"Any one of them met Amran Ismail?"

"I was just coming to that. At about nine P.M. last night, we managed to get though to Eric Kan, who was, I believe, second to last on our list of people to whom we had not yet been able to speak. As soon as I mentioned the name of Mr. Ismail, Eric gave a cry of recognition."

"What did he say?"

"He sort of said, 'Yes,' or perhaps, 'Yup,' in the Singaporean style."

"No. What did Kan say to Amran Ismail? Where did he tell him to go?"

"Ah, right. Yes, of course. That's the key bit of information. Well, let me tell you. Ismail apparently told Eric exactly the same news that Madame Xu and I heard, about this girl Clara being due to die this week. And then Eric looked through the papers that Ismail had brought. Eric did pretty much the same feng shui calculations as you did. And he came to the same conclusion that you did. Eric said that he should head north from Singapore."

"North?"

"Yes, north. He said that Madeleine's luck was extremely bad here, but would be better if he headed north. I think he actually gave a suggested compass destination—like nor'nor'east 358 degrees or something. I can't remember. Chong Li wrote it down. Then Ismail asked what would be the worst destination. Interesting, huh?"

"Yes. And . . . ?"

"And Eric Kan told him that whatever he did, he should not take her southward. Tell your friend not to even think about going to Australia over the next few days, he said. He probably said it as a joke. He said it would be the worst place—as you yourself said at lunch yesterday."

"I see."

"Then Ismail gave him a small cash tip, thanked him profusely, and headed off. No doubt straight to a travel agent to buy a pair of tickets to Sydney. Now let me just look at my notes. Um. Ah, that's right. Amran Ismail saw Eric on Wednesday at about ten-thirty in the morning, and the travel agent said that he bought tickets to Australia for that evening's flight just after lunch on the same day. That afternoon, no doubt he made up some cock and bull story to tell to Clara that Australia was the safest place for her, and off they went."

"Thank you. Did Eric say where in Australia to go? Or just say, Australia?"

"He just said Australia. So I'm sorry. It doesn't narrow it

down for you. Oh, the only comment he made was some sort of joke. He told me he said something like: Don't even think of sitting under a hanging knife in a graveyard in Australia. In other words, he was telling him to avoid bad feng shui spots in Australia. So I would suppose that if he had gone to Sydney, he would find the worst feng shui spot in Sydney. I mean, that's logical. It's not a very big clue, as far as clues go, I'm afraid. Is that any help?"

"Yes, yes, of course." Wong was about to thank Sinha and ring off when the elderly Indian astrologer spoke again.

"Then there were the other chaps who came round about teatime to help with the search. I presume you put them up to it, Wong?"

"Ah?"

"The other chaps."

"Other chaps."

"What was the guy's name? Jackie Something was the leader. He had a couple of friends who didn't say very much."

"*Mm-mingbaak.* Don't understand." Wong wondered if Sinha was getting confused in his old age. "Don't know any Jackie Something."

"These guys turned up at Madame Xu's door—we were doing all the calls from her place, so as to be coordinated—and said that they were looking for Madeleine Tsai. Chong Li said she had no idea who Madeleine Tsai was—she is so forgetful, that dear girl. I of course pointed out that Madeleine was the name that Clara used when talking to Joyce. So I presume that Jackie Something must be a friend of Joyce."

"Jackie Something. Funny name. *Gwai lo?*"

"No, he was Chinese. I'm not saying his name was Jackie Something in the sense that his family name was Mr. Something. I'm saying that I can't remember what his family name was. Maybe Madame Xu can remember. You could give her a call. She should be at Sago Street now. Although perhaps not awake yet. It's not yet six here."

"Jackie is name of girl in most places. In Hong Kong, it is name of boys. This man: He was from Hong Kong?"

"Yes, I think he probably was. He had that sort of hard-nosed slickness that the Hong Kong young men have. Not soft and fat like Singaporean boys. So did his friends."

"What did he look like?"

"Very elegantly dressed. Dark suit, probably Zegna or something like that. Dark glasses. Like a movie star. He was, I can honestly say, almost impeccably well dressed. There was just one thing wrong."

"What?"

"It was quite amusing, really. Everything was perfect in every detail—but he had unfortunately forgotten to cut the fingernail on his pinky. It stuck out a good half-inch, maybe more. Maybe an inch."

"*Aiyeeaah,*" said Wong, closing his eyes.

"He seemed a perfectly charming young man, although he spoke English with a very strong accent, presumably a Hong Kong accent. I don't think there is anything to worry about. He said he considered himself a brother to Clara."

"Big brother?"

"That's right."

"*Aiyeeaah.* What did you tell him?"

"I told him that we had no idea where Clara was. But I told him that she was somewhere in Sydney and that you and Joyce had gone to find her. I told him that Joyce was her big buddy, and knew her personally. He said he would get on the next plane to Australia to lend you guys a hand. I gave him the name and address of your hotel. I thought it would be helpful. He said he would go straight to the airport. If he managed to get a plane last night, he's probably already in Sydney now. He'll probably have been on the first flight to have arrived this morning."

Wong dropped the phone and raced to find Joyce.

❖

The young woman had just finished getting dressed when her bedside phone rang.

"C. F.?" she asked.

"Ms. McQuinnie?" asked an Australian female voice.

"Yes?"

"This is reception. There are some young men here to see you." The voice spoke to someone else: "What name shall I give, sir?" The receptionist returned to Joyce. "The name is Jackie Sum. Shall I send them up?"

"Jack what?"

"There's a young man named Jackie Sum who is here with two other gentlemen."

"To see me? Are you sure they want me? I'm Joyce McQuinnie, in room, er, 706?"

"That's right. That's who they asked for. Do you want to speak to one of them?"

"No worries," said Joyce, slipping back into the Australian lilt that she had had as a child. "Just send 'em up."

She had not missed the fact that the receptionist had specified that they were young men. She raced to the mirror to see if she looked all right. She dabbed some perfume under her ears and on her wrists, and started trying to get her hair into some kind of order. Who could they be? Must be friends of C. F.'s. Actually, he had talked about getting in touch with the local feng shui masters here in Sydney. It must be them. Wong was sometimes a surprisingly fast worker. That was the advantage of being an early riser, she supposed.

Two minutes later, there was a knock on her door.

Joyce took one last look in the mirror, and then went to open the door. "You're a fast mover, Mr. Sum," she said. "Oh. It's you."

"Yes," said Wong, stepping into the room. "Good you woke up. We have plenty work to do. Must get started. Must leave immediately. Right now."

"Yep. I'm ready to rock 'n' roll." He gave her a look. "Not literally," she added. "Even I don't go dancing at this time of the morning." She strolled over to the desk and started picking up things to put in her handbag. "Ready to start searching, I mean."

"Quick. We must leave now. Who is Mr. Sum? You mention Mr. Sum. When I came in."

"Isn't he one of your friends?" Joyce replied. "He phoned from downstairs. He and his friends are coming up now."

"Must be mistake."

"You don't know him? Could he be a Sydney feng shui man?"

"I didn't call any yet." His expression was becoming increasingly concerned.

Joyce shrugged her shoulders. "Anyway, we'll find out in a minute. I think reception said his name was Jackie. Funny name for a guy."

At this news, Wong seemed to jump out of his skin.

"Jackie! Come," he said. "We go. Quick!"

He grabbed her hand and tugged her violently toward the door.

"Wait. Let me get my bag. What's the deal here?"

"*Fai-dee!*" he shouted.

They raced out of the door, Wong pushing her unceremoniously like a peasant shoving a reluctant bull to a cart.

"The elevator's that way," Joyce said.

"I know. So we go this way."

Escaping from a hotel is much harder than it seems in the movies. After running down four flights of stairs, both Joyce and Wong slowed to a crawl. And there were still three more stories to go. They could barely move.

"Phooo!" said Joyce. "It's a—long—way—down. Let's—take—the—elevator." Each word came out as a gasp.

"Okay," agreed Wong, his chest rising and falling as he took deep drafts of air. "Maybe there is service elevator."

They went through a couple of swing doors and eventually found a metal elevator the staff used to transport baskets of laundry and other goods between floors.

It trundled slowly and noisily down toward the ground floor, but stopped at the second. The doors opened, and a chambermaid entered. She was fortyish and had rosy cheeks. "G'day," she said. "You've come the wrong way. This is the staff elevator. You should use the main elevators. They're much nicer." There was a strong smell of disinfectant from her basket.

"He's a feng shui man," Joyce explained, pointing to her companion. "He won't use the other elevators because they have bad feng shui."

"Oh," said the woman. "Really?" She looked around at the ugly non-slip steel plates of the cargo elevator in which they stood. "But this elevator has good feng shooee, does it? Does that mean it gives me good luck to use it?"

"Definitely," said Joyce.

"That's good. I go up and down in it a hundred times a day if at all. Mind you, it hasn't brought me any good luck yet. Does it take a long time to come through?"

"Um. Paint your room pink and drink a glass of orange juice every morning," ad-libbed Joyce. "The good luck will start to flow."

Thanking her, the woman advised them to get off at the first floor and go through a door on the right. "That leads you back into the hotel main lobby. Or you can turn left and go to the back of the hotel, to the place where the buses pull up. I'll get some orange juice straight away. Thanks for the tip."

They thanked her in turn and raced out of the back door of the hotel into the car park. The morning air was cool and reviving.

"Come on," said Joyce. "We can sneak out through the side gate and get a taxi around the front."

"Where to?"

"I don't know."

Instead, Wong insisted they walk at a brisk pace to the right, where he vaguely recalled from his morning walk that there was a narrow alley leading to a busy main road. It seemed to be a good route for people who wanted to quickly leave the immediate area of the hotel and get lost in the rush-hour crowd.

Wong looked at his watch. It was 8:49. The pavements were fairly busy, and the pair quickly blended in with office workers racing to their workplaces. They found a small park and sat on a secluded bench, watching pigeons peck at the ground.

"So who IS Jackie? You'd better tell me what is going on."

Wong looked nervously around. "I think he is Big Brother."

"Maddy's brother? That's nice. So why are we—"

"No, Big Brother. *Goh-goh, daai-lo*. It means—"

"Step brother? Adopted brother?"

"Let me talk. You know what is a triad?"

Joyce thought for a moment. "Yeah. They're like bad guys—I saw a Chow Yun-fat movie once. Like the mafia?"

"Yes. I think Jackie Sum is a Hong Kong triad. They are looking for Maddy. He is called Big Brother. He is senior rank."

"They want to rescue her?" Joyce asked hopefully.

"They want to kill her."

"Oh."

She appeared not to have believed her ears. She repeated: "They want to *kill* her?"

"Probably."

Joyce was speechless. She froze like a statue. She seemed to have stopped breathing entirely.

Silence descended. They watched the pigeons peck at the ground. There was a chiming sound, like an old-fashioned ice-cream van in the distance. Somewhere, a duck quacked. A child's voice could be heard shouting: "It's over here. Mama. *Mama.*" The traffic lights in the distance changed color, triggering a roar of vehicles.

A flood of questions burst out of her. "Why did they want to come up and see me? Where did they get my name? How did they know we were in Australia? How do they know who I am? What are they doing here? I don't understand any of what is happening. Why are we running? Why do they want to kill Maddy? Do they want to . . ." She trailed off, unable to finish the sentence.

"No. They don't want to kill you," he answered quietly.

"So why are we running from them?"

The geomancer sighed. "It all start to make sense to me now. Maddy comes from family who is involve with triads in Hong Kong. 14K is name of big triad group, one of the biggest. Remember Cady Tsai-Leibler?"

"Maddy's cousin."

"Yes. Owner of the flat in Ridley Park. Wife of dentist."

"Yes, yes, I know."

"Now I remember something what she said. She said that she had friends in Hong Kong could sort out problems—any sort of problems—but not ghosts. She said many strange things. I think she is from triad family. I think Maddy also got mix up with triads. I think she was girlfriend of one triad. Senior triad. Name Jackie Sum. She is young, pretty. What they like."

"So if she was one of them, why do they want to . . . kill her?" She clearly found the phrase hard to say.

"There is one thing no triad girlfriend is allowed to do. She did it, I think."

"What is it?"

"Leave."

"Oh." Joyce contemplated this for a while. "So they're cross with her because she wanted to leave the triads and be, like, a normal person?"

"I think so. So she leave Hong Kong. She go to Malaysia. She change her name. She move around only at night. She hang out in underworld in Malaysia. She meet Ismail. He looks after her. She is happy for a while. But Ismail is also difficult person, dangerous person. Also ho marfan—much trouble. After he found out that she had much big bad luck coming—then again she is in danger."

"Huh. The moral of this story seems to be don't date dodgy guys from the underworld. They may be cool guys with cool shades but they eventually try to kill you."

Wong nodded. "Too bad."

Silence returned. Joyce had become increasingly nervous. Her shoulders were hunched. She appeared to be shivering. Every time someone walked by, she followed them with her eyes. Every time someone glanced at them, she tensed herself, ready to spring up and start running again. Every time she heard a car engine roaring, she imagined a group of men with guns jumping out of the car and running toward her.

"You didn't answer my question. Why were they coming to see me? Why me? I'm nobody. I'm a schoolgirl. I'm nothing."

"I don't know. They have been looking for Maddy for long time, I think. Their contact in Singapore maybe see her or her boyfriend visiting home of Madame Xu. So they go to see Madame Xu yesterday, after we go to airport. Dilip Sinha is there. He tells them that Maddy is a friend of yours. He gives them our names, name of our hotel. So they fly to Sydney on next plane. They arrive early this morning. They go straight to hotel. They want to see you, because they want you to tell them where Maddy is."

"But I don't know where Maddy is."

"Yes," said Wong. He didn't want to tell her what he thought the most likely outcome would have been had they been caught: that the triads would have beaten or tortured them half to death in a bid to find the slightest clue to Madeleine Tsai's whereabouts.

The feng shui master felt odd. He was uncomfortable, fidgety. He wondered for a moment whether he was coming down with an illness. But then he looked at the young woman next to him and realized that the unfamiliar feeling was more emotional than physical. His hostility had waned, and had been replaced by a small spark of sympathy. Interns are not normally required to deal with triad death threats.

Again, the quietness flowed around them. The small park seemed such a natural, peaceful place. It was strange and terrifying to be talking about evil and murder in a sunny, green spot so filled with freshness, flowers and chirping insects.

"C. F.," said Joyce, without looking around at him.

"Yes?"

"I'm scared."

Wong nodded. "I too."

She turned to him. "You know, when you see this sort of thing in the movies, the hero gets more and more determined to risk everything to save the person in trouble. He'll, like, go out on a limb. He'll give up his own life, even."

He looked at her with curiosity. What was she about to suggest?

"But it's not like that in real life," she said. "Is it? You know what I wanna do?"

"What you want to do?"

"Go home."

Wong nodded. "Me too."

"I hardly know Maddy. Why risk my life to rescue her? It's kinda dumb really if you think about it."

"Kinda dumb, yes."

"She's probably hung out with these sort of people all her life. She's an underworld person. She knows how to handle herself in these situations. I don't. What do I know? I'm experienced at nothing. I'm experienced at being in school. And working in a tax office. I know the names of all the members of N'Sync. Those are the only things I'm good at. I'm out of place in, in, this situation."

"Understand."

She turned pleading eyes to him. "I wanna go home. Please, C. F.?"

"I think it is good idea," he said. He started fumbling inside his jacket. "Wait first." He pulled out a large envelope that contained what Joyce recognized to be ticket folders from Susan Leong's travel agency. Wong studied the writing on the tickets. "Hmm," he said. He ran his fingers over the wording and mumbled in Cantonese. *"Ho marfan."*

"What?"

"Some problem. I bought cheap tickets. Cannot change date. Can fly home tomorrow only. Not today."

"Can't we just buy new tickets?"

"No. Very expensive. Very wasting. To not use these tickets. Cannot."

Joyce was annoyed. "I'll pay for them."

"You have money?"

"No."

"You have credit card?"

"No. Dad says I can get one when I'm eighteen."

"So how you pay for the tickets?"

"You pay on your credit card. Daddy will pay you back."

"I got no credit card. Credit card bad feng shui. Makes money move away, cannot see it go. Very bad."

This stumped Joyce. "That is like *soooooo* dumb. Whoever heard of a grown-up without a credit card? I didn't even know it was *allowed*."

Wong grit his teeth and folded his arms.

She bit her nails and thought for a while before flashing a grin. "I know. I've got it. Some of my family from my dad's side still live in Australia. I've got an Aunt Su in Sydney. She'll give us some money."

She grabbed the geomancer's forearm. "If I get money from my family, can I buy two tickets out of here on the first plane?"

Wong, depressed about the collapse of this case and the remuneration he had been hoping for, unconsciously put his hand protectively over the wallet in his inside jacket pocket. "Maybe we can leave early. But only if you pay. I already spend too much."

Just under an hour later, they were knocking on the door of a small house somewhere between Redfern and Chippendale. Wong was intrigued by the suburbs. He stared open-mouthed as the Sydney buses ferried them past street after street of neat little houses in tidy rows. Each one had its own small, square front garden, one bay window on the ground floor and two windows on the first story. On some streets, almost all the houses seemed to have identical hanging baskets dangling by the front door.

"*Ho daw,*" exclaimed Wong. "So many."

After traveling past eight or nine streets of tiny houses, Wong had started to sketch a small home in his notebook. "Houses pretty-pretty. I think in China these houses very good. Very popular. Can have many home in small place. So many people can be inside. China has many people. China has small homes, but not so pretty."

Joyce pulled her goggle-eyed employer off the bus at one street that appeared indistinguishable from all the others. Then she dragged him by the arm to a house close to the middle of a long row of what he had seen described as terraced cottages.

"I think this is it," she said. "Number seventeen." They had been unable to phone Auntie Su in advance because Joyce couldn't recall her Aunt's surname. All she knew was that she wasn't a McQuinnie or a Smart. But she had been to the house several times as a child.

She took a deep breath. The air in Sydney tasted wonderfully different from that in Singapore. She had become used to high humidity and always being too hot or too cold. The temperate, dry, breezy air of Australia was deliciously refreshing.

Stepping up to a chipped front door painted a faded shade of leaf green, she rang the bell and waited. There was no response. Joyce lifted up the knocker to make a bit more noise, but stopped as she heard noises from within the house. "She's there. I can hear her."

They heard the sound of locks being fiddled with and a chain being put in place. Then the door opened about three inches.

"Yep?" said a male voice.

"I'm looking for Auntie Su—I mean, Mrs. Susilla. I'm her niece. My name's Joyce McQuinnie. Is she home?"

"Nope." The door was shut with a considerable degree of violence.

Joyce banged the knocker.

The door opened again—the same three inches.

"When will she be back? We've come a long way. We're from Singapore."

"Singapore," repeated the voice. The door swung open another two inches and a somewhat aquiline nose looked out. Hooded eyes on either side of it peered at Wong.

"Are you one of her relatives? Are you a cousin of mine?" said Joyce, trying to elicit a warmer welcome. "I'm Auntie Susilla's niece."

"Maybe," said the voice.

"Can we come in?"

"Okay." The door was wrenched open with such force that the chain tore from the jamb. This elicited a string of curses. "Pardon my French," said a stocky man in his early twenties, waving his hand like a traffic cop to usher them into the tiny vestibule. He was unshaven and was wearing a sleeveless shirt. His muscular arms were thick and there were scars on his skin. He didn't smile. Despite the perfunctory gesture of welcome, his expression remained faintly suspicious.

"Mum didn't say to expect anyone. She'll be back this arvo," he said.

"I don't know French," Wong whispered to Joyce.

"He's speaking Australian," she hissed.

"But he just said—"

"Never mind what he said."

There was an uncomfortable period where the visitors stood in the hallway waiting for further prompting. Their host eventually growled again. "Suppose you want tea or something. Kitchen's on the left."

Wong nodded his thanks, and they took seats around two sides of a little square table set against one wall.

Joyce said: "Got any green tea? He likes green tea."

He considered this for a while. "Nah. Got Gatorade. That's blue."

Joyce pondered. "He's got Gatorade," she needlessly repeated to Wong. "It's blue."

The geomancer shook his head.

"Thanks, but I think, no," she said. "Ordinary tea will do him. Make it with no milk and no sugar. Just dip the teabag in three times, that'll be strong enough."

The young man busied himself with a kettle and some teabags, only dropping the spoons on the floor two or three times. It wasn't a complicated operation, but Joyce was quite impressed. Most of her older sister's boyfriends would have been unable to accomplish such a task.

"You're good at domestic stuff then," she said.

"Yeah. Can roast a chook even," he said proudly with an involuntary smile. "Want anything to eat? A sambo?"

Wong decided to attempt to enter the conversation. "Your mother is where?"

"Down the bingo."

"Dunabingo. Is that in Sydney?"

"Course." He gave him a quizzical look. Wong decided he would leave the conversation to Joyce.

The man looked at Joyce. "She didn't say anyone'd lob in."

"She didn't know we were coming," she said.

There was a silence. Their host's smile had quickly disappeared again. "Your dad's Martin McQuinnie, right? My mum doesn't like your dad, does she? Calls him a rich bloody bastard who doesn't look after his own."

Joyce nodded. "Yeah. They never really got on."

"She says all your side of the family are good-for-nothing bludgers who care for nothing but money."

"I guess she hasn't really spoken to anyone on our side for a long time. Like years and years."

"She says you got no hearts," he added, undisguised bitterness in his voice. "The McQuinnies got cash registers instead of hearts, she says."

Joyce was struggling to keep smiling. If she wanted to borrow money from this family, she would have to keep on good terms with them—but this hectoring was becoming increasingly hard to take. "That's her opinion. But it's probably all from some like misunderstanding or something. You know how people fall out?"

"Yeah," the young man said. "But your old man did pretty well with the property business, we heard. Never shared any of his loot, did he?"

"I think he made most of his money after your folks fell out with him. They'd stopped talking to him, so he could hardly go and hand them a load of cash, could he?"

"Don't see why not," he said in a mumble. Involuntarily, he looked around at the small, shabby room. "I could have done with a better upbringing. This is bloody scungy." As if to demonstrate his anger, he bent the teaspoon into a neat right angle.

Joyce had a set speech she had made a couple of times about how she would have swapped all the family fortune and huge empty apartments to have had a humble home containing a loving mother and/or father. But she decided that this was not the time. And looking around the sad room, she realized with a start that it might not even be true. She couldn't even begin to imagine growing up in this tiny place.

The tiny sprig of sympathy that threatened to sprout within her was quickly crushed by their host's now-naked hostility.

"Of course we wouldn't have taken any of the money, even if you had offered it to us. Since it comes from a tainted source. Property being theft and all that."

Joyce was about to reply when Wong interrupted. "Must not stay too long. Must get business done. Move on. Go home."

She nodded. But how could she ask for money from this resentful, spiteful young man? Maybe Aunt Susilla would be more reasonable. "Your mum and my dad must be a bit friendly. I used to come around here when I was a child. You don't remember me, do you? I remember you a bit. You had floppy hair and always wore a Superman suit. Your mum sent me a book of Australian mammals once for my birth-day. When will Auntie Su be home?"

"Dunno," he said. "What are you here for, anyway? Wanna borrow money?"

"Course not," she said, blushing immediately. To cover her embarrassment, she blurted out: "We're on a mission. We're here to rescue a kidnap victim."

Their host looked up suddenly. He seemed unsure of whether he had heard her correctly.

"A kidnap victim," Joyce repeated. "She was brought to

Sydney on Wednesday night by a bad guy from Malaysia. She's a friend of mine. So we came to find her. We often do this sort of thing. We help the police. I saw a dead body once. We got involved in all sorts of exciting cases. A woman was found dead in bed yesterday morning. A woman from one of our cases. We were consulted. The superintendent of police comes to talk to us regularly. I've spoken to him loads of times. We often have to deal with these sorts of things quite a lot. That's what we do."

He was amazed at this drama-laden speech—as was Joyce herself.

"So you're bloody heroes or something, are you?"

Joyce didn't know what to reply. "Sort of," she said. "In a manner of speaking."

The young man eventually revealed that his name was Brett, which rang a vague bell in Joyce's memory. She recalled him as a thin, unsociable boy with lank hair who wouldn't let her play with any of his toys. His surname was Kilington. This came as more of a surprise to her. She had never really thought of Aunt Susilla having a surname.

Brett said he hated his name. "They used to call me Killer at school. I killed a guy once. Well, a dog. I hate names. I wish we all had numbers. When I was a kid I tried to just use a number. Nobody would use it. Bastards."

Wong shifted uncomfortably in his chair. "Joyce. I don't think we will get any—you know. I think we go back to old plan. Look for girl. Stay tonight. Leave tomorrow. You have telephone book? I want to make call," he said.

Brett still had his suspicious eyes firmly on Joyce. "So you some sort of agents, then, are you? Special forces or something?" Rising to his feet, he looked at the teenage girl and the skinny old man. "You don't look like special forces. You look like . . ." He trailed off, evidently unable to decide what they looked like.

"We are, er, a civilian division, you could say. We help the Singapore police, but we're not *actually* police ourselves in a manner of speaking," Joyce explained.

"Phone?" repeated the geomancer.

Brett beckoned to Wong to follow him. "This way. Phone's there. Book's under. Got it?"

"Thank you."

He returned to the kitchen, intrigued with what Joyce was saying. He had a nervous habit of banging his left fist against the kitchen counter. There was a bandage over the knuckles of his right hand. "So let me get this straight. You and the old geezer are here to rescue a kidnap victim. Where is she?"

"Can't say," said Joyce, mysteriously. Then she decided that she had better be more honest. "Don't know exactly. Do you know what feng shui is?"

"Yeah," he blinked, apparently taken aback by the abrupt change of subject.

"Well the guy who has kidnapped her is a *bomoh*. That's a Malaysian mystic, like. We think he'll take her to the worst feng shui spot in Sydney."

"Where's that?"

"Don't know. We need to contact local feng shui people to find out what the worst place is. Because that's where we're likely to find her. See? Simple, really, when you're experienced at this kind of thing."

Wong returned, muttering. "No feng shui master in phone book," he grumbled. "Bad place. No wonder so many economy problems in Australia."

"There's got to be feng shui people in Sydney," said Joyce, directing her questions to Brett. "Do you know any?"

"Feng shui is a load of wallaby balls if you ask me. But my mum's got this friend who is into weird new age stuff. She runs a new age shop just off Cleveland. Why don't you phone her?"

Eight minutes later, they had had a brief conversation with the proprietor of a new age shop, who gave them the name of two local practitioners of feng shui. The first number they called produced a disconnected line signal. The second was a wrong number. They called the new age shop again, and were given two more alternatives. The first of these produced a cheery female voice with an English accent. The woman introduced herself as Martina Bircka, Sydney feng shui specialist and interior decorator.

When Wong asked her for help on the case on which he was working, she said she never did any work over the phone, and would only speak to them if they made a booking with her. "Fifty dollars a reading, paid in advance."

Joyce grabbed the phone. "Hello," she said. "I'm Joyce McQuinnie. I'm working with Mr. Wong—the guy you just talked to. Listen, we need some urgent information. This is police business." She paused to let that sink in.

"Oh, I see. Right. Yes," said Mrs. Bircka, suddenly formal. "What can I do for you, Miss, er, Officer?"

"We have reliable information that a known villain called Amran Ismail is in Sydney and is heading to the place in Sydney with the worst feng shui. He may be like contacting local feng shui masters to find out what that place is. Have you been consulted by anyone of that description in the past forty-eight hours?"

"No. I haven't been consulted by anyone in the past forty-eight days to be honest."

"Whatever. We'd like you to do two things for us. One is to tell Mr. Wong, who is a feng shui consultant from Singapore, where you think the strongest negative feng shui force would be in this city. And the second is to help us make a list of feng shui people in Sydney so we can call them and find out if Mr. Ismail has called any of them."

"Ooh, I don't know all of them."

"Just as many as you can."

"I'll try."

They spent two hours at Susilla Kilington's house, phoning every feng shui practitioner in Sydney. None of them admitted to having been consulted or called by anyone resembling Amran Ismail. By the end of this period, Wong felt that they had achieved nothing. They had to just get out on to the streets and start looking for the girl.

But as they stepped out of the house into the warm sunshine, he realized that they had done one thing: they had convinced Joyce's cousin that her seemingly wild story about saving a kidnap victim was true. It was clearly the biggest excitement he had had in years. He had immediately joined the team.

Joyce and her cousin—who was actually her second cousin—had a long chat while C. F. was on the phone, during which she discovered some of his history. Brett, who was born in Edinburgh, had been five years old on the day that he last saw his father. His mother Susilla Kilington packed up all her belongings and left the house immediately—moving across the world back to her native Brisbane. Brett had grown up as an Australian. He went to school in Brisbane, eventually moving with his mother, who was a painter of medium skill, to Sydney. He had not thrived at school, and had got a temporary job in his late teens as a clerk in a small organization based at the Opera House. He had eventually given that up and had started a dotcom business, providing a site for rock-climbing hobbyists.

"It didn't work that well. Then, just for a laugh, I started a site with pictures of dead bodies. Corpses-R-Us.com.au. All of a sudden I was getting 400,000 hits a month. Real eyeballs." His eyes gleamed with pride. "I was a millionaire, sort of. Well, that was what my company was valued at by my mate who had a dotcom valuing company. But then it all went down the toilet," he said. "The newspapers sued me for nicking their pics. Corpses-R-Us went down. My mate's company went down too. Bastard."

Brett said that he had finally come into his own a year ago when he left Sydney and went to work as a bush guide, eventually becoming part of a travel company operating around Uluru in central Australia. This had transformed him. He had become strong, independent, self-possessed and had developed specific skills—he was an expert climber and tracker.

But he had lost his job on Uluru—he called it The Rock—two months earlier, and had moved back to Sydney the previous week. "My mum thinks I'm just bludging for a couple of weeks. Or taking a long sickie. Haven't told her I lost my job. It's hard, you know," he said. "She'd have a fit."

"Yeah. I can imagine."

"I was bloody upset when it happened. But I think I'm okay now. Kinda came good a day or so ago."

"What happened?"

"I was just listening to Limp Bizkit and suddenly I thought bugger it. I'm not going to be bloody miserable for the rest of my life. I punched the wall—made a bloody great hole in the brickwork of my room. Wanna see it?"

"Er, not now."

"But I also fractured the knuckle of my index finger. See? Had to go to the emergency. After that I was all right. Got it out of my system."

"No, I meant what happened on the Rock?"

"Had a big row with the boss cocky. You know how it is." He gazed at the floor. "Trouble is there's not much work in Sydney for mountain climbers. I've been looking at the classifieds in the *Herald* but can't find anything. Funny, really."

"Yeah. Funny. Something will come up."

"Yeah. Maybe someone will build a mountain in Kings Cross or something." He laughed nervously.

"Something will come along eventually. Might take a while," said Joyce, gingerly putting her hand on his upper arm. It was like a boulder. He moved away, evidently suspicious of human contact.

Looking at him, Joyce suddenly realized just how much she had changed. It seemed impossible to believe that just a few years ago, they were two kids playing on the floor of the same house.

Now he was five feet eight inches of angry Australian machismo nicknamed "Killer," while she was . . . what? A soft, lost creature, drifting and directionless, a citizen of everywhere and a citizen of nowhere. She realized that she no longer felt remotely Australian. For a start, his speech patterns now seemed odd and unfamiliar to her. She spoke international English, Americanized English—she'd noticed that she had at some point started saying "cookie" instead of "biscuit" and "Santa" instead of "Father Christmas." Yet she wasn't British or American. And she certainly wasn't a Hong Konger or a Singaporean. So what was she?

C. F. entered the room and announced that he had finished studying the notes he had made from talking to local feng shui practitioners and was ready to hit the road.

Brett leaped to his feet. He was excited. "Where do we go first? Are we working with the Sydney police or what? Do we get a patrol car?"

Neither of the visitors vouchsafed an answer. They just looked at each other.

"How did you travel to our place?" Brett asked.

"Uh. A senior agent dropped us," Joyce lied. Admitting that they had come by the Glebe shoppers' bus would have been too disillusioning. "This is a top secret mission. Most of the local cops know nothing about us. The contacts were made at top level. As far as the local officers go, we're on our own. We're kind of undercover if you know what I mean. Low-key, like."

In the end, they borrowed Brett's aging, dented Mazda 323. "It's low-key," Joyce said approvingly.

After umming and ahhing for almost a quarter of an hour on the phone, Martina Bircka had told Wong that the most significant feng shui spot in the whole of Sydney was the Sydney Harbor Bridge. "It's a big, arch-shaped thing. A lot of intensity, especially in the middle and underneath. And this great surge of energy as all those lanes of traffic go through the center of it. I mean, I don't really know if it is good feng shui or bad feng shui, but it must be the most intense feng shui spot in the city."

Brett had gone upstairs and found a postcard of the bridge to show Wong. "We call it the Coathanger," he had said. "D'you see why?"

"Ah," Wong had replied. "Interesting. Certainly it must have a very great concentration of *ch'i*. There is no doubt about it."

Half an hour later, they arrived at the bridge.

It was an awesome sight. It stood slightly too high above the general skyline of the city, a towering edifice linking two sides of a sprawling urban conurbation. There was a classic, almost Victorian grandeur about the massive buttresses of pale brown concrete and granite on either side, soaring ninety meters into the air. And this was dramatically contrasted with the relative modernity of the angled steel girders that gracefully looped between them. The heart of the bridge was teeming with traffic—eight lanes of cars and buses, plus two railway lines, a pedestrian footpath and a bicycle path.

They drove around the roads on one side of the bridge, and then crossed it to prowl the streets on the other side. They crossed the bridge again back to the downtown area, before doing what Brett called "a sharp yewie" to get back on to the bridge heading northward.

"What are we looking for?" said Brett. "Are we just going to drive up and down the bridge all day?"

"A Malaysian guy dragging around a girl aged nineteen? She's Chinese but she's got streaky hair, black, brown and reddish." Joyce sat in the passenger seat in the front of the car, watching everyone they passed on the left. Wong was in the back seat behind the driver, looking at people on the right. There was no sign of Amran Ismail or Madeleine Tsai.

After a wasted half-hour driving up and down the bridge, Brett suddenly stopped the car abruptly. "Bugger me up the outhouse wall! I've got it. We're looking in the wrong place."

"What you mean?" asked Wong.

"They're not going to be at the bottom of the bridge. They'll be at top. There's walking tours over the top of the bridge. I bet he'll have taken her up there."

Brett turned the car around and took it to a vantage point where they could see a point at the zenith of the south tower. "You go and meet the bridge climbing guides over there. Then they take you up. They guide you over the catwalks and up ladders and things. You have a special suit. It takes several hours. There's railings to hold on to. All the touroids do it. I'll take you to the bit where you have to sign in. I'll bet they'll be there."

"Of course," said Joyce. "It's perfect. They can get up there and he can push her off. To her, like, you know . . . death." Her voice dropped to a whisper.

"I think you have to wear a harness or something. It's actually quite safe. Mum's done it."

Wong nodded. "Joyce is right. He can put his arms around her. Open her harness. Or cut her rope. Push her. She falls. Dies. Everyone thinks is accident. Perfect murder."

"We'd better hurry. Lemme see. I think you have to book in advance really, but some people come and take a chance," said Brett. "We'll just have to get in line."

He parked the car at Harrington Street and then led the visitors to an office emblazoned with the name Bridgeclimb. Although there was a high wind blowing, the weather was warm and bright, and there was a string of tourists heading the same way.

Joyce kept looking at her watch. "*Geez*. Friday is running out fast. I hope they're here." They were.

The three searchers came upon a large gaggle of about forty or fifty people more or less in a line outside a doorway. Almost immediately, the young woman squealed. "There they are! There! C. F. See?"

"I see."

"Ya beaut, Killer. What did I tell you?" said Brett, congratulating himself. "Where?"

"There," said Joyce, pointing at a queue of tourists. Halfway down the line were a pair of East Asians, one of whom was abnormally tall.

They stood out from the crowd because of their posture. Neither looked like relaxed vacationers waiting to see a national monument. Amran Ismail stood stiff and tense and excited, his chest rising and falling fast as the minutes ticked by on this long-awaited day. Madeleine Tsai, like a crumpled bird, pressed herself unhappily into his side under his left arm.

Brett took a huge breath, flexing his pecs and biceps. "Are they dangerous? Is he armed? Shall I tackle him. That bloke is it?" He looked at the Malaysian and quickly exhaled. "Bloody hell. He's big, isn't he? Bigger than me."

"He is big," agreed Joyce.

Brett suddenly appeared to be looking for a way out. "I think we should call the police. That's what we do in Australia, if we see a killer or anything. We call the police. We don't tackle them ourselves. I think it is against the law to tackle them yourself, maybe."

"I'll do it," Joyce said, discovering hidden reserves of energy at the sight of her friend. "She won't know you guys from Adam. She knows me."

She raced toward her friend. "Maddy! Maddy, it's me. It's me."

Madeleine turned around. "Joyce?" The young Hong Kong woman's face broke into a puzzled smile. "What are you doing here? How did you find us?"

She started to move toward Joyce, but Ismail grabbed her shoulders and held her back. "No! Don't move," he said. "*Alamak!*"

"She's my friend. Her name's Joyce. She's from Singapore."

"No. She's with them," he said. "With Big Brother."

"She's my friend," Maddy repeated, but with less conviction.

"She's with your Big Brother. How else she can find you? They got people all over. Don't go near." To Joyce, he shouted: "Stay away."

"Joyce! How did you find us?" Maddy said.

"I—"

"Big Brother told her," interrupted Ismail.

"Maddy, don't listen to him. He's lying. We're here to rescue you. Don't trust that man. He's lying. You're in danger."

"*Alamak!* I told you already," spat Ismail. "She's big trouble-lah. She's trying to separate us. She's with Jackie."

At the sound of that name, Maddy winced. She folded herself under his large arm. "I don't want Jackie to find me."

C. F. Wong appeared behind Joyce.

Ismail, looking alarmed, grabbed Maddy's arm and abruptly pulled her out of the line of tourists. He started marching her briskly to the exit.

"Stop them," Joyce told Wong.

The feng shui man merely looked at her. She compared the geomancer's tiny skeletal frame with the *bomoh's* towering one. "Okay, he's big. But we have to do *something*. We can't just stand here and watch them leave after coming all this way to find them."

"Mr. Ismail. Need to talk to you," Wong called out. "About your predictions."

Amran Ismail continued to walk away.

"Can save Ms. Tsai, if you want her to be saved," the geomancer added.

At this, Madeleine turned around to look at Wong, but Ismail tightened his grip on her upper arm and yanked her violently away.

As the tall Malaysian broke into a jog, there was an unexpected shout. "Halt!" said the voice of Brett Kilington. "You're under arrest. Sorry, mate."

McQuinnie and Wong watched with amazement as her Sydney relative cantered up to Ismail and Madeleine, followed by two police officers. "That's the man, officer," said Brett to the taller of the men in uniform. "He's kidnapped that girl. Arrest him. I would have done it myself, but I was worried that I might hurt him." He was trying to look calm and unsmiling, but his face was glowing with pride at being part of a major disturbance, a public spectacle. "Those guys behind them, there—they have the evidence. They're with me," he added.

"Ohhh," said Wong. "I don't think this is good idea."

❖

He was right. It turned out not to have been a good idea, Joyce decided soon. The police herded them all into a van and took them for questioning. There was no immediate evidence that a crime was in the process of taking place, but that didn't seem to worry the officers concerned. She realized that since the man making the accusations was an ordinary Sydney citizen, he inspired a degree of trust, while three out of the four other people involved were foreign, and all seemed rather odd to say the least.

Brett told her that there had been a couple of major security scares recently. These days the laws were being interpreted in a way that enabled police to take a reasonable amount of liberty in detaining suspicious-looking individuals loitering around major landmarks—especially after the destruction of the World Trade Center in New York.

Arriving at the police station, Joyce was painfully aware of the suspicion in the eyes of the officers dealing with them. But she understood it. The young Chinese woman had visible scars on the inside of her arms—apparent evidence of drug-taking. The tall, dark-skinned man was menacing and vaguely resembled the Muslim militants one saw on television. And the little old Chinese man spoke broken English and didn't seem to make much sense. Add in a lot of confused-sounding talk about imminent death at a major tourist landmark, and you had a recipe which got police officers very excited indeed.

They were separated in the station. Joyce tried desperately to tell a senior officer a long and involved story about why the tall man should be detained. But she saw from the listener's face that he felt the facts didn't seem to fit the picture. She soon found herself being interviewed by the officer in a small room with a woman constable sitting nearby as chaperon.

"So. You are saying that he intends to kill her." The interviewer had a clear complexion and an upright stance, but he looked tired and never smiled. He had pale gray eyes and a jaw that was too large.

"Yes. I keep saying."

"But you have no evidence of that."

"He's taken out loads of life insurance on her life."

"My wife's taken out life insurance on my life. So does that mean she is trying to kill me? I'd be a bit upset if she was."

"Of course not. But this is different. He's a bad guy. He really is. I just know he is."

The officer, whose name was Denton Gallaher, and who had just been refused a promotion for the second time, sighed. His fingers tapped nervously on the desk, as if he were longing for a cigarette.

"Okay, let's go back a bit. How is he planning to kill her? I didn't really understand that when you told it to me the first time. By supernatural means, right?"

"He thinks she is going to die today. You see, he's a *bomoh*. Like what you might call a fortune-teller sort of thing. He's predicted that she will die today. So he's just waiting for it to happen."

"But how has he predicted she is going to die? Will she be shot with a laser beam by some visiting aliens? Will she spontaneously combust? Will she be eaten by a giant shark leaping out of Sydney Harbor right to the top of the bridge?"

"He didn't say how she would die. He just said she would die. We don't know how she will die. Someone might kill her. Or she might just . . . die."

"You believe him, do you?"

"Well . . . yes, I suppose so."

"You don't sound very sure. Now you just said he was a bad guy. Why should you believe him? If he's such a bad person, he may be lying, right?"

"We had her fortune checked by a lot of different people. Including my boss. They all said the same thing."

"The old Chinese gent."

"Yes. They all agreed that this was a really bad day for her."

"Well they're right. I'll tell you something else, without a crystal ball, neither. This is a bloody bad day for me, too. We all have bad days. Or haven't you noticed?" Gallaher leaned back in his chair and toyed with a pen, clinking it against his shiny front teeth.

"Look. I didn't ask you to arrest him." Joyce was becoming irate.

"Your cousin did."

"Yeah. Well it wasn't my idea."

"So what do you think we should do?"

"Let us go so that my boss can save the life of the girl."

"So you think I should just let everybody go?"

"No. You need to detain the Malaysian guy. Amran Ismail. You have to lock him up. Just for one day, even. Just until the end of today. Then Maddy will be safe. The danger period will be past." Even as she said it, she realized just how stupid she sounded. She was amazed at herself. How had a sharp, skeptical, sassy teenager somehow been transformed into this pathetic creature who sounded like a gullible tea lady, running around trying to spread terror about what sounded like gypsy predictions?

Gallaher leaned back in his chair. "Now come on, little lady. You say you lived here when you were a kid. In Australia we don't lock people up without evidence. That's just not the way we do things."

"So you are going to let him go free?"

"I am almost certainly going to let him go. We're running a few checks, but as far as we can tell, Mr. Ismail and Ms. Tsai are a legitimate pair of tourists who have come here for a legitimate purpose—to do some touristing. They have committed no crime, nor is there any evidence that they are in the process of committing any crime. They were visiting the Sydney Harbor Bridge, which is a recommended activity for tourists, and boosts our economy. Indeed, it should be a compulsory activity for tourists, if it was up to me."

Joyce, unhappy and confused, looked around desperately for help. The room had no windows, but the door was slightly ajar, drawing her eye. No one passed by. She glanced to her right, where the woman police officer sat, quietly taking notes. She was deeply frustrated with herself for being unable to communicate her fears intelligibly. Then the feeling suddenly changed to anger.

"Okay, let him go then," she snapped. "You'll regret it if you read in the *Sydney Morning Post* tomorrow that a young Chinese visitor was killed."

"*Herald. Sydney Morning Herald*. That would be a surprise, and yes, I guess I would rather not see that headline in that paper or any other. But I see no signs that Mr. Amran Ismail is likely to do anything terrible to his young Chinese fiancée. He says so, and he seems to make sense—much more sense than you and Mr. Wong do. The young woman herself is not talking very much, but it is clear that she seems to feel very unsafe whenever we take her away from Mr. Ismail. And you and Mr. Wong can only give me a wild story that some undefined supernatural destiny has decreed that she die today. And Mr. Kilington is a bit of a bloody silly goon who will probably end up wearing his underwear on his head in my humble opinion. It's not much to go on, now, is it?"

"So you're not going to do anything? You're just going to let everyone go?"

"I didn't say that. I said that I was going to let Mr. Ismail go. And his fiancée. They have committed no crime. I'm rather sorry to have wasted their sight-seeing time. They might, conceivably, sue the police for that. They've done no harm to anyone. But I'm afraid I can't say the same for Mr. Wong, Mr. Kilington and your good self. You see, wasting police time is a very serious crime in Australia. It's a particularly serious crime in my department, because we are criminally understaffed, thanks to the stinginess of the government. And it is the most serious crime of all when I am the individual whose time is being wasted, because I am a bloody impatient bastard who doesn't like being monkeyed around with by people playing silly buggers. Do you get my point?" His voice had risen in pitch and volume throughout this speech and the last words were uttered in barely repressed fury.

"Yes," said Joyce in a tiny voice, suddenly terrified. She didn't trust herself to say anything else, but sat and squirmed. She waited for him to continue, but he appeared to be enjoying her discomfort.

After rising to his feet and strolling around in a circle for a minute, he sat down again.

"Do you understand," he whispered, putting his face

close to hers, "that I could lock you up and throw away the key for what you are doing?"

"Ahem." The female officer coughed. She apparently did not approve of physical closeness between her boss and the young woman being questioned.

"Gotta bad throat?" Gallaher snapped at her.

"She's a minor," the woman said. "She's under eighteen. Go easy. We should really have a social worker in here."

"This is unofficial. Just a little chat." Gallaher turned his face back to Joyce's. He continued to speak very quietly. "I'm going to go and have a cup of tea. And then I'm going to decide what to do. If I were you, I would be saying my prayers. I would be praying that that nice officer Gallaher enjoys his cup of tea and that it leaves him in a good mood. Because if it fails to lift me out of the bad mood you have got me into, it could be very bad news indeed for you and Mr. Wong and Mr. Kilington."

He stormed out of the room.

Joyce burst into tears. "I wanna go home," she wailed.

The woman constable handed her a tissue.

Two hours later, C. F. Wong, Joyce McQuinnie and Brett Kilington were released. They were not charged. Nor were there any further interviews. The lengthy delay seemed designed merely to punish them for wasting police time. Gallaher had given them a severe lecture, telling them that if they stepped one inch out of line again—"And that includes crossing the road one nanosecond before the green man has started flashing"—they would be hauled in and charged with a lengthy assortment of crimes which he, personally, would compose for the purpose.

Wong took a long, deep breath of cool, free Sydney air as he stepped out on to the street. In truth, he was astonished at how unviolent their experience in the police station had been. While Joyce—judging by her continuing sobs and sniffs—had found the session traumatizing, the geomancer had found it fascinating and rather uplifting. Although he had spent many hours in the offices of police officers and detectives in Singapore, this was the first time for many years that he had been on the wrong side of an exchange with the law.

Some thirty years ago he had spent several uncomfortable days negotiating with corrupt members of the Public Security Bureau in a town near Guangzhou after his parents had had a dispute with neighbors. He remembered none of the details—but he would never forget the feeling of utter powerlessness that the officers of the PSB had conjured up inside him. These men had the power to destroy people's lives at a whim, and they went out of their way to demonstrate this to anyone who fell within their clutches. And it wasn't just financial or social ruin that they could bring about. They were not above physically harming, maiming or killing individuals who did not do exactly what they wanted. But what was worst of all was the evil in their faces: the higher the rank of the officer, the less humanity in his eyes.

What a contrast with the Australian constables. These men were large, firm, hard-nosed, and even menacing—but throughout the meeting, it was clear that they did everything according to the book. There was an underlying sense that they were working toward examining evidence and establishing the truth—two issues that simply were of no interest whatsoever to the mainland officers who had arrested him. And they had been polite, too: there was no hitting, no spitting, no cursing, no blood-curdling threats of torture and death. How on earth did they ever get confessions out of people in Australia?

In contrast, the police with whom he had dealt in China almost never failed to get confessions—whether they had detained the right people or not. Nor did they care. Trials were quick and predictable in China. The lack of a proper legal system was the biggest single curse of the mainland, he decided. It spread corruption and fear. Again, he recalled the thin, piggy eyes of the chief PSB officer at that station in Guangzhou. Wong had never experienced such terrifying coldness from a human being again until some years later, during the time he lived in Hong Kong, when his small office had been visited by triads—but that brought up other painful memories.

The geomancer shivered and made a conscious effort to change the flow of his thoughts. They had to rethink their mission.

"What do we do now?" Joyce asked.

"Yes," said Wong. That was the question. What did they do now?

"I wanna go home."

"Yes."

Her eyes were still wet and she had acquired a sniff that wouldn't go away. "If you pay for the tickets, I'll get Daddy to pay you when we get back."

"Must think first."

"Naaah. You can't go home now. We have a girl to rescue. Or did you forget?" This was Brett. Unlike the two visitors from Singapore, he was still on a high. He had loved being the instrument of arrest at the Sydney Harbor Bridge, despite the fact that the police had unaccountably and immediately decided that the good guys were the bad guys and the bad guys were the good guys. What's more, he had been thrilled to have spent almost three hours in the police station. Important people in uniform were taking note of what he was saying. Sometimes they were literally jotting down his words as he uttered them. And not just any old cop shop, but a police station at The Rocks, in the heart of Sydney. He had become part of a human drama. It was so refreshing to belong again after two months of unemployment.

"So what do we do now? We get them ourselves, right, mate? The police won't get them so we have to arrest them ourselves and take them into custody. And then get some evidence. Right?" he asked, looking from one to the other.

"No. I'm tired," said Joyce, who was still weepy. "I wanna go home."

"I guess I'm a bit hungry too," said Brett. "Wish I'd bought those sambos. Fancy getting a feed or something? Chips? Mackas?"

"Let's go and have a nice cup of tea," said Joyce. "I think that's what we need. That's what I need. Somewhere quiet and far away from any bad guys?"

"Cuppa sounds fine," said Brett. "After all, we are rels."

He slung his thick arm around Joyce's shoulders. Her eyes widened with alarm.

The two of them headed to a café on George Street. Wong said he wanted to go for a walk, promising to return in half an hour. He took Brett's cell phone. "You have any problem, you call me. I come back quick," he said.

The geomancer decided to walk back to a little garden he had seen earlier that morning. He thought he could locate it from where he stood. But after walking for seven minutes and failing to find it, he decided to look for another spot in which he could sit and think. A few minutes later, he found the perfect place: a grassy knoll under a tree in the middle of a nearby park called the Domain. The roads were reasonably distant, and formed an embracing circuit that pulled energy toward the spot, but without swamping it completely: an ideal place to make a decision.

Should they go home to Singapore or should they stay? Wong knew exactly what he wanted to do. He wanted to race to the airport and get on the first plane back to safe, boring, secure Singapore. Australia was all too dramatic for him—there were too many unpredictable, difficult things needing to be dealt with at once: a young woman with a terrible clash in her pillars of destiny who had to be helped against her will, a giant *bomoh* who had to be found and restrained, a traumatized intern who needed to be sent back to her father, a group of murderous Hong Kong triads who had to be avoided at all costs. These all added up to one thing: serious bad fortune. Logically, they should leave at once.

He recalled the wonderful lesson in the *Book of Chuang Tzu* on the importance of non-involvement. Fire, the sage wrote, is its own enemy. It destroys itself. Similarly, the cinnamon tree grows into such a delicious spice that it must be chopped down and consumed. The sage Chuang Tzu, while thinking on these things, was saddened by the way that powerful things contained the seeds of their own destruction. But that night, in a dream, he saw a Chinese sacred oak, the wood of which is not good for carpentry and is never used for building. The tree said to the sage in the dream that it had spent thousands of years acquiring the ability to be entirely useless. "Now all the other trees in the forest are regularly chopped down but I am not," the tree said. "When danger is all around, becoming entirely useless becomes the only condition which is of any use at all."

The lesson was clear: If preserving life is the end goal, you must be neither greatly evil nor greatly good. The evil soon comes to a bad end—but heroes also often come to a bad end. Better to be neither.

So why did he not immediately agree to go to the airport when Joyce had suggested it? He tried to locate, within himself, the precise emotion that was preventing him from taking that step. "It's because I know," he said out loud. "Because I know what the *bomoh* will do. I know where he will go."

His mind went back to the trip in the back of the police van from the Harbor Bridge to the police station. As the vehicle had moved along the roads, Wong had noticed that something outside had suddenly caught Amran Ismail's eye. The tall man's head had jerked to one side and stopped moving. Wong had followed the direction Ismail's eyes were facing, and then he had seen it too. Both mystics were transfixed. There, in the distance, was a structure that had an extraordinary amount of *ch'i*: and it was all bad. "*Waaah,*" Wong had breathed to himself.

It was a massive building on a platform that seemed to cut into the water. He had noticed it vaguely an hour earlier as they had crossed the bridge. But now he got a better look at it. Clearly it was built on some sort of plinth that jutted into the harbor. Somehow, it appeared to be falling over. He had never seen anything like it: a huge pile of massive bowls that had tumbled down, and then been frozen at the point at which they smashed into the floor. Huge, curved, shell-shaped walls jutted almost vertically into the sky. They were arranged in series, as if the pile of bowls had shifted to one side, each bowl moving individually, before the whole pile crashed. As a building, it must be totally impractical. The sharp curves would create enormous problems with shaping the rooms in the upper storys.

But the worst thing of all was the cutting *ch'i*. It was a

feng shui master's worst nightmare. A series of angles cut deep into the central area of the structure—it would be like a series of chopping blades, or axe-heads pointed at whoever was in the middle. The feng shui of the building must be atrocious. There was no doubt at all in Wong's mind that anyone who spent much time in that building would suffer enormous upheavals, arguments, fights, and possibly sickness or death.

As the lights had changed and the police van had moved further along the road, Wong noticed that Ismail's head moved to keep the monstrous building in view. Although not a trained feng shui man, Ismail, as a mystic, would surely realize that the ugly thing on the waterfront was the perfect spot in which to conjure bad fortune for Madeleine Tsai. If anything tumultuous were going to happen to a person in Sydney, that was the place where it would happen.

And this was the crux of Wong's dilemma as he sat in the park, trying to decide what to do next. He reckoned there was a better than 90 percent chance that Amran Ismail, upon being released from the police station, would immediately have taken Madeleine Tsai to that monstrous falling-over structure that had so firmly caught his eye.

The question was this: since he, Wong, knew where Ms. Tsai would be, was it incumbent upon him to rescue her?

No. He had no obligation to do so. There was no commission, no contract, and no deposit had been paid.

So that led to another point: what happened next was his own free decision. What did he stand to lose or gain by staying to help her? It appeared likely that if he could find and possibly rescue her, or even help her just a little bit, he stood to gain a great deal out of it. Wong visualized a traffic accident about to happen during the approach to the monster building, and him, following surreptiously, snatching Ms.

Tsai out of harm's way. He was anxious to intercept her, if at all possible, before she reached it. The building was a feng shui man's worst nightmare. There was no way that he would enter it himself.

The crux of the matter was this: the fates had given him a unique chance to help someone very, very rich. And that meant that he would be rewarded, for sure. Her father, he knew, was wealthy beyond imagination. The gift would surely be huge. And Old Man Tsai would surely cover expenses, too. He could send the tycoon an invoice which could cover his and Joyce's fares to Australia—he'd pretend that they always traveled first class—and then add on a day rate of thousands of dollars a day for each of them. U.S. dollars, perhaps. He could earn a fortune.

But if they went home now? Things would be very different. He would have to pay for new air tickets. Even if Joyce's father reimbursed him for those, he would still be out of pocket. The invoice for the old tickets would arrive from Susan Leong's travel agency next week. He would get no payback whatsoever for this whole wild goose chase. And then there was the hotel bill, for which he had paid cash. All in all, he stood to lose everything he had made from Mrs. Mirpuri this week. He felt physical pain at the thought of this. He clenched his fists so tightly he almost gave himself stigmata.

So what was it to be? If they stayed one more night, at least there was a fair chance that they could earn some money from Tsai Tze-ting. What if they stayed, but failed to find the girl? Even then, there would only be one pair of airline tickets to pay for, which, hopefully, Joyce's father would be persuaded to cover. Maybe he would pay Wong back for the hotel as well? After all, this whole trip had been his idiot daughter's idea. A misguided mission to find her friend, which he, Wong, had gone along with only out of the kindness of his heart. If Joyce's father would cover such charges, most of the money from Mrs. Mirpuri could be retained as revenue. And if the dentists paid as much as he hoped they would, this could still turn out to be a good week for him.

"We stay," he decided. "Finish the job."

❖

The next two hours were spent in a blur of frantic activity—which again achieved nothing at all. Joyce, at first, was upset that Wong had changed his mind about heading straight back to Singapore. And she was even more annoyed when he revealed that financial considerations were his main reasons for doing so.

"For many years I want a reason for Old Man Tsai or someone like that to owe me favor. Now it has come. I cannot let opportunity go," he said.

"So this girl's a tin-arse," Brett commented. "Interesting."

Incensed, Joyce announced that she was going on strike with immediate effect. She flatly declared that she would refuse to provide Wong with any further help in any way, or even accompany him on his mission to catch up with Madeleine Tsai and Amran Ismail—much to his delight.

"I'm going back to the hotel," Joyce snapped. "Oh—maybe not." She recalled that the triads knew the hotel in which they were staying, and knew her name and room number. "Well, I'm still not going to help you get that guy. It's like *totally* dangerous. I could get killed. I'm too young to get killed. I don't like this job anymore: triads, police—they're all horrible. I used to work in a tax office. A tax office is really nice. Nothing happens."

"I don't want you to get killed," Wong assured her. "I will

go and search for Ismail myself. No problem. No need for you to come."

"I know!" Joyce said, suddenly brightening up. "I'll go to Aunt Susilla's. If the triads find me there, Brett will protect me, right? Got any guns?"

Brett looked at her. "Maybe. But sorry," he said. "I'm going with Mr. Wong. He needs me. Right, Mr. Wong?"

"Er," said the geomancer.

"This is a job for men," Brett added. "Rescuing a young woman from bad guys." He snapped a fork and flung it over his shoulder, where it landed in a double-tall cappuccino.

"A damson in distress," put in Wong, straining to recall a phrase from *How's Tricks: Colloquial English II*.

"But I need *protecting*," pleaded Joyce. "That's a job for men, too. I don't wanna be left alone in your house or in a hotel or anywhere. I need looking after. You're supposed to be gentlemen. I'm a female. I'm a minor. You should be fighting over who gets to look after me."

"Yeah, yeah, yeah. But we can't waste my sort of skills on being a nursemaid," Brett said. "I know where I'm needed. For finding these bloody bad guys, you need a man. You need an *Australian* man. Mr. Wong doesn't know how to get around. He doesn't speak English—not so's anyone could understand it, anyway. There's only one alternative for you, Joyce."

"What?" she said, crestfallen.

"Go to the police. Tell them you're in danger. Ask for protection. You'll be apples."

"As if. No thanks," she said quickly. "Oh geez. I'll come with you. But I wanna guarantee that there's going to be no danger. I don't wanna get killed. Daddy would be like *furious* with me. Totally."

"Me too," said the geomancer, sighing. "Cannot risk my retainer."

Brett patted her on the head, to her disgust. "That's my girl. I know you're a bit stroppy, but it'll be fun. It's no good being a bloody sook."

Stepping out of the coffee shop into the bright afternoon light, Wong noticed a store called Dymocks that had a window full of books. He asked Joyce and Brett to wait while he collected some information about the big ugly building.

He entered and pointed to a postcard. "What is the name?" he asked the shop staff member.

"Of that? That's the Opera House," she replied.

"Oprah House?"

"Yep."

He thought about this for a moment. "I saw her on TV. In Singapore. I'm from Singapore. Visitor."

"Welcome to Sydney. Is there any particular book you are looking for?"

"I want a book on Oprah."

"Sure thing." The woman had then found him the autobiography of an American television talk-show host. He flicked through it, frustrated to find there were no pictures of her house.

"You have any book with pictures of her house? Or only postcard?"

"I don't think so. Unless there's a picture of her house in there."

"I want floor plans of Oprah's house. Her house in Sydney."

At this comment, the woman began to look worried and retreated back toward the manager's office. Disappointed, Wong had moved as if to leave the bookshop but was delighted to find a book on a table near the front of the shop with the dangerous building on the cover. He made further inquiries from another staff member and was guided to a shelf with several books featuring the building on the cover. He bought one that had photographs, plus a floor plan and a detailed history.

Outside the bookshop, Wong shared his feelings about the Opera House with the others. Brett was initially insulted to hear Wong talk about the bad feng shui of the building.

"Whoa," he said. "This is an Aussie icon, mate. Perhaps the number one Aussie icon. You'd better not say anything bad about it to other people. I mean, you better remember that I am an unusually understanding sort of Aussie. Not everyone is as easygoing as I am. Slagging off the Opera House. That's probably an arrestable offense these days. You'd better not let Gallaher hear you saying anything like that. He'd have your guts for garters."

The feng shui master understood almost nothing of what Brett said, but had simply nodded and asked to be led to the car. The young man drove them to a parking lot at Circular Quay East Street. A few minutes brisk walking took them to the site of the Opera House. Wong had gasped as they approached. The huge building, with its massive jutting curves standing into the sky, horrified him. "*Waaah,*" he gasped. "So strange."

The feng shui master flatly refused to go past the guard station at the main approach. "I wait here," he said. "You go find her. Bring her to me. If they come this way, I will try to stop her." He refused to move any further.

Joyce and Brett walked around the building. It took them quite a while. They tried to inspect every seat in every eating place—there were at least five restaurants and cafés. They walked through all the public areas. They poked their heads into the performance spaces, several of which were empty. Then Joyce proposed doing the entire circuit again.

"It's too slow us all going together. We should split up, search the place and then meet again here in about, say, half an hour," said Brett. "I used to work here. There are more than a thousand rooms."

"I don't wanna be left alone," squealed Joyce. "There are men with guns looking for me. I don't like men with guns. Why didn't you bring your gun?"

"Didn't want to. In Australia it's not recommended."

They did another round of the main restaurants. By 4:33 P.M., Joyce was beginning to lose hope. There was no sign of Madeleine. If she was here, she was so well hidden that there would be no way of finding her without a search warrant which would allow them to march into the private offices, rehearsal spaces and dressing rooms. She knew there was not the slightest hope of the police helpfully providing such a document.

The two of them returned to the guardhouse where Wong was still staring with a considerable degree of fear at the angular structure that disturbed him so deeply.

"You have to come and help us," Brett said. "She won't leave me, so we just keep going round and round and we may be missing them. We'll go one way and you go the other way. That way we should be able to zero in on the buggers."

Wong shook his head. "No. Cannot. This building very bad. The design is broken rice bowls. Broken rice bowls is the worst symbol. Very bad fortune." He backed away from them as he spoke. "Cannot," he repeated. "Cannot."

Why was the Malaysian not there? The geomancer wondered if he had got it wrong. Perhaps Ismail had merely been staring at a remarkable sight, and had not specifically decided that this was the spot at which Madeleine should die. But how could he have come to such a conclusion? The Opera House was far more dramatic than the bridge—there was a twisted, moving feeling about the place. The design made it a building in motion—and thus it produced an astonishing concentration of swirling *ch'i*.

The position of the building on the waterfront added to its negativity, as the map in his book clearly showed. It was on Bennelong Point, which jutted directly into the sea, causing a dramatic interruption to the natural flow of the waters of Sydney Harbor, the fundamental source of the city's fortune. The natural interchange of waters between Sydney Cove and Farm Cove was interrupted by the platform on which the monster building stood.

Brett was still unconvinced. "This building is adored, mate. It's loved more than any other place in the whole bloody country. It can't be such a stinker as you make out."

Wong said he wanted to step further back, so he could see the structure as a whole and try to get some idea of what the architect had in mind.

Joyce decided to join him. "I'm coming, I'm coming. Every time I see a young Chinese guy I think it must be Jackie Sum. How am I supposed to spot him? I don't even know what he looks like."

As Wong marched backward away from the building, his expression suddenly changed.

"Ah," he said, a smile breaking out on his face.

"What, what?" asked Joyce.

"There! Now I see."

"You mean you see what the architect meant to do?"

"No," said Wong. "I see Mr. Ismail."

The next ten minutes were spent arguing. Amran Ismail had somehow taken Madeleine Tsai up on to one of the huge, curved roof sections of the Opera House. How he had done it, none of them could work out. There was no walkway visible from the ground to the roof. They could see no railings or paths or ladders intended for people climbing up from the lower levels to the outside of the alcove windows under the overhangs. There were no access doors to the roof. The upper surface of the building was off-limits to everyone. The windows that looked out on to bits of the upper surface areas—which were not contiguous since each was separated from its neighbor—were clearly not designed as doors onto the roof.

"I think there are some steps you can get to somewhere," said Brett. "I remember meeting some buggers whose job it was to clean the windows. But I wouldn't know how to get up there. Not legally, anyway."

Joyce surmised that Ismail must have told the young woman that it was the safest place to be, while he knew that it was the opposite.

"He must have smashed a window and climbed out onto the surface," Brett had said. "Or perhaps scaled up one of the sides where the curve comes right down to like ground level. Or found some steps which are supposed to be off-limits."

Wong had spotted the Malaysian just as he reached the zenith of one of the less steep roof sections. As they watched through binoculars hastily retrieved from Brett's car, they saw that Ismail was dragging his terrified companion along. Maddy may have been calling for help, but her small voice was lost in the wind. They watched as he pushed her down into a sitting position. She kept glancing back the way they had come, but seemed unwilling to leave her companion. She sat next to him, helpless and apparently frozen with fear. The big man sat down next to her and waited.

Neither Joyce nor Brett could think of anything to do to get Madeleine down from her perch. The obvious thing was to call the police, but their experience earlier that day meant that was no longer an option. Nor was there any hope of Brett or herself talking to the *bomoh* about the bad feng shui of the location and persuading him to come down.

No, they needed C. F. Wong to do it. He was the only one who could speak to Amran Ismail in the language of mysticism and negative energy and so on—and persuade him that this was not going to be the last day in the life of Madeleine Tsai. But the geomancer clung to the guardhouse and flatly refused to move. He appeared to be in mortal terror of the building, visibly quaking every time he looked at it.

After a round of fruitless discussions, Brett suddenly took matters into his own hands—literally. He put his arms around the skinny geomancer's back and grabbed him by the shoulders. He then lifted Wong six inches off the ground and hustled him toward the building.

"Come on, Jo," Brett said, walking at speed toward the Opera House. "This is the only way we are going to get him over there."

Joyce, shocked, put a hand over her mouth.

"Stop!" Wong barked. "Put me down. Stop. Joyce! Tell him. Stop him or you lose your job. *Now.*"

Joyce tried not to laugh as she trotted helplessly alongside Brett and his struggling cargo. It was difficult.

"You are fired!" shouted Wong. "*Aiyeeaah.*"

They received puzzled attention from passersby. When a guard approached them, Joyce smiled innocently and announced: "Don't worry. It's—uh—just a game sort of thing. We're doing like street theater?"

In less than two minutes, Wong had been heaved up the main staircase at the entrance to the building. By good fortune, a quartet of Chinese musicians was performing in the foyer. The eerie whine of the erhu seemed to comfort Wong.

He stopped wriggling and Brett gently lowered him to the ground. "Sorry, mate. But we need you here, not at the bloody entrance miles away."

Wong, scowling, brushed the sleeves of his jacket where Kilington had held him. But he didn't run away.

Brett Kilington was struggling with himself as he went to his car to fetch his climbing gear. He was a rock climber. He had been a guide on the Rock. He had won a bronze for barehanded climbing. He had some basic gear, including a climbing gun, in the boot of his car. And he had a general level of familiarity with the layout of the Opera House. If anyone could get up on to almost any portion of the roof, he could.

But was it right to do so? Was it against the rules? Was it, in short, an arrestable offense? It was certainly a good and right thing to go and arrest a large man who was holding a young woman against her will in a highly dangerous place. But at the same time, he had already made one strenuous effort to bring the man to justice and the police had been oddly unappreciative of his efforts—as had the girl. More than that, a senior officer had warned him that if he strayed a toe off the straight and narrow any time in the next fifty years, he would be down on him like the proverbial ton of bricks.

Yet here he was, on the very same afternoon, seriously considering doing something that would go directly against all the rules with which he had grown up. In the days when he had been a clerk at the Opera House after leaving school, he was told to take a certain route to and from the mailroom every day—and he had abided by it rigidly every working day for the entire six months he had been there. But here, five years later, he was being asked to throw out the rule-book by entering one of the private areas, smashing a window, and climbing out on to the roof. Or by using his climbing gear to mount the roof from below. It was ludicrous. He couldn't do it. He would be locked up for sure. What would mum say? Worse, the image of Officer Gallaher loomed over him like a storm cloud.

"Oh pigs! I'm sorry," he said to Joyce when he got back. "I can't bloody do this. I can't break rules. When I was small I wanted to be a cop."

The young woman looked at him with her head on one side. "I've sussed you out," she said. "Never mind the muscles. You're a wuss."

"I am bloody well not. I just don't like breaking rules, that's all. I'm a Catholic. It's just me. I'm like that. But I'll help you do it if you want to go ahead."

"No way. I'm not going up there."

The feng shui master, now he had managed to remain within the shadow of the broken rice bowls building for several minutes without being struck dead, decided that the fates were safeguarding him. He was going to be all right. He should act. This was his moment.

"I am," said Wong. "Going up there. Ms. Tsai is in danger. No one is helping. I must help her. Here, please do this."

Joyce blinked down at a small yellow box he had handed her. It was a disposable camera. "What's this for?" she said.

"Take picture of me, please. One here. Then take picture of me up on roof, when I rescue her. Or when I try to rescue her."

"So you can send these to her dad, get a big reward?"

"Must have evidence."

"You are so mercenary."

"Mersal—?"

"Mercenary. It means, er, like obsessed with money."

"Yes. Thank you. Come."

This last word was aimed at Brett.

Wong raced off. Brett followed behind, the equipment in the box rattling.

"Oh pants," cursed Joyce, and set off after them, camera in hand.

❖

Amran Ismail was simultaneously exhausted and filled with the greatest elation he had ever known. It was a curious compound of feelings, and it left him unsteady and almost delirious.

Madeleine Tsai clung to his arm, shivering with fear. "I want to go back. I want to go *back*," she said.

He lazily turned his head to look at her. "Later we will. Later."

"I want to go back *now*. I don't know why we are here. This is so dangerous. Please, Amran, I'm scared. Take me back."

"*Takboleh*. Cannot. Very soon it will be over. I promise you," he said. "Wait awhile only."

She looked at the terrifyingly steep slope at their feet on either side. A sob came from her throat.

"*Aiyoh!* Don't look if it upset you to look," Ismail snapped.

Madeleine closed her eyes and pressed her wet face against his shoulder.

He gently pushed her head away. "Careful. Don't push me. Balancing very difficult. Better just sit still and wait only."

They sat there together, not saying a word. The high winds were whipping her hair around, flicking it into her face. Occasionally there would be a sudden strong gust, which would flatten their clothes against their bodies.

"What time is it?" Maddy asked.

"*Alamak*, you keep asking already. Less than twenty minutes to go only. It'll go quickly. Should have bought something for you to do, distract you. Why not you just sing a song or something? Tell me a story. Or you like I tell you one? I can tell you about my children. The children in my home. I am going to do such wonderful things for them. And for Zahra. Ah, all my little ones. So cute. So *choon*."

She shook her head. "You keep talking about them. I don't want to talk about them."

"Sleep then."

She dropped her head on to her knees, but kept a tight hold on his arm. She began weeping more loudly. "You shouldn't have made me do this. I'm scared. I hate you."

"Afterward you realize. All the fortune-tellers said the same thing. Those *bomohs* in K. L., the Great Bomoh in Melaka, that fortune-teller woman in Singapore, that old Indian guy, whatever his name was. They all said very bad luck coming. Must go through this. Everybody confirmed. But Allah is so kind. He sent me to help you. You already dead for sure if you stay in Malaysia and Jackie find you. Allah is great. He sent me to you. Now if can just stay here until end of tenth hour of daylight, then *inshallah*, all finished. Done. Move on."

He looked at her. She didn't move her head. Without looking up, she said: "When can we go back?"

"A little while more only-lah."

They sat in silence again. After a while, he peeled her fingers off his arm—not without difficulty.

"What are you doing? I want to hold on to you."

"It's okay, it's okay," he said in a reassuring tone. "Maybe I just hold you more tighter."

She was sitting on his left. His long, thick left arm snaked around her shoulders. His other arm held her right upper arm tightly. She was entirely in his grip.

The wind rose higher, making conversation difficult. She wept quietly as they waited.

"Mr. Ismail. Mr. Amran Ismail!"

The *bomoh* spun around. There was a voice in the wind. Someone calling his name? How could that be?

"Ismail-*saang*."

He arched his head further back and was astonished to find the head of the old Chinese man—one of Maddy's friends—emerging from over the slope.

"Die already! Get away," the angry *bomoh* spat. "What you want?"

Maddy squealed. "It's Jackie."

Ismail held her shoulders tightly. "Don't be scared. Is not Jackie. Just one of his men."

Wong carefully climbed the slope until he was about six yards from them. "You're in danger," the feng shui master called. "Come down. Not allowed to be here. Very against the rules."

"Go away," Ismail snapped. "Don't come."

"Only want to help. Young lady she is scared, I think. I help her come back to door. You, me, together. Then she will be safe. All safe."

"Go die."

Wong moved another yard closer to the couple.

Madeleine shrieked. "Stay away from me," she shouted.

"Only try to help," Wong said.

The *bomoh* growled. "Don't be scared. I warn you . . . *Koyak-lah!* Go now!"

Wong sat on the same ridge. But slowly he shuffled along on his bottom, getting closer to them, inch by inch.

"Ms. Tsai. I come to help. Mr. Ismail, he does not really want to help you. He want you to die. This very bad place. Very dangerous. Not good to be here. Very bad feng shui. Also, for you especially, very bad time. You must be extra careful at this time. Not go into extra-dangerous place like this. Must come down off roof with me, come inside."

"Finish! He's lying," Ismail said. "Shut up already-lah."

"Come inside," said Wong.

"Don't come near me," the terrified young woman squealed. She tried to move away from Wong, and temporarily lost her balance—and screamed again.

Ismail grabbed her shoulders. "*Aiyoh!* Go back, old man. You making her nervous. You making this situation dangerous, not me."

Wong stopped moving. He appeared to be thinking about what Ismail had said. Then he nodded. "I think you are right. I do not want to cause harm to the girl, scare her, make her fall off. That would be very bad. I go back."

He started shuffling the other way. Then he flipped over on his hands and knees and gingerly clambered, spider-like, out of sight.

"Thank God he's gone," Madeleine said. "Maybe that was it. Maybe he was the danger."

"What do you mean?"

"Maybe he was the danger that I was to face at this hour. Now that he's gone, maybe it's all over. Can we go down now?"

"Just wait. Little more time only," said Ismail.

They waited in painful silence. He looked at his watch. "Not long now. A few minutes and it will all be over."

Two minutes passed as slowly as hours. Ismail murmured:

"Nearly finish—oh no!" This last comment was elicited by the sight of another head appearing over the curve of the roof. "*Alamok,*" cursed the *bomoh.*

"Go away," said Maddy.

Then she gasped as she saw Joyce. The teenager was trembling from head to toe. Behind her, Wong was trying to pull her back. He was holding her arm so tightly that the skin of her forearm was white. "Come back. Must come back. You fall off, I will be in big trouble with Mr. Pun. Please," the geomancer said.

"Omigod-omigod-omigod-omigod," Joyce was chanting like a mantra. "Dear Jesus. Dear dear dear *dear* Jesus."

"Joyce?"

"Maddy! Come in. You can't sit out here. It's like sooo dangerous. Come in *now*. Pleeeease."

"Amran says I have to—"

"Don't listen," ordered Ismail. "Don't talk."

"You come back," Wong ordered Joyce. "Crazy girl. Go down."

"Never mind what any of those stupid guys say," the young woman shouted. "Use your brain, Maddy. Is it dangerous to sit out here or what? Come *on*."

"Something terrible will happen to me right now unless I'm really careful. It's in my stars. I know it sounds crazy but I believe it," said Maddy.

"I believe it too," said Joyce.

"You do?"

"I do. And I can tell you exactly what the bad thing is. The bad thing is that you have ended up in this incredibly dangerous place with a dangerous guy. Talk sense, Maddy. Come on."

"Don't listen," Ismail repeated, tightening his grip on her.

"He's the dangerous one," said Joyce. "Not me. You know that's true. Deep down, you know that's true, don't you? Don't you? Answer me. I'm going to stay out until you come back."

"No," said Ismail.

"No," agreed Wong. "You come inside now. I am your boss. I order you. Come down now. Otherwise I fire you."

"No, you're not," snapped Joyce, turning to him. "You fired me already, remember?"

"Oh. Okay, I give you your job back. Then I fire you."

"It's too late."

"Please. *Must* come in."

There was silence. Wong and McQuinnie turned to stare at each other. Both were dimly aware of shifting dynamics.

"I'll come in but I want promotion. I want the title of Personal Assistant. Intern sucks."

"Okay. You are Personal Assistant Intern Sucks. Now come inside." Wong was angrily hissing his words from between clenched teeth. "I am in big trouble with Mr. Pun if you fall off."

"I want my own business cards."

"Okay, okay, own business cards, anything."

"I want the desk by the window."

"Okay, can do, no problem. Now come in."

"I want my own cell phone."

"*Aiyeeaah*—too expensive. No." He flung her arm down in disgust. "Maybe better you fall off."

Glad to be out of his grip, she shuffled closer to where Ismail and Madeleine were perched.

Alarmed, Wong lunged forward and grabbed her arm again.

"C. F.?"

"Yes?"

"I really, really want to stay out here and wait for Maddy to come in. Please?"

Wong was exasperated. "She will not come in. Already I tried."

"Well, *I* wanna try."

"Waste of—"

He was interrupted by Madeleine's voice. "Joyce? You're not with Jackie, are you?"

"Of course I'm not."

"Did you find that girl you were looking for?"

"Dani? Yeah. We rescued her. It was in *The Straits Times* on Thursday. They didn't print my name. Her mum took all the credit, but—"

Now it was Amran Ismail's turn to lose his temper.

"You girls stop talking now," he shrieked. "Talk, talk, talk only. This is not the right time. Please go away you people. We don't want you here. GO NOW." The last words were bellowed in apoplectic fury, his eyes bulging at Joyce.

Joyce folded her arms. "Whatever. I'll stop talking," she said quietly. "But I'm not going anywhere. I'm going to wait for my friend. If she stays, I stay."

Madeleine looked over to Joyce—and flashed a smile. She mouthed two words at her: *Thank you.*

C. F. Wong didn't know what to do next. So he waited.

The four of them sat on the roof of the Opera House, an odd quartet with nothing to say to each other. Just hanging on took considerable effort. The wind buffeted them in short, unpredictable bursts with the force of flying fists. The gusts carried odd snatches of sound with them—people talking at ground level, the sound of police cars, the chug of passing boats.

"*Aiyeeaah*." The feng shui master made the mistake of looking down at the ground, a dizzying distance below. He was tingling from head to toe. His limbs appeared to have turned to stone yet at the same time his muscles were tensed, ready to spring to safety. There was a whiteness creeping through his mind as he looked down. His thoughts moved in slow motion. He was breathing in short, shallow gasps like a dog.

But as the minutes passed, he realized that the fear that was gripping him was gradually being shot through with strands of a completely different feeling—something akin to triumph. As he scanned his immediate environment, he slowly shook his head with amazement: he was astonished at what he had achieved in the pursuit of doing a favor for Old Man Tsai. Not only had he approached the monster broken rice bowls building but he had clambered on top of it. What more graphic example could be imagined of a feng shui master conquering his most nightmarish fears?

He wished Dilip Sinha and Madame Xu and Superintendent Gilbert Tan could see him now. He thought for a moment of asking someone to take a photograph of him—he still had the disposable camera in his pocket. But one hand tightly gripped a railing on the roof and the other was holding Joyce's forearm. He daren't let go of either.

The geomancer carefully turned his head to sneak a sidelong glance at his new Personal Assistant, who was staring at the boats in the harbor. He was equally stunned by her behavior. He had tried hard to persuade Madeleine Tsai to come in off the roof and had been abruptly rebuffed. Yet Joyce, acting against his express orders, had stupidly climbed out on the roof to try the same thing—and appeared to be making headway. At least the Chinese girl had listened to her and responded in a trusting way.

Joyce McQuinnie was still a totally unknown quantity, he decided. How could this *mat salleh* child who couldn't even speak intelligibly, manage to connect with this Cantonese young woman, when he, who was a member of the same sub-group of the same race, had so miserably failed to do so? It was remarkable. He shook his head. Truly there are strange things on heaven and earth.

The uncomfortable notion floated into his mind that Joyce could have been *meant* by the gods to be his assistant. Together they might just be able to achieve things that he could not do by himself. It was not impossible that her very differentness could even be a direct advantage to his operations. To distract himself from this horrific thought, he quickly cast his eyes over the broad horizon that stretched terrifyingly before him.

This morning, he had been unable to locate the mountains that usually cluster around a prosperous city. These were important—centuries before Western scientists had started to think about dinosaurs, the philosophers of China had dug up their swirling bones and had named them mountain dragons. But now, from this high vantage point, he could at last see Sydney's missing dragons. There was a huge rolling ridge of mountains in the distance, slightly shrouded in smog.

He saw how the urban settlements had spread toward the distantly undulating landscape. Closer at hand, it was clear that the city's immediate *ch'i* came from waterways. *The Water Dragon Classic*, written by Chiang Ping-chieh in the Ming Dynasty, identified the ways the water dragon carries *ch'i* through natural conduits. Wong noticed the series of bays cutting steeply into the Sydney waterfront, two of which surrounded the spot where he sat.

He was confused by the defensiveness that Brett Kilington had shown for the broken rice bowls building, an obviously ugly monstrosity. But it was possible that the Opera House in context, at the heart of the sprawling city, might have a charm that he could not see. Gingerly looking downward, he saw streams of visitors approaching the building on foot and in tour buses. Dozens of people were taking photographs. Some had spotted them sitting on the roof and were taking pictures of them. Could he arrange to get one to send to Old Man Tsai? Probably not. How to contact the people down there? Not possible.

Yet Brett had a point. The building appeared to be greatly admired, beloved even. Perhaps something had evaporated the bad *ch'i* its evil form produced? Perhaps he was wrong.

The thought further humbled the feng shui master. Here he was, fifty-six years old; yet what a lot he had still to learn.

Madeleine Tsai turned to Ismail. "I want to go with her."

"No," said Ismail. "You ruin everything. Must stay out here. Until it happens."

"Come on," said Joyce, suddenly excited. "I know this market in Sydney where you can get really cool stuff. And it's cheap. Better than Clarke Quay. Come on. I know Sydney really well. I'll take you to the Paddo Village Bazaar. It's on tomorrow."

"I'm going with her," said Madeleine, shaking her shoulders out of Ismail's grip.

"No," he shouted.

"Get your hands off me. I'm going with my friend."

Twisting downward and yanking herself out of his grip, she quickly scuttled out of his reach and started to carefully track on her hands and feet over to where Joyce sat.

"NO!" shouted Ismail. He leaped to the side and grabbed her, his arms wrapping themselves around her upper body. She lost her balance.

Wong and Joyce both reached forward at the same time— but neither of them could reach her.

Maddy screamed as Ismail held her tightly and pulled her away from them. The two of them fell across the railing separating them from the steeply pitched roof.

"Let her go," Wong shouted. "You're falling."

Ismail managed to stop them falling. He roughly shuffled away from them, keeping the young woman in his arms, his forearm around her throat. "Get away. Get away from us!"

The geomancer started to move toward them.

"Get away," said Ismail again.

Wong continued to approach.

"Stop," said Ismail. "Stop or I *throw* her down. I'll do it."

"Amran," gasped Maddy, breathing with difficulty. "Let me go."

"I throw her down," Ismail repeated in a furious growl. "I will. I drop her. Take one more step closer to me only and she goes down. She dies."

Wong stopped moving.

"Amran!" Maddy screamed.

The geomancer crept forward again.

"Stop. I drop her," Ismail said. "You move one more time, she dead already."

"Amran!" Maddy shrieked.

The young woman stopped kicking. She turned her face to his. "I thought you loved me?" She spoke in a dreamy voice, suddenly a child. "They're telling the truth, aren't they? You are the danger."

"Shut up."

Ismail continued to gradually move away from Wong and McQuinnie, dragging his victim with him. "I've won. I'm sorry, but I have. She's going to die and then all finish."

"We'll tell on you. We'll tell the police," shouted Joyce, the schoolyard phrases sounding odd as soon as they had left her mouth.

"Police don't like you. Think you are *chi-seen*," said Ismail. "They like me better. I think they believe me, not you. I tell them all your fault. I tell them I try to save her. Officer Gallaher—he is my friend."

"Let her go, you beast," said Joyce.

Ismail turned his forearm and looked at his watch. "Almost time," he said. "Almost time to say good-bye."

"I thought you loved me," repeated Maddy in a thin, high voice. "I thought you were going to save me."

"I do," said Ismail. He looked down at her face and the granite hardness in his eyes disappeared. "I do love you. But no one can change fortune. No one can. The only thing is make the best of it. Everything I do is for you."

"You lied to me."

"I am like a doctor who not tells patient that she is dying. I bluff you because I want you to be happy."

"I saw the papers. I saw them on your desk."

"Papers?"

"The insurance. You took out all that insurance. You will make money if I die. You love money, not me."

"No!" Ismail was suddenly furious. "No. Don't love money instead of you."

"I saw the insurance papers."

"You are going to die. No one can change your fortune.

No one. Not me, not Joyce's friend, no one. Very sorry. Insurance I got so something good comes out of your death only. Is for memorial to you, understand or not? When I got the money I will use it to start a foundation-lah. To help young people."

"Zahra? And the kids in your home?"

"Yes. Zahra will be first. She must get surgery. Very expensive. My *pak-mak*, no money. I need money to send her to Singapore, get good hospital. The other children too. All need money. They will pray for your spirit."

"You want money more than me."

"No choices are left. You must die. Is it better you die only? Or better you die and Zahra lives? Other children also?"

"Amran. I don't want to die."

"You must. No choice only. Not just me saying that. Joyce's friend say the same thing."

Ismail suddenly looked over at the feng shui master and his assistant, clutching the roof four yards away.

"Tell her," the *bomoh* shouted. "Tell her she must die today. You say you know her fortune. I went to see a feng shui man in Singapore myself: Eric Kan. He told me that she is a wood person. At five o'clock today, metal and fire and water converge on her sign. Very bad. Here and now. True or not? Come on, true or not?"

The feng shui master looked at them, but said nothing.

"True or not?" Ismail repeated as a shriek.

"Is true," said the geomancer. "But feng shui does not predict time of death. Only bad factors and bad times. You can do things, you can fight bad fortune."

"See?" Ismail crowed to Madeleine. "Metal and fire and water. Death. He knows the truth. All finish now. Go quietly. I make sure they will remember you. The Maddy Tsai Foundation I call it."

The latter words in Ismail's speech were difficult to hear. Suddenly the wind had risen to a deafening volume. The roof started to shake. There was a rumbling sound. There were shouts from below. A ship's foghorn sounded. The roar of air traffic seemed to be all around them. Vibrations made it difficult for them to continue holding on to the ridges.

Ismail's eyes darted from side to side. He tightened his grip on Madeleine. Tremors ran through the roof.

Wong struggled to maintain his grip on the shuddering surface beneath him. "Earthquake?" he said to Joyce.

"This is it," said the *bomoh*. "The end is here."

There was an ear-splitting roar as a helicopter appeared over a ridge on the curved landscape of white ridges that surrounded them.

"It must be the police," Joyce shouted into Wong's ear. "Brett must have phoned them." She looked suddenly distraught. "Oh no," she said, her chin beginning to quiver. "Officer Gallaher."

Ismail froze. Madeleine Tsai pulled away from him and grabbed Joyce McQuinnie's outstretched hand. The two of them and Wong raced off the roof at high speed. The *bomoh* stayed where he was. He appeared traumatized, unable to keep up with events. "Come back," he yelled. "Must come back. Few minutes left *only*."

Minutes later, Wong, McQuinnie and Madeleine were racing down the steps and then down the promenade, heading desperately for the street where Kilington had parked his car. Joyce was running the fastest, her terror of the police officer lending speed to her blurred feet. The deafening, fluttering roar of the helicopter appeared to be following them.

Instead of disappearing into the distance as they raced away, it got steadily louder.

"No good," Wong shouted. "Following us. Helicopter will get in front of us. Cannot escape."

Within minutes, all three had stopped running as the aircraft passed over their heads and then spun round, lowering itself gently between them and the only road out of Bennelong Point.

As the helicopter gently touched the ground, a sob broke from Joyce's throat. "I can't—I can't—I don't want to be arrested again. By that man."

"It's okay, Joyce. I'll talk to them," Madeleine shouted. "They'll help us. I'm sure they will. They're okay with me." She lowered her head and stepped with difficulty toward the cabin of the shuddering craft, leaning forward into the gale-force air that still blasted them.

As she reached the helicopter door, it swung open.

Smiling, Jackie Sum reached out and cut off her scream with a black-gloved hand before tugging her into the craft and ordering his pilot to lift off again.

The feng shui master moved forward to help her, but he was too late.

Jackie Sum, a broad smile below his thick sunglasses, shouted a single word down to Wong through the open door: "Thanks."

Madeleine screamed again as the door was slammed shut.

Joyce McQuinnie watched transfixed as the triads' helicopter lifted itself gracefully into the air. Wong stood baffled, buffeted by the winds from its rotors.

Within seconds, a group of four security guards and two police officers arrived at the spot. The young woman instinctively recoiled from them, but soon realized they were interested only in the escaping aircraft. To them, she was only one of several dozen open-mouthed passersby watching the scene.

The helicopter, angled slightly nose-down, turned in the air and then started moving directly northeast.

Joyce's heart was in her mouth. She turned to the feng shui master. "What are they going to do to her? Are they going to . . . ?"

"I don't know."

"Is there anything we can—?"

"I think no. Can call police. But police already know."

The helicopter skimmed the top of the Opera House before moving over the water to the northwest of the building. A tiny figure standing on the roof of the building watched it sail past.

Joyce sniffed, overcome by disappointment and helplessness. "We tried, didn't we, C. F.? We really tried."

The geomancer put a hand on her shoulder. "Yes. We tried."

As they watched, they noticed the helicopter rocking slightly. It veered to the right and then pulled sharply to the left.

Brett, his puffed out pecs hoisted proudly in front of him like a shield, trotted up to where the two of them stood. Now that nothing obviously illegal was going on, he was happy to rejoin them. "Amazing. Like something out of a bloody movie. Looks like your friend is putting up a bit of a fight," he said, pointing high in the sky. "See how the whirlybird is rocking?"

The fluttering aircraft jerked suddenly to one side and then righted itself. As they continued to watch, they saw the door of the helicopter swing open. Then a body fell out.

"Bloody bastards!" said Brett, shocked. "The buggers have thrown her out. Geez, what a way to go."

Joyce put her fist to her mouth.

The body seemed to fall forever. All three of them held their breath.

Then it hit the waters of the harbor with a splash they could see but not hear.

"I can't believe it," said Brett. "Pushing her out."

"No," said Joyce. "I don't know. Maddy was on the swimming team at school. I think she jumped."

Joyce's inclination was to race toward the water to see if Maddy could be rescued but the others persuaded her that she had landed much too far away.

"The police'll get there long before we do," said Brett. "She's landed near Circular Quay. I hope she hasn't landed on one of the ferries. That would hurt."

The young Australian told them that while they had been on the roof, he had sat down and read through all of Wong's book about the Opera House. He was fascinated to report that the geomancer had been right—it clearly had been a place of great negative energy. The history of the Opera House was one of constant arguments. The original architect had stormed off the project and his replacements had found that no part of it could be brought into being on schedule and within budget. Even after it had been opened, the performance spaces within it had been a matter of dispute, with some rooms changing designation repeatedly.

Wong's attention was still on the harbor, as he anxiously waited for Madeleine's head to bob up out of the water. Without looking away from the scene, he accepted Brett's compliments, and then graciously pointed out that the millions of visitors who had visited the Opera House over the years would have done a great deal to alleviate the building's negative energy and leave it with a positive air.

The mutual back-patting session was interrupted by Joyce. "Excuse me, guys," she said with infinite sadness in her voice. "The police are coming this way. I think it's our turn to be arrested again. Oh dear."

❖

The next series of interviews with the police took a little over five hours. They were described by officer Denton Gallaher as "debriefing." Although neither Wong nor McQuinnie were familiar with the word, it was clear that they were no longer seen as sources of trouble. Instead, they were perceived to be key sources of information regarding a highly unusual disturbance at the Opera House.

Gallaher's face was white and set. He was in a state of shock. He found it hard to accept that the group of inconsequential weirdos he had held in his office that afternoon had suddenly become a major item on the television news.

His colleagues had contacted him with a string of bizarre revelations. The Malaysian man he had shared tea with earlier that day had refused to come down from the roof of the Opera House for several hours and appeared to be in a demented state. A group of visitors from Hong Kong had hired a helicopter and landed it at the approach to the building—and then had used it to abduct the young Chinese woman who was allegedly "destined by the stars" to die on that day. She herself had then jumped—or been thrown—out of said helicopter from a great height into the water, and was missing, presumed dead. She had not emerged from the water, nor had her body been found.

The helicopter had eventually landed on a small airstrip north of the city and the individuals inside detained. None of them was being in the least bit helpful. A Cantonese-speaking police specialist in international triad activity had been summoned back from an organized crime conference in Melbourne to help question them.

Meanwhile, initial witness statements appeared to indicate that the people he, Gallaher, had identified as the real troublemakers—Wong, McQuinnie and Kilington—had not committed any specific crimes. Indeed, there was some evidence to suggest that their behavior had been exemplary. Witnesses said they had appeared to be attempting to talk the Malaysian man and his Chinese fiancée down from the Opera House roof, and Wong had later been seen by several officers trying to stop the helicopter abduction of the young woman.

Gallaher found the whole thing almost impossible to take in. Not a day goes by without police officers encountering lunatics making ridiculous allegations. Such claims *have* to be dismissed. Normal police business couldn't proceed otherwise. But wacko predictions aren't normally fulfilled almost immediately afterward.

He decided he was ultimately livid with God/Destiny/Fate for having played such a vile trick on him. The fact that the accusations made by Wong and McQuinnie turned out to have been right was just one of those huge, horrible coincidences that showed that whoever ran the universe had a sense of irony the size of Uluru.

In the end, after hearing the entire bizarre tale a dozen times over, Gallaher came to his own conclusions. The weirdos from Singapore were convinced that Madeleine Tsai would die today. By spreading this fear around, they somehow managed to bring it about. It was all explicable by normal, scientific means. It was a prediction that had fulfilled itself thanks to group hysteria. He was absolutely convinced that the troublesome visitors had brought it all upon themselves. But, unfortunately for him, they had not done so in a way that enabled him to charge them with specific offenses, except very minor ones, such as trespass.

It was infuriating, but it looked as if he would have to let the crazy old Chinese guy and his mad young assistant go.

"I've never been so tired in my whole life," said Joyce, as a police car dropped them back at their hotel at 10:41 that night. She gave a yawn that was so large it hurt her jaw and made her close her eyes. "Dear God," she said. "Poor us. Poor me. Poor Maddy." She sniffed and her red eyes filled with tears again. "She was only a year older than me. Can't we go and help them look for her? She was a champion swimmer. She *told* me. I really think she could have jumped deliberately."

"I think better we decide that Madeleine Tsai is dead. Sydney coroner will probably write down open verdict, presumed dead. Most bodies in harbor waters are recovered. Some are not. But if she is officially dead, that means that triads will not come find her. Jackie Sum will not look for her. This is good. Old Man Tsai will not come find her. She doesn't like her father. This is good. Australian immigration officers will not come find her. Also good. No one will come find her."

"But if she is still alive . . ."

"If she is alive, she can start again. Fresh. Clean. New. New country. She is young, clever. She knows how to look after herself."

"Will that horrible guy get the insurance money? Her boyfriend?"

"Don't know. Maybe. He said he wants to spend it on sick children. Maybe he is telling the truth. Spending money on sick children is good."

As they stepped into the elevator, the young woman said: "If like she's officially dead, then it all works out fine for everyone, in a way, doesn't it?"

"Not fine for everyone," said Wong. "No one to pay me."

THE USE OF HUMAN HANDS

THE GHOST groaned, right on cue at seven o'clock. It was a sad, whimpering exhalation: *"Unhhh."*

"There it is," gasped Joyce McQuinnie, standing in the doorway.

"I'm going home," said Lai Kuen, grabbing her handbag and trotting stiffly out of the office on her high heels.

The two dentists stood in the waiting room, while Lai Kuen waited in the corridor, trying to cram her fist in her mouth. They had all come back to the still-shut office on Monday evening to watch C. F. Wong deal with the ghost.

The geomancer's face was set, but with exhaustion rather than fear. The long weekend holiday he had craved had turned out to be nothing like a vacation. It would be impossible to imagine anything less relaxing than to fill three days with two long-haul flights, divided by a long day of breathless action—especially since the non-flying hours had been significantly oversupplied with painful police interview sessions.

And although they had arrived back in Singapore on Saturday evening, he had been unable to relax on Sunday. The unsolved case of Amanda Luk and the ghost at the dental office had been preying heavily on his mind. Words related to "death" had been too much in evidence in his waking hours recently. Madeleine Tsai was gone and with her the chance of a big reward from Old Man Tsai. And although Amanda Luk had lost her life, the assignment at the dentists' remained unresolved. In all, the past week had been far too stressful. He desperately needed to get back to his quiet, safe world of floor plans and ancient calendars. But first, the unquiet spirit had to be dealt with.

On entering the offices, Wong had noticed that both Liew and Leibler had changed noticeably since the events of Thursday morning. Both seemed years older. The tall, angular Liew Yok Tse was stooped and shrunken, and appeared to have lost weight. He and Cheung Lai Kuen stood close together, apparently taking comfort from each other's presence. She held on to his arm.

Gibson Leibler had lost his strut. There was no spring in his step. His head was bowed. He shuffled on his feet, his face unshaven and his eyes looking sore. Wong noticed that the surgeon's collar was standing awry on one side and his left ear contained a spot of shaving cream. The implication was that this was a man who was living alone. Had he walked out on Cady? Or had she thrown him out?

Both of them watched from the waiting room as the feng shui master entered the haunted room holding his *lo pan* and another, smaller device, which was encased in plain wood and had unusual markings on it. He walked carefully around the room once with his *lo pan* and then put it down on the tray next to the dentist's chair.

"He's in the chair," whispered Joyce. "The ghost. He's in the chair. I can hear him."

Wong picked up the other device.

"What is that?" asked the young woman, who was watching carefully from behind the outward-opening door.

"Feng shui metal finder."

"Never heard of that before."

"It is for finding unseen metal. These days usually you can get a floor plan. Will show you where metal pipes are. This is good when you need to find metal not on floor plan."

Wong carefully went around the edges of the room and stopped when he got to one of the side walls. He slowly lowered his compass to ankle level and then lifted it up as far as he could reach. Then he brought it back down again, roughly to shoulder level.

"Here," he said. "There is metal here which is causing the problem."

"*Ahhhh,*" moaned the ghost. "*Owww-unhh.*"

Wong marked the spot on the wall with his pencil and then reached down into his bag. He lifted out a drill with a fine point and plugged it into a socket he found near the sink.

"What are you doing?" This was Dr. Liew.

"Getting rid of the ghost," said Wong.

"Don't! That stippled wall covering cost a fortune," said Lai Kuen, holding on to her boss's arm. "Amanda got her friend to do it. I don't know if we will be able to replace it. Look, this is ridiculous, can't you stop him?" That last comment was aimed at Dr. Leibler, who showed no reaction.

"But shouldn't you find out what the metal is?" asked Joyce. "What if it's a water pipe or something? Or something electrical? You could hurt yourself."

"*Ohhh,*" said the ghost.

Wong said nothing, but turned the machine on. The whine of the drill in the small room was so loud that all conversation had to stop. The geomancer used two hands to steady the machine as it bit into the plaster. He pressed harder, and the drill head slowly sank in, millimeter by millimeter, with the sound rising a tone as he put pressure behind it.

"Nearly there," he shouted.

"Stop!" yelled Lai Kuen.

Suddenly the drill changed tone, as it hit something inside the wall. There was a metallic splintering sound.

Wong turned the drill off. It took a few seconds to whirr to a halt. Silence filled the room. *Complete* silence. The ghost had gone.

The feng shui master turned to his assistant. "Did you bring invoice book? Is invoice time. Then dinner."

More than two thousand years ago, the great sage Confucius was sitting and talking to four young scholars about what would bring happiness to them.

The first said that he would achieve happiness if he achieved the rank of Minister of Defense.

The second said that he would have ultimate joy if he became Minister of Finance.

The third said that he would reach the peak of human pleasure if he became the Emperor's Master of Ceremonies.

The fourth student was bored by the discussion. He played his lute.

Confucius said to him: "Tseng Tien, I want you to answer the question."

The young man said: "Happiness is to be with a group of friends, bathing in the River Yi in late spring. A cooling breeze blows through the rain altars. We sing at the tops of our voices as we stroll home."

Confucius said only Tien understood anything about happiness.

No wisdom has ever surpassed that of Confucius. But one who may have been equally wise was Lao Tzu, Blade of Grass. Two and half millenniums ago, he said: "He who is satisfied, is rich."

*(Some Gleanings of Ancient Chinese Wisdom
by C. F. Wong, part 351)*

❖

"What IS that thing, anyway?" Madame Xu stared suspiciously at the dish on the table.

"I'll show you," said Joyce. She flicked through a book on Australia that Brett Kilington had given her. "It's that." She held the book up and showed Madame Xu the image. "It's called a kangaroo."

"But what IS a kangaroo?"

"It's a native of Australia."

"Really," said Madame Xu, amazed. "And to think my nephew married one of those to get a passport."

Joyce had brought some kangaroo meat and a box of macadamia chocolates back as a souvenir of Sydney. Ah-Fat had agreed to stir-fry the kangaroo meat as long as he could have a portion himself out of curiosity.

"Tastes like venison," said Joyce.

"I'm not really sure if I want to eat it," said Madame Xu. "It's got such fat legs in the picture. I'm worried it might give me fat legs."

"If eating this stuff makes you fat, we'd better force-feed C. F. with large amounts of it," said Dilip Kenneth Sinha. "He looks skinnier than ever. It must have been all the stress of your adventures in Australia."

"Australia very nice place," mused Wong. "But very shocking things happen there. Police they arrest you all the time. Every five minute, almost. Worse than China even. But policemen not so bad as some China policemen."

"Don't be ridiculous," said Joyce. "The first time they arrested us it was because of Brett. And the second time, they did have a pretty good reason for detaining us and talking to us. They thought we were landing helicopters on their most famous national building."

"It all sounds much too dramatic and exciting for me," said Sinha. "Thank goodness I wasn't there. Sampling this kangaroo meat is probably enough excitement for me."

"It's full of crocodiles too," Madame Xu said. "And arboretums."

"Aboriginals," Joyce interposed after some thought. "That's what we call the native peoples of Australia. It's a good place. If you ever go down there, I'll give you a list of places to visit. Nightclubs, shops, everything. Fab CD shops. They've got it all."

"Why don't we plan a joint excursion?" Sinha suggested.

"This is not a meeting to plan our holidays," said Madame Xu. "This is a working dinner. And we can get to work now, because the final member is here."

Superintendent Gilbert Tan hurried into the night market. "So sorry, so sorry," he said. "I'm very late, is it? Helluva rude of me. Ordered already, good, good, then we can start eating right away."

"Try this," said Madame Xu. "It's special. Joyce brought it from Australia."

"What is it?" the police officer asked.

"It's slices of Australian natives. Apparently everybody eats them down there. It's allowed. They are known as arboretums."

"Sounds yummy, but perhaps I go for something more

familiar," said the Superintendent, pushing the dish away and reaching for a dish of *char kway teow*.

The police officer suddenly stopped, mid-grab. He looked over at Joyce. "Before I forget, I just want to say I'm sorry about your friend, Joyce. The girl who died in Australia?"

"Poor dear Clara," Madame Xu said.

"Madeleine," Wong said.

"It's a terrible thing but I knew she would die the moment I saw the picture of her hand," the fortune-teller said. "It was tragic but it had to be."

"Er, thanks." Joyce quickly wiped the smile off her face. "It was, er, very sad. But I think she's in a better place sort of thing?"

Madame Xu put her hands together prayerfully. "A paradise where there is no more laughter and no more tears."

"Whatever."

There was little conversation for the next fourteen minutes, and the members of the investigative advisory committee of the Singapore Union of Industrial Mystics did justice to the creations of Ah-Fat, the night market's best chef. Despite his protestations, Superintendent Tan consumed most of the kangaroo, which had been cooked *rendang* style.

Only when all appeared to be reaching a point of satiety did thoughts turn to matters of work.

"Now," said Gilbert Tan. "What do we have to report?"

He looked from face to face.

"I want to hear Wong's story about the dentists," said the fortune-teller. "So what happened? I am all on tenterhooks. Is the ghost exorcised?"

"Hmm?" Wong looked up from his journal, in which he had started scribbling again. "It was quite simple. But I had to put some different things together."

"I helped," said Joyce proudly. "In fact, if not for me, he might not have been able to solve the thing, right, C. F.?"

The geomancer gave her a sidelong glance. "The problem was not too difficult. Simple mathematics. A matter of putting one and one together."

"Two and two."

"What?"

"Two and two," said Joyce. "The phrase is, putting two and two together. Not one and one."

"Same-same." The geomancer turned to Madame Xu. "You see, it was easy for someone like me, who always has pen and paper and is scribbling. I wrote down the times of the visit of the ghost. Saturday at one afternoon, Monday at nine morning, Tuesday at six afternoon, Wednesday at four afternoon. You see?"

Sinha jotted it all down. "No, I can't see any pattern. No, wait, hang on . . . Yes. No. No, I don't get it."

"I cannot do sums," said Madame Xu. "Concepcion does all the household accounts for me. I don't know where I would be without her."

"Aha!" This was Sinha, who had continued to scrawl in a tiny hand. "I've got it. The ghost was on a timer. It went off every eleven hours. So it *also* went off, let me see, at eleven P.M. on Sunday morning, ten P.M. on Sunday night, eight P.M. on Monday night, seven A.M. on Tuesday morning and five A.M. Wednesday and, and, three A.M. Thursday, but no one was there to hear it at those hours. Those not being office hours."

"Yes," said Wong. "Regular yet not regular."

"Suspiciously regular for a ghost," said the Indian astrologer. "Or to put it another way, suspiciously irregular, since the ghosts I know prefer to appear at the same time every year. Certainly not in eleven-hour cycles."

"Can I tell them my contribution now, C. F., please?" said Joyce excitedly.

"Okay."

"Well, it was like this, see? We were in the airport in Sydney and he was telling me all this about the ghost arriving and the fact that it seemed to be on an eleven-hour cycle. We noticed that the time from when the ghost started moaning to his last groan was always an hour and fourteen minutes. You know what lasts exactly an hour and fourteen minutes, don't you? Only one thing in the world."

There was silence.

"The last act of *La Bohème*?" offered Sinha.

"Part one of *The Sound of Music*?" suggested Madame Xu.

"No. Do you give up?"

Sinha put his fingertips together. "We do not. Let me think. The exchange of vows at an Indian wedding? A business lunch at Raffles? A taxi drive from Tampines to Sentosa during rush hour?"

"No. Now do you give up?"

"I do," said Madame Xu.

"I most certainly do not," said Sinha. "I can never resist a challenge and I will never give up. Let me think. Oh, I don't know. I give up too. Do tell."

"A minidisk," said Joyce, clapping her hands together with glee. "You know. Seventy-four minutes?"

There was silence.

"A minidisc," repeated Joyce. "You know, the recordable disc players from Japan? Like CDs but small, teeny things, squarish?"

The astrologer looked at the fortune-teller.

"This thing." She fumbled in her bag and handed over a square of metal.

"We used to call these pocket transistors," said Sinha.

"Yes, but they don't call them radios anymore," said Madame Xu. "Concepcion's daughter has one. They call them Walkie-Talkie-Men or something, right?"

"Er, sort of," said Joyce, "Anyway, the discs that you get with these machines, they are always seventy-four minutes long. So we worked out that the ghost was made of one of these things hooked up to an eleven-hour timer. It was buried in the wall."

Madame Xu was confused. "But why did the sound come from the middle of the room when it was really from a machine in the wall? C. F. said that the moaning came from just above the chair."

Wong explained: "The machine was hidden away. Two speakers were buried in the wall. One on one side, one on the other side. Special effect. If you stand in the front of the room, sound seems to come from in between. New invention. Called stereo."

"It's not a new invention. My dad's had a stereo for years," said Joyce. "It must have been invented at least ten years ago. Maybe more. Anyway, there's this thing called stereo imaging. They've had it years, only these days they do it better and with smaller speakers. My dad's—"

"I'm afraid I don't understand," sighed Madame Xu. "I am really far too old for all this."

"Here," said the young woman, pulling a magazine from her sack. "I bought this from the airport bookshop to explain it to C. F. There's an article in here which will explain."

Madame Xu looked at the magazine: "*Rocksoff.* I don't think I subscribe to this particular journal."

"You should. You'd really like it. There's a column on page sixty-two called High End Audiophile. It's about spatial imaging and all that stuff. You should read it. It's a good magazine. My dad gets it. I'll lend that one to you if you like."

"That's really very generous of you, dear."

Wong interrupted to interpret. "The sound comes from both sides, two speakers. But if you use correct speakers, correct volume, from some parts of the room it sounds like sound comes from middle of room. Between speakers instead of from speakers. Very clever. Special effect."

"Ah. I see," said the fortune-teller.

"But who did it?" asked Sinha. "The American I suppose? Wanted to scare off his Singaporean partner and nab the business for himself?"

"I don't know," said Wong. "I am only feng shui man. Not police man. Superintendent Tan is looking at the case. He will tell us in good time. It was not Dr. Leibler who organize the ghost, I think."

"C. F. and I talked about this on the way here. We reckon it might not have been the dentists at all," said Joyce. "It was probably that woman Amanda Luk, who was killed last week. Sorry to speak ill of the dead and all that. Thank God I never met her. It would be awful to meet someone who died. But she redecorated the office, remember? Before they moved in. She got her friends to install that sound equipment there while they did the place up. Maybe."

"What was the motive?" asked Sinha.

"We don't know," said Joyce. "She wanted to get rid of Dr. Liew. Scare him off. That's what I think."

"But do you have any idea why she did it?"

"Dunno. My theory is that she had something going with Dr. Leibler, but Dr. Leibler won't divorce his wife and marry her because he doesn't have enough patients. Not enough income. Getting divorced is the most expensive thing you ever do in your life—that's what my dad says. So I reckon Amanda Luk cooked up this scheme to get rid of Dr. Liew, so Dr. Leibler gets more patients, marries her and they live happily ever after?"

"So who or what killed Amanda Luk?" This was Madame Xu.

"Don't know," said Joyce. "But I know it wasn't a ghost. Maybe it was Dr. Liew. Or maybe the other woman assistant at the dental office did it."

Wong winced. "You must not say such things. This is libel and slander. Very bad. Cannot say without proof."

Madam Xu nodded. "He's right, Plum Blossom. It is libel and slander. You mustn't say these things."

"Let me ask you a professional question, C. F." This was Sinha. "Could you really locate that recording machine so precisely behind the plaster purely by using your feng shui metal-detecting equipment?"

"Well, not just the feng shui compass. I also read the magazine of Joyce."

Joyce beamed.

"*Rocksoff*," said the astrologer, picking it up and looking with grave distaste at the sweaty guitarist on the cover.

"Well, this proves one thing, in my book, anyway," said Joyce. "Vega was right. There's no such thing as ghosts. It's all just mumbo-jumbo. I don't know how people can seriously believe such dumb stuff. People are like soooo gullible. I wonder if Seth can teach me how to do channelling?"

The geomancer lowered his chopsticks and caught the eye of the police officer.

"I have a suggestion," said C. F. Wong. "Just an idea. Unofficial."

"All our discussions are unofficial, you know that."

Wong pulled at the straggly hairs on his chin. "We think

ghost was organize by assistant, Amanda Luk, who died."

"Yes."

"Remember how Dr. Leibler had lawsuit from man named Joseph Oath? But Mr. Oath died just after lawsuit started?"

"I do."

"I think maybe you ask your friends in Hong Kong police force to open old file about Mr. Oath. You see, this happen little while after Cady Tsai-Leibler married Dr. Leibler. She thought she marry a rich man. Successful dentist. But then she find that he faces lawsuit, maybe will lose all his money. Too bad. But then problem solve itself. Man with lawsuit dies." Wong leaned forward. "That's the story. But now we know something that before we do not know."

"Which is?" Tan smiled expectantly.

"That Mrs. Tsai-Leibler is involved with triad groups. Death of Joseph Oath may be happy coincidence for her. Or maybe not. I think you reopen old files. Ask some questions. Maybe interesting. Maybe not. Don't know."

"I understand." The police officer scribbled down some notes. "When you put it that way, it does sound like something that needs to be looked into." He finished writing and scanned their faces again.

Wong continued: "Then another person make trouble for Mrs. Tsai-Leibler: Amanda Luk. She meets her husband in hotel when he is staying here. They make friends. He gets her a job as receptionist in his dentist office. She maybe wants to have affair with him. Maybe she already has had affair with him. I don't know. Then she dies too."

"Interesting," said Sinha, who was picking a sliver of kangaroo *rendang* out of the crevice in the middle of his teeth with a toothpick. "Seems that people who cross swords with Mrs. Tsai-Leibler soon get put out of action."

"I'm with you," said the police officer. "Thank you, Mr.

Wong. I shall pass these extremely interesting deductions to the gentlemen in my office in charge of this case. I shall, as usual, take full credit for them myself. Anything else to report?"

Sinha leaned forward. "But if Mrs. Tsai-Leibler was the evil person behind the deaths of Mr. Oath and Ms. Luk, that still leaves one crime unaccounted for. Who tried to burn the house down and kill Mrs. Tsai-Leibler? Was it really the ghost of Mr. Oath, as she said? It surely wouldn't have been Ms. Luk? I can imagine a young woman having a fling with someone's husband—but it's a big jump to go from that to burning down a house with a family inside."

"I think it was not Ms. Luk," said Wong. "I think Jackie Sum sent agent down to kill Madeleine Tsai. When house-burning failed, Jackie comes down himself to finish the job."

Joyce put up her hand, a school habit she had yet to lose.

"Yes, little lady?"

"I went down to The Hole with Danita last night and she told me something interesting. That horrible fat man who locked her up? Well, you know he turned out to be this guy who had like seen her once or twice in the shop and really, really fancied her and all that and decided to kidnap her?"

"Yes," said Superintendent Tan.

"He may know who you are talking about but we don't," said Madame Xu.

"Well, he was the kidnapper. Remember on Wednesday we had to rescue this girl?" Joyce said. "Well, he worked in this photo studio and he locked her up in his darkroom?"

"We remember, I think. Do we?" said Madame Xu.

"We do," said Sinha.

"Anyway," said Joyce. "Dani told me some stuff. Here's the interesting bit. On the Tuesday, Fatso goes into the dark-room to deliver her breakfast. Danita can't resist boasting about her clever way of getting a message to the like outside world."

"She tells him about it?" Wong asks, suddenly interested.

"Yep. She's like, 'So did you find a letter on the ground and mail it yesterday?' He's like, 'I dunno.' She's like, 'Well, is there a letter on the ground in the revolving door or just outside?' And he's like, 'No.' And she's like, 'Well, you or your assistant must have picked it up and mailed it. Which is why your ass will soon be grass. Because it has all sorts of incriminating stuff in it which will cause a friend of mine who works closely with the police to come and rescue me.' Are you following me?"

The superintendent nodded.

"Anyway, Dani tells him that the letter has been mailed to Mr. Wong of Telok Ayer Street. So he comes around snooping, trying to intercept the letter or take it back. He must have got a good look at us."

"Maybe followed you around," said Sinha

"Yep. Which is why, when I walked into the shop on the Wednesday, with C. F. walking behind me, he suddenly yelps and runs out the back. So now we know how he knew who we were."

Wong suddenly sat up straight. *"Waah!"* he said. "Now I know something too."

"Know what?" Joyce asked.

"Now I know what happen to our air conditioner."

"What?"

"Fat bottom man go upstair. Sneak into our office early morning. Sneak in because Winnie forgot to lock it. Often she forgets. He go looking for letter to recover. He looks on your desk. He leans down in your drawer. His fat bottom hits air conditioner. He is very heavy. Very fat. Metal holding thing—what do you call it?"

"Er, bracket?"

"Bracket very old, very . . ."

"Rusty."

"Very trusty. Bracket very trusty. His big bottom push it, air conditioner fall out of window. Make big noise falling on ground. Fat kidnap man very nervous, run away. Letter still on Winnie desk. Also, I think he drop his watch. Something is tipping in our office."

"Ticking," said Joyce.

"Ticking, yes. I hope is Rolex."

"So he should pay for the new air conditioner."

"He should. But I think will not. Maybe we can sell his watch. Anyway, is no problem."

"Why do you say that? It's sweltering in that room. We aren't going to be able to work without a new air conditioner."

"This morning I send invoice to Dr. Liew. I phone him to make sure he got it. He will pay no problem. I ask him to pay cash. He is rich. For a little while, we also a little bit rich," said the feng shui master, rubbing his hands together.

"Good," said Joyce. "Let's go shopping. I need a new chair. And the clock in the office doesn't work. I need to get some business cards designed and ordered, remember? 'Personal Assistant.' Sounds good, right? And you need to buy two new cell phones. One for the office, and one for me."

"Study catalog no need. Want one of these, is it?" said Gilbert Tan, pulling out a small chunky device in a leather pouch. "Combined mobile plus PDA. Latest must-have for true Singapore chuppie. Even can receive and send remote E-mail. Internet, everything got. It's helluva small and so nice, man."

Joyce moved to a stool next to the officer to jealously examine the gleaming machine. "Wicked. Can I see? How do you do it? Can I check my Hotmail account?"

"Easy." Tan chewed his bottom lip as he concentrated on stabbing the tiny buttons with his fat fingers.

Sinha turned to Madame Xu and spoke quietly. "Fancy a walk in Fort Canning park tomorrow? We could feed the ducks if it's a nice day."

"Do they have ducks there?"

"I don't rightly remember. But if they do, we could."

"What do ducks like to eat? I have some *laksa* in the fridge that's last week's."

"Ducks adore leftover *laksa*. That is, if they have any taste. Stale bread is also good."

She frowned. "I don't have any stale bread. How does one make stale bread?"

"Good question. I've never really thought about it. I suppose one just gets fresh bread and then waits for a while."

"How long?"

"Hard to say. Many hours, I should think."

"We'd better get started."

Their conversation was interrupted by a gasp from Joyce. She was staring at the tiny screen on Superintendent Tan's communicator with her palm against her mouth.

"Bad news?" asked Tan.

She shook her head, unable to speak for a moment. After slowly exhaling, she looked up at him. "It's nothing. Just an E-mail from—from a friend."

Joyce turned to the feng shui master. "I've just got a message from Australia. From a friend at a guest-house in Uluru, you know, the big rock?"

"Ah," Wong said. "From your cousin? Gone back to work?"

"No, it's not from Brett," said Joyce, her face beaming. "It's from someone else we know in Australia."

"Oh." He nodded. "And how is she?"

"Okay, I think. Okay!" She turned to the police officer. "What do I press to reply?"

He took the phone from her and peered at the screen. "I think you press this, and then this . . ."

Wong, pleased to have a few minutes of peace, turned away from the others and opened his journal. It had been a good week, but he had not written as much as he would have liked. He had hardly added anything at all over the weekend. It wasn't just exhaustion from the drama of Friday and the long trip on Saturday. He felt oddly guilty. The classic tales he recorded in his journal were always so full of altruism and high morality. Yet he always felt so much under pressure to earn money, pay rent, cover the bills, make a living. And most ironic of all, he knew that one of the main motivations for his writing a translation of the tales of the sages in English was that he hoped it would sell to a Western publisher and earn him some real cash.

But perhaps this moral dilemma was not something that could be escaped. The sages and the gods gave us tales of high morality as a model for life from heaven. Yet we live on earth and have to deal with the petty needs of our earthly bodies as well. Maybe the job of bringing heaven and earth together was the true work of man during his brief breath of existence?

He was reminded of a tale of one of the few female sages, and he picked up his pen and started writing.

❖

A woman in Ta-yeh county led a good life in a city of evil. She prayed and sacrificed. She was a vegetarian. Her name was Niang Tzu.
She was rewarded for her goodness with a vision. A celestial messenger told her that the city would be destroyed on the

*day that the stone lions at the great hall in the center of town
wept tears of blood.*

*She spent days marching around the town. She told people
about her vision and asked them to change their ways or face
doom.*

*The people laughed. They said there was no way statues
made of stone could weep tears of blood. But Niang Tzu
said that she trusted the celestial messenger.*

*One day, the pork butcher in town decided to play a trick on
her. He smeared tears of pig blood under the eyes of the
stone lions.*

*Niang Tzu was amazed. She fled town and camped on a des-
olate hill nearby.*

*The celestial messenger saw the tears of blood on the stone
lions. That night there was a great earthquake and a river
burst its banks. The city was destroyed in a flood—all except
for the hilltop on which Niang Tzu sat.*

The waters wiped the tears from the faces of the stone lions.

The gods do a great many things. Some are ordinary. Some are
miraculous. But one thing should always be recalled, Blade of
Grass: they do all things using human hands, never their own.

*(Some Gleanings of Oriental Wisdom
by C. F. Wong, part 352)*